Also by MaryJanice Davidson

BeWere My Heart

Bears Behaving Badly
A Wolf After My Own Heart
Mad for a Mate

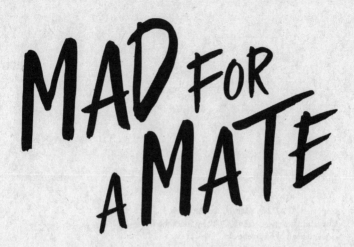

MAD FOR A MATE

MARYJANICE DAVIDSON

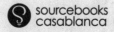

sourcebooks
casablanca

Copyright © 2022 by MaryJanice Davidson
Cover and internal design © 2022 by Sourcebooks
Cover design by Sourcebooks
Cover art by Aleta Rafton/Lott Reps

Sourcebooks and the colophon are registered trademarks of Sourcebooks.

All rights reserved. No part of this book may be reproduced in any form or by
any electronic or mechanical means including information storage and retrieval
systems—except in the case of brief quotations embodied in critical articles or
reviews—without permission in writing from its publisher, Sourcebooks.

The characters and events portrayed in this book are fictitious or
are used fictitiously. Any similarity to real persons, living or dead,
is purely coincidental and not intended by the author.

All brand names and product names used in this book are trademarks,
registered trademarks, or trade names of their respective holders.
Sourcebooks is not associated with any product or vendor in this book.

Published by Sourcebooks Casablanca, an imprint of Sourcebooks
P.O. Box 4410, Naperville, Illinois 60567-4410
(630) 961-3900
sourcebooks.com

Printed and bound in Canada.
MBP 10 9 8 7 6 5 4 3 2 1

For my children, Christina and William, who think nothing of going out of their way to make the world a better place.

Chapter 1

SOMEONE HAD DUMPED ANOTHER BODY IN THE GARDEN.

Magnus Berne swallowed a sigh with his coffee, one of the things Americans did better than anyone else. Oh, aye, arguments could be made for café au lait and chicory and espresso, for café breve and affogato, for the long black and the flat white, but in terms of turning a bitter beverage into a lush dessert it was socially acceptable to gulp down at 8:00 a.m., no one beat the Yanks.

Besides, it was too early for hard cider. He had today's bottles all lined up in the icebox: Hoppet and Cran Dry from Thor's Hard Cider.

He trudged out the back door and through the yard, heading for the property line. His loathsome seasonal allergies had kicked in and the wind was going the wrong way, so he wasn't getting much in the way of a scent, but he was betting this new body would be like the others. Limbs strewn about, a bad wig, or no wig, faceup, and looking at the sky with the frozen "look at this, aren't I elegant?" expression of the store mannequin.

Why someone kept pitching mannequins into his yard, he hadn't a clue. Was it malice? Or affection, the way cats laid mice on pillows? Was it a game? Or a mistake? A courting ritual? A dare? An environmental protest? He knew he should be taking some sort of action, but it was such a weird, ridiculous problem. He had the vague hope it would resolve itself but didn't especially care if it did.

It took effort to care about much since Sue Smalls had been foully murdered.

He tried to wrench his mind back to a relevant track—the dummy pileup—but it was hard to find the motivation to come up with a plan. Set up motion detectors? Stay up all night guarding the yard with a shotgun across his knees like a rancher worried about poachers? Let the bodies pile up into some sort of macabre structure, as opposed to hopping in the boat and lugging them to the dump?

Was it a neighborhood thing? Specifically, a new-neighbor thing? A deeply fucked-up welcome wagon thing? A Stable thing? He didn't know. He couldn't know. They didn't do this *shite* in Scotland. They did entirely different shite in Scotland.

Regardless, it was past time he took steps. He might be too puzzled to come up with a strategy, but he could still do what anyone would when they discovered a body in their back yard: call an accountant.

He blew his nose on a wad of Kleenex, stuffed them back in his robe pocket

(*fucking allergies*)

and then pulled his phone out as he reached the dummy, dumped on its front and abandoned like trash. Pale as a pearl, short, with slender limbs and shoulder-length dark-red hair so wet it looked like black cherry soda with a healthy shot of grenadine. He gently prodded a toe into her ribs, and nearly screamed when she flopped over on her back and her eyes popped open. Shrieking wasn't remotely dignified, but damn.

He dropped the phone. On her face.

"Ow!"

"You're not a store mannequin!" he blurted, wondering how he could have missed something so patently obvious.

Her rebuttal was swift: "Idiot!"

Fucking allergies.

Chapter 2

SHE CLAMBERED TO HER FEET (NUDELY!) AND SLAPPED his hand away (also nudely) when he tried to help her up. "Jesus. Get one of the smaller phones, pal, that one felt like an Etch A Sketch when it nailed me on the forehead."

"I like the bigger screen," he said, already shrugging out of his robe and doing his damnedest not to notice her sweet, plum-sized breasts. Her head came to his Adam's apple; if he pulled her into his arms, she would fit perfectly.

"So if someone asks you for a wake-up call, do you just whip your phone at their face?"

"Almost never," he replied deadpan.

"Ha! Okay, that was—" *Whack!* "Stop trying to help me up. I don't need your help and also, I'm up."

"This is amazing. You don't have a bad wig. You're not bald!"

Given her expression, he could have been trying to hand her a pile of dead snakes instead of a robe. "Did you just tell me I'm not bald?"

Magnus ground his teeth. He loathed the "did you just say something I definitely heard you say?" question, which wasn't a question at all. Her American accent was nice, though. The midland patois always sounded friendly to him. "Are you all right? What are you doing here? Did the dummies foretell your coming?"

"Dummies. Jesus."

"Did your boat sink? Or were you trying to get away from someone? Should I call nine-nine-nine?"

"Knock yourself out, but I don't think it'll help. We don't call nine-nine-nine in America, you British weirdo."

The naked mannequin thinks I'm *the weirdo?* "Scottish weirdo," he corrected. "Would you like to come in for tea? Or coffee? I think the last owner left a bag of beans."

"Hot water run through old, abandoned beans does sound tempting." Her pale brow furrowed. "What time is it? I didn't get a chance to check your phone as it careened into my forehead."

"It's seven thirty a.m."

"What? Did you just tell me it's seven thirty?"

"Yes," he replied through gritted teeth. What came out was *Yzz.*

"Shit on toast, I'm late!" She batted his robe-laden hand away again and dashed away like a pretty, profane White Rabbit.

"Wait! Where are you going?" He had to raise his voice as she widened the distance between them. "I have a boat! You don't have to swim away!"

Nope. Gone. He had a last glimpse of a pert bottom before she splashed into the bay.

His phone squawked at him. "—nus? Magnus? Hello? You okay, big guy?"

In a few strokes, she was just a bobbing head, far out and getting farther. Reaching land meant a swim of about three kilometers; thank God it was a calm, sunny day. She'd be exhausted by the time she hit the shore. Especially if she'd swum round trip.

His phone let out a demanding "Maaaaaaaaaagnus!"

"A beautiful dummy just came to life and swam away," he blurted.

"Uh. What?"

"What is happening?"

"Excellent question."

"I don't understand what's going on."

"Me neither! Magnus, *you* called *me*."

"It was some sort of bizarre Alice-in-Wonderland situation," he explained. "If Alice were naked. And a grown woman. And an utter nutter."

"Uh. That doesn't sound—are you okay?"

"Good point—it's not right. It was more a White Rabbit situation."

"Sure. Sure. Your standard White Rabbit event. Totally normal thing that happens all the time. Not weird at all."

"Is this something you Americans do?"

"Not this American. I'd have to check with the other three hundred and thirty-one million, though."

"I have to think about this." Magnus broke off to sneeze into his elbow. "Sorry t'bother you, lad."

"Magnus, wa—"

"Goodbye."

Fucking allergies.

Chapter 3

THE SEVENTH SQUIB, WHO ALSO WENT BY VERITY "TAKE No Shit" Lane, splashed out of the surf (not that Lake Minnetonka had much in the way of surf) and hoped like hell her car was nearby. The latest Damp Squib challenge had stipulated booze, relay swimming, and stuffing random mailboxes with teddy bears; she was pretty sure the others had dumped her car in the lot on the south side of the lake. If not, she was in for a fifty-mile walk. Naked. Or a ten-minute walk to her phone and, ultimately, Uber. Also naked.

Either way: places to be.

The brisk swim had left her equal parts exhilarated

(*I did it!*)

and tired

(*gah, this is taking forever; did I fall into the English Channel by mistake?*)

and starving. She could murder a dozen Pop Tarts; no need to cook them first. Or a dozen eggs; no need to cook those, either.

At this hour, the only people on the beach were a couple of Stables in Phi Delta Gamma sweatshirts, one blond and stocky, one brunette and also stocky, whose jaws dropped lower the closer she got. A pity they weren't Shifters; her own kind wouldn't have questioned why she was swimming naked in the wee hours.

"Uh…" Blond and Stocky began.

Verity waved. "Good morning!"

"Are you okay?" Brunette and Stocky managed, because Stables weren't just stuck in one form, they were nosy, too.

"Never better."

Stocky Blond cleared his throat. "Walk of shame?"

"Not even close." It was, in fact, her fourth Damp Squib challenge. The exhilaration made it worth the inevitable aches and pains. It could be argued that the pain was the point.

She could only see a third of the parking lot from where she was, so she scrambled up some brush and a tiny dune for a better look, slitting her eyes against the aggravating early sunshine.

"Do you. Um. Need a ride?" Stocky Blond's voice cracked on *ride*, which was too cute. "Or a coat?"

"Actually, I might take you up—nope! Never mind. There it is. Thanks anyway, guys."

"Okay, I'm Travis and this is Biff—"

"Really? A little on the nose, doncha think?"

"—you sure you don't need anything? Like, a cop?"

"Nope."

"Maybe you should take our numbers," Biff put in. "In case you need help."

"Nope."

"What's your name?" Travis asked.

Verity "Second-Class Citizen" Lane, she thought. *The Seventh Squib.*

"And how come you're naked in a lake at, like, seven a.m.?"

She didn't answer them. One, lack of time. Two, where to even begin?

Chapter 4

"TA-DA!"

Every head whipped around to behold her, then they came as a mob and engulfed her in greetings.

"I'm amazed you're alive now!"

"Thought we might've lost you, Verity."

"Don't take this the wrong way, but you smell…uh, not great."

"I didn't know you were in Phi Delta Gamma."

"I'm not. Fraternities are weird." She returned Jerry Hart's hug. "But I didn't have any clothes, what with being naked in a lake and all." She poked at the sweatshirt. "I dunno what kind of fabric softener this guy uses, but I want it."

"That explains the towel, then."

She grinned and looked down at the SpongeBob SquarePants towel knotted around her waist. "Give me a break, Jerry. I wasn't in a position to complain. Also, frat guys named Biff are super nice."

Les Mearn, their de facto leader, was at first rigid with surprise then let out an exuberant yowl, pushing through the others to give her a welcoming whack—

"Ow! Easy, I'm sore all over."

—on the shoulder. "Thought we lost you, kiddo. Great to see you."

"Don't call me *kiddo*, we're the same age, and I'm crushed by your damning lack of faith. Are you gonna eat that?"

Les held the croissant out of her reach, because he was

a dope who courted death everywhere he went. "Don't you dare, it's the last one. There's a bunch of jelly doughnuts on the other table."

Verity wrinkled her nose. "Stuffed doughnuts, ugh."

"I've seen you eat garbage, Verity," Les said, like it was weird or something. "Literal garbage."

"That was for a bet. Fine, I'll choke down one of these puffy, oozy monstrosities." She poked at the swollen pastries. "Any fruit?"

"This has purple in it," Maggie Rule said, pointing. The petite—she was even shorter than Verity—brunette with the deep tan was a *Simpsons* superfan; 100 percent of her dialogue was lifted from episodes. The show had been on so long, Maggie rarely had trouble coming up with appropriate phrases. "Purple is a fruit."

Verity snorted. "Dammit, Maggie, one of these days a situation will present itself that *Simpsons* dialogue can't cover, and I really, really want to be there when it happens."

Maggie grinned and shook her head so hard, she ruffled her crew cut. "Not a chance."

"All right!" Les said briskly. "It's great that Verity's not dead, but—"

"I feel like you could end the sentence at that point," she said around a mouthful of doughnut and purple, ahem, "fruit."

"It *is* great, but we've gotta address more pressing questions. For example, at what point in the evening's festivities did you misplace your clothes?" Jerry asked. A head taller than she was, Jerry was the most amiable were she'd ever met. Verity tried to sidestep stereotypes, but Jerry was a slim and gangly vegetarian with the big brown eyes and reflexes of a mildly sedated deer and wouldn't yell if someone set him on fire. Which, as he was a werehart, made sense. He had a headful of shaggy, reddish-blond hair, an explosion of freckles from forehead to chin, and a scraggly neck beard he scratched when he didn't think anyone was looking. He clutched his ubiquitous, dirt-stained notebook and continued, "And where'd you end up?"

"Berne's den."

"Whoa! That's on the far side! And Lake Minnetonka isn't exactly a pond."

"Tell me." Twenty-two miles at its widest part. She only had to swim about six, thank God.

"No," Jerry corrected. "You tell *me.* Did you talk to him? Did he yell at you to get off his land like some coot farmer? What's he like?" He pulled out a pen. "Inquiring minds want to et cetera."

"You really do need a decoy notebook. The real one and the one you don't care if your little sister reads."

"Don't change the subject. Good idea, by the way, she's super nosy. What was he like?"

"Big. Deep voice, cool accent. Super startled to find me on his lawn. Clumsy. Surprised I wasn't bald. No yelling. And I gotta say, that man can rock a baby-blue robe."

"A class act all the way," Maggie snickered.

Berne was the bear everyone knew but no one had met. Werebears were rare bears—she could count on both hands and one foot how often she'd met one in two decades—and when one moved into the territory, word got around. It was probably just as well Stables had no idea Shifters of any sort—wolves, lynxes, harts, wolverines—were living snout to snout with them. And if they ever found out werebears were a thing, Stables would set the planet on fire. As a species, they weren't known for their restraint.

Unlike most Shifters, she didn't feel especially sorry for Stables. *"Oh, no, poor things, locked into one shape all their lives, poor luckless bastards..."* Nope. There were worse things than not being able to shift. And yeah, Stables couldn't shift, but they were apex all the way, and not just because they had the numbers. There wasn't a more gluttonous, bloodthirsty species anywhere in the world. She didn't pity them. She feared them. And so did any Shifter with half a brain.

She accepted warm congrats from the others, all squibs she knew less well than Jerry and Maggie: Norm Hansen, bespectacled werebadger, and Darcy Linn, werewolf.

"I knew you'd be fine," Norm said, beaming. "And isn't that what all this is for? We're not genetic throwbacks in need of protection. We're formidable on our own."

"Or, better, in a group," Darcy added. "One of these days, there'll be dozens of us, all who think the same way. Who knows what we'll accomplish?"

"Careful, Darcy, you're giving off some SAS vibes right now," Jerry warned.

Darcy took exception, as Darcy does. "I'm not a speciesist," she snapped. "There's middle ground between refusing to team up and signing on with a bunch of slack-jawed terrorists. We can create a formidable group without turning into the Shifter version of the KKK."

"That's not what I meant," Jerry protested.

"Then what *did* you mean?"

"I forgot, you're scary right now. SAS is gross. I think we can all agree on that, right? Which is why it's so aggravating that they're the sect of Shifters that thinks squibs are valuable."

Verity rolled her eyes. Back in the day, SAS would openly recruit squibs for spying. A Shifter who could never shift (and thus could never give themselves away, inviting all sorts of dangerous and inconvenient speculation) was a valuable commodity.

But only to terrorists. As for "back in the day," for all she knew, SAS was still recruiting squibs for their species war. At least their numbers were dwindling since their uncool heyday and Bullshit Race War anniversary.[1] Everyone in the room yearned for the day when the reaction to someone talking about SAS was "What the hell is SAS?"

"All right, all right," Les said, hurrying to the front of the room and flipping the whiteboard over, revealing the new and improved damp dares. "Settle down. Let's get back to it."

They gave him their attention, because Les tended to do things like pace and whine and wring his oddly small hands when he fretted he didn't have the room. Verity wasn't sure if all werecoyotes were like that or if it was a trait peculiar to Les, but the more he paced and worried and whined, the more she had to fight the urge to knock him over and sit on him until he quit with the fidgeting.

Les was crossing off and erasing and writing on his beloved whiteboard. (It wasn't even his only whiteboard! Who keeps a spare whiteboard in their trunk?) The dry eraser wasn't much smaller than his hand, and the fluorescent lighting picked up reddish highlights in his sand-colored hair, which was annoying: Why did men get all the effortless highlights? And the long eyelashes? So many men had Elizabeth Taylor lashes, while she needed several coats of mascara or she looked like an angry seal. "So Verity did all

---

1. The gory details of the Bullshit Race War anniversary can be found in *A Wolf After My Own Heart*.

the shots, blitzed the playground, snuck in and out of Stable Central, swam across Lake Minnetonka with no equipment of any kind—"

"Gotta hand it to you," Jerry murmured, sketching a playground in his notebook.

"Busy night," she whispered back and nearly giggled. She'd never been simultaneously giddy and exhausted before joining these adorable weirdos. She squashed the urge to hug Jerry, a man she'd only known for five months, who had in that time become the best friend ever, not least because he'd introduced her to the group.

"—and made it back by the time today's meeting started."

"I can do that, but I don't wanna." From Maggie.

"And so." Les held up the holiest of holies: a tiny gold star, the kind kindergarten teachers licked and then pressed on their students' papers. The room was hushed as he solemnly walked over and stuck it in the middle of Verity's forehead.

She rolled her eyes in a vain attempt to see the shiny star. "I've…I've never been so happy."

"No one deserves it more," Jerry said warmly. "Except everyone else in this room."

"This must be how Sir Ian McKellen felt when the queen knighted him. Or Mark Hamill!"

"Mark Hamill wasn't knighted."

"Yes, he was, Darcy!"

"This is what the SAS should have been doing," Norm observed. "Handing out gold stars instead of plotting genocide."

"That's enough about SAS," Les ordered.

"Are you gonna forget you've got a gold star in the middle

of your forehead and walk around getting funny looks for the rest of the day, like last time?"

"Fuck off and die, Jer," she replied happily. "I need my phone. I need to take a thousand pictures of my forehead. Ten thousand!"

"Darcy, do *not* give Verity's phone back," Jerry ordered. "Nobody's got time for you to immortalize your forehead."

The argument might have raged for a while, except someone chose that moment to pointedly clear their throat. To Verity's intense surprise, Magnus Berne was hovering in the doorway of Radisson Blu's conference room B, looking confused and sheepish and intrigued at the same time. Or perhaps he was just constipated.

"Am I interrupting?"

Chapter 5

"YOU KNOW YOU ARE," VERITY REPLIED WHEN IT BECAME obvious no one was going to answer him. "It's completely obvious that we're doing something and that you're interrupting the something we're doing."

She watched Berne approach and was annoyed to feel her pulse jump at the man's increasing proximity. He'd ditched the robe for cargo shorts, sockless loafers, and a navy-blue polo shirt. His thick, dark hair was standing up in spots, like he'd been raking his fingers through it; his jaw bloomed with dark stubble. There were shadows beneath his deep-brown eyes; the guy was either big-time stressed or not sleeping. Or both.

"Are you all right?" he asked in a voice that wasn't deep and sexy at all.

"Why does everyone open with that? And how'd you even find me?"

"Because I can drive faster than you can swim. Barely," he added in a mutter. He even had the gall to look put out.

"And why'd you even find me?"

Magnus didn't answer. He was too busy looking around the room, taking in the whiteboard, the wide-eyed group of strangers (none of whom had uttered a word), and the, ahem, fruit-filled doughnuts. "What's going on?"

"Private business," Verity snapped. "No outsiders, so scram."

He blinked. "Private? You're in a conference room at the Radisson Blu."

"Great. So if a hotel hosts a wedding reception, anyone can just barge right in?"

"Uh…yeah. I mean, it happens all the time, lass."

Adding to the list of annoying qualities: sexy Scottish burr.

"And why *not* the Blu?" she challenged. "It's inside a huge mall, there's tons of people around to provide cover if we have to ditch—"

"Why would you have to ditch?"

Verity ignored his reasonable-yet-nosy question. "Plus, free Wi-Fi. Pitchers of ice water. And the food court is *right there*."

"The only court we can never be in contempt of," Maggie added.

Les cleared his throat and stepped forward. "Hi. I'm Les Mearn. We're the Damp Squibs."

"Whoa!" Verity yelped. "Whatever happened to 'the first rule of Fight Club is coincidentally the first rule of Damp Squibs, only with croissants'? Don't talk about Damp Squibs!"

"And she's the Seventh Squib," Les added, because he'd lost his fucking mind.

"Magnus Berne," Magnus Berne replied, ignoring her outburst in favor of shaking Les's proffered hand. "Sorry t'barge in on your little group here. I found th'lass on my property and was wurred."

"I'm fiiiiiiiiiiine!" Verity all but yowled. "Everyone stop worrying right this second!" She turned back to Magnus. "I'm fine, we're all fine, literally every single thing is fine. Help yourself to a purple pastry and run along."

"A word, please?" Before she could reply, Les had clamped

a hand around her bicep and pulled her to the front of the room. "This could be huge for us," he said in a low voice.

"He can hear us, Les."

Les leaned closer, his breath redolent of Crest and croissant. "I think we should show him around, let him see who we are."

"He's seen everything. Your whiteboard is right there. We're all here in this twenty-by-thirty conference room. Which he has also seen. That's the tour, basically."

Les took a page out of Magnus's book and ignored her on-point points. "I think if we explained some of what we're up against, Magnus could be a real ally."

"Again: he can hear us, Les. There was no need to haul me up to the front of the room. We could have had this conversation from where we were. If we were in the ballroom, that'd be one thing, but—"

"He can legitimize us!" he hissed.

She drew back at that. She had never, not once, *ever* thought such a thing would come out of Lester Mearn's mouth. "No," she replied, incredulous. "He can't. That's not up to him. It's not up to anyone but the people in this room. Besides Magnus. Anyone in the room besides Magnus Berne."

"That's not what I meant. I'm betting we could recruit more squibs if they saw a bear like Magnus was on board. If he's with us, we're not just a tight little pack of malcontents who can't shift."

"Whoa!"

"We have allies, and those allies know we're doing what needs to be done. Aren't you tired of all the stereotypes?"

"You know I am."

"He can help us show people we transcend them."

There was a low rumble as Magnus cleared his throat. "For what it's worth, I would like to see what you're about. Verra much."

"See? He heard every word." To Magnus: "Nuh-uh."

"It's nothing bad," Jerry ventured. "Well. It's nothing really *really* bad. Laws are occasionally, um, flouted."

Les was almost shoving Verity toward Magnus. "Why don't you guys go grab a cup of coffee and get acquainted?"

"Jesus, Les." Verity shook off his clammy grip. "Have you secretly been the host of a dating game show this whole time?"

"And why would you do that?" Maggie added.

"I could buy you some suitable clothes," Magnus added, because for some reason it was suddenly 1952.

"I don't need you to buy me shit, and I resent your petty judgments on my attire of choice. All *right*, Les, don't *push*."

Three seconds later, they were on the wrong side of the conference room door.

"What just happened?" Verity wondered aloud. And, when Magnus opened his mouth, "Rhetorical."

"I was about tae buy you some clothes."

"Forget it. As an honorary member of Phi Delta Gamma"—she indicated the sweatshirt—"I will cherish these forever and possibly be buried in them. I'm starving. Let's nosh."

He didn't reply, just stood there blinking at her like a big, ~~yummy~~ irritating dumbass.

"Swimming back to the mainland from your island paradise burned up a shit ton of calories, and I hate the purple stuff lurking inside those doughnuts, so let's eat. It's not a date. It's a non-doughnut breakfast meeting so we can talk about things that, until five minutes ago, were never to be spoken of with outsiders. Also, I think Les might be running a fever. Something's up."

"Oh. No! No, no." Magnus shook his head like he was trying to dislodge a wasp. "No, definitely not a date, lass."

"Okay, then."

"I would never take you out," he continued because he was a great big dope. "Nothing like that at all, I can promise."

"Got it."

"I canna put this too strongly. I am not taking you out."

"I like how you keep emphasizing that a date with me would be an all-around terrible idea."

"Not terrible," he replied, still shaking his head. "It just shouldna happen. And willna happen."

"Thanks for clarifying. Now my self-confidence is skyrocketing! Just kidding. My self confidence isn't dependent on you."

She marched away, head held high—as dignified an exit as was possible in flip-flops.

Chapter 6

THE MALL OF AMERICA WAS THE PERFECT ENCAPSULA-
tion of America: lots of space, a dizzying array of things to choose from, people of all shapes and genders and skin colors, busy but not crowded, and a little too much.

"I'm not answering any questions," Verity said, munching her way through something called a Cinnabon.

He couldn't decide which eye was prettier, the green or the brown. "I—I didna say anything."

"It's all over your face, pal. Do you play poker? You should stop."

Hmm. He *was* a poor poker player, come to think of it. He'd assumed it was from disinterest rather than an utter lack of poker face. Something to ponder, perhaps.

"I've never seen anyone devour a pastry the size of their head before."

She laughed. "You should see how many marshmallows I can fit in my mouth."

Is that an offer? "And you ordered extra-*extra* frosting," he marveled, putting the mental image of her cheeks bulging with marshmallows out of his head with no small effort.

"I know! I'll definitely need a nap later. That's the price you pay when you dance with the 'Bon." She chewed, chewed, swallowed. Eyed the remnants. Took another bite, chewed more. "So. About our little club. You remember— the one you barged in on?"

"I remember," he replied dryly.

"We're adventurers."

"And?"

"That's it." She spread her hands. "Nutshell."

"Then why the secrecy?"

"Because it's nobody's business," she snapped. "And there's hardly any criming. And they're victimless crimes."

He gritted his teeth over the absurdity of turning nouns into verbs. "You trespassed on my private property." Well. His landlord's property.

"Which victimized you how, exactly?"

"The mannequins were starting to unnerve me," he admitted.

"What are you talking about?"

"Dummies."

"Whoa! Totally uncalled for."

He sighed. "I meant someone's been dumping store mannequins in my yard. But not you guys," he realized by her dumbfounded expression.

"Jeez, no." Her tone was equal parts astonished and intrigued. "Of course not! Who's got the time? And to what end?"

Excellent questions. "So your little club hasn't been messing with me."

"Oh, *man*, the ego on you."

"It's not about ego!" He was almost sure. "Someone's been leaving naked lady mannequins in my yard. And then you were in my yard."

"Also naked." She nodded. "Okay, fair assumption." She laughed. "No wonder you shrieked when you turned me over."

He grinned at the memory. "Would you believe it was a shout of surprise? A deep, manly shout?"

"I believe you screamed like a tiny, tiny girl."

"Fair," he admitted. "Give me points for a prompt recovery at the least."

"Never. Maybe your friends are pranking you? If you. Um. Have any? On this side of the pond, I mean," she added hastily. There was a dab of frosting on her nose. He had to actively suppress the urge to wipe it off. Or kiss it off. It would be worth the felony assault that would surely follow. "I'm sure you've got gobs of friends in Scotland."

"That would be an incorrect assumption." Well, there was his neighbor, the Earl of Stair, John David James Dalrymple. Or was it David John James? They'd been neighbors for twenty years, nice fellow, that John David or David John. They got together all the time. Well. Some of the time. In fact, his best mate John David or David John was the one to tell Magnus that coyotes and wolves were being reintroduced to Scotland. Sure, he was more interested in finding a market for his ewes before predators descended than in getting a pint somewhere, but the fact remained he had friends, at least one friend, and his name was John David. Most likely.

And there was what's-his-name, too, from Armchair Books in Edinburgh. Whenever Magnus came to pick up an antique, the fellow was always friendly. Though it could be argued that *friendly* wasn't a synonym for *friend*…

"Okay, so maybe you don't have piles of bosom buds. That's okay."

"I know it's okay," he almost-but-not-quite snapped.

"Simmer. And trust me, whoever's doing that weird thing with nude, bald dummies, it's not us. What would be the point?"

"What's the point of your little club?"

"Wow, you really put a condescending spin on that, didn't you?"

"Fair. I apologize. But whatever you're called, at the end of the day, you're just kids acting on dares."

"Yep." He must have looked as surprised as he felt, for she added, "What, was that my cue to hotly deny it? And talk about how it's *not* immature and *not*, at least on some levels, silly in addition to being dangerous?" She shrugged then glugged the rest of her milk. "That's the Damp Squibs in a nutshell. But you can cram the 'kids' thing. I'm twenty-five."

A child, he thought from his lofty age of thirty-four. "You're a bear." Not a question; he'd know one of his own kind anywhere. Verity smelled like moss and sunshine and her own essential self and carried herself like a predator so high up, she hadn't much to worry about. And yet, something was…not "off," and certainly nothing negative, but there was something here he couldn't quite figure. "Maybe one of the wee ones?"

"Florida black," she replied shortly.

"Kamchatka brown." He'd never met a Florida black werebear but assumed they were a smaller, cuter sub-species. The novelty of such a creature was the only reason he opened his mouth and heard utter nonsense escape. "Lass, you don't haveta run around looking for dares to keep busy. You can come to my island if you're needing room to romp."

"Room to romp? Magnus, if that's a sex thing, you're about to get a face full of Cinnabon frosting."

Ack! He'd never get the smell out of his hair. "No, no."

"You're right. That was a bluff. I'd never waste frosting

on your face. I'd just smack you in the balls seven or eight times."

The thought made him blanch. She was small but seemed entirely capable. "I just meant…you're obviously looking for something you don't yet have."

"You've got that part right, at least."

"And you wouldna need to worry about being seen in your other form. It's verra private."

She let out a bark of laughter. "Of all the things I'm currently worrying about—and they are legion—being seen as a bear is not one of them."

"I don't even have to be there if it would make you uncomfortable," he persisted.

"Where would you be?" she asked sweetly. "Organizing your dummy collection?"

"It's not *my* collection." *Don't pout. It's not a good look.* "It's someone else's."

"Possession is nine-tenths of the law, pal. Well, this has been fascinating," she announced as she pushed her tray back. "But I have to nap and then eat and then maybe work, I dunno, I'll have to check the schedule. Just kidding! I'm the one who makes the schedule. Just kidding! I don't actually have a job." Her nostrils flared and she turned. "Hey, Jerry."

"Hey." The lanky hart had come up behind him (fucking allergies), one hand stuffed past the wrist in his pocket, the other clutching a battered blue notebook, a quizzical smile on his face.

"Ach! Y'scared me, lad." To Verity: "Allergies."

"Really?" she replied, sounding delighted. "But you're so big!"

"I don't think size is, y'know, a factor," Jerry said. "My mom gets allergies this time of year, too. She swears by Benadryl and vodka."

"There isn't enough Benadryl in the world for mine," Magnus said ruefully, and they laughed.

"Okay, sorry to interrupt. I was just wondering if you wanted a ride home."

Magnus opened his mouth to offer but was cut off by Verity's "Soundsgreatlet'sgorightnow." To Magnus: "Gotta run."

Indeed. It seemed to be a characteristic: dashing off when things started to get interesting.

"And d'you need a ride to the memorial?" Jerry added.

"No" was the curt reply, and she was already getting up.

Magnus raised his eyebrows. "Memorial?"

"Uh, yeah." Jerry looked a bit taken aback at Verity's throat-slashing motion and Magnus's sharp, sudden question. "For Andy Bray. He died—hey—died last month—don't do that, Ver—but the memorial wasn't until now—ow, don't *pinch*—anyway, he's dead."

"Jerry! What are you doing?" she cried.

"He's supposed to be in the loop!" Jerry replied. He scratched his beard in his agitation. "It's why you're having a breakfast date! Isn't it?"

In unison: "It's not a date!"

"Died...doing one of your wet dares?" Had to be, Magnus realized, or the woman wouldn't be having a minor nervous breakdown before his eyes.

"Damp Squib, yeah," Jerry replied. "He slipped."

Magnus was on his feet before he knew he'd moved. "Your childish dares are getting people killed?"

"He was an adult" was Verity's short reply. "We all are. And it was his choice. What's the point—"

"Precisely!"

"—if you're not putting something on the line?"

"*Something* on the line?" Christ. And here he thought *he'd* been cavalier about living lately. Not to mention back in the day.

(*No, don't think about that; the past is long gone except for the nightmares.*)

"You have to stop doing this immediately!"

"Just her?" Jerry asked. "Or all of us?"

"All of you!" Magnus jerked a thumb in Verity's direction. "But especially her!"

Verity snarled and batted her tray aside. "Les was wrong and this was a bad idea and Les should feel bad on account of all the wrongness." She glared while adjusting the SpongeBob towel across her hips. "You can't help, and even if you could, it's none of your business, and we have to go. I don't know what I was thinking, and I definitely don't know what Les was thinking. The only saving grace of this not-a-date was the Cinnabon, bye."

"You don't *have* to go," Magnus replied, trying not to sulk. "You don't have a job."

"My cats don't feed themselves, Magnus Berne! Except they do because I bought one of those automatic cat feeders. Just kidding, I don't have cats! And don't you dare!" she added, snatching at the small container of frosting on her tray.

"I wasn't! And you can't possibly still be hungry," he snapped.

"This is for tomorrow's toast or maybe a post-nap frosting shot!" she retorted, then grabbed for Jerry's—

"You'd better not pinch me again, or no car ride for you."

—hand and dashed away, and all he could do was stare after her like an addled adolescent.

And then swear when he realized that in all the nonsense, he had never gotten her full name.

Chapter 7

A CELEBRATION OF LIFE...

On Sunday, July 22, there will be a memorial service for Andrew Bray, son of Lillian and Peter Bray, to commemorate Andrew's life and indomitable spirit.

Andrew passed away last month after a fall from Minnehaha Falls in Minneapolis. He had just completed his master's degree. He was twenty-six.

The service will be held at Unity Church in Saint Paul at 10:00 a.m. A livestream of the memorial can be found on Unity Church's website.

May his soul rest.

Chapter 8

"I THINK HER NAME MIGHT BE JESUS. SHE SAID THAT A lot."

"No, that would indicate she thinks *your* name is Jesus. It's not, though. Right? You'd tell me if your name was secretly Jesus? Magnus? Right?"

Magnus rubbed his eyes. "Lad, I'm trying to think why I came t'you…"

"We're all wondering that," Lila said cheerfully.

Thoroughly nonplussed, Magnus had left the Mall of America and found himself in Lilydale. He'd had no destination in mind when he'd settled behind the wheel, only realizing where he was headed when he passed the purple house with the purple birdhouse. Twenty seconds later, he was pulling into the driveway of a century-old house, deep gray with brown trim and a large front porch, where the fireplaces worked but were never used, the garden shed was a hot chocolate hideaway, and the front and back doors were always locked but immediately unlocked for friends.

Five minutes after that, he was having breakfast with Mama Macropi, Oz Adway, Annette Garsea, and Lila Kai herself: the first Stable friend he'd ever had. Well. *Friend* might be an exaggeration… They'd only known each other a couple of months. Not like the years he'd known the Earl of Stair, John David James. Or David John James.

Fond acquaintance? Pleasant companions? Well, *pleasant* wasn't right…for him *or* Lila… Anyway, he'd found himself telling them the whole story, from discovering the lass on his island to her exit at the Mall of America.

"So that's what your weird call was about," Oz said. "I was worried you were having a series of small strokes. Not worried enough to, y'know, actually do something, but still."

"No such luck," he replied gloomily and decided not to notice how Oz and Lila traded glances. "So now the daffy lass is off again, no doubt looking for more lethal trouble."

"Daffy? Watch your mouth, Magnus," Mama Mac mock scolded then leaned over to fork five more pancakes onto his plate.

"Noted." Magnus made a concerted effort not to inhale the pancakes; he hadn't touched a thing on the not-a-date breakfast date. Too busy gaping at…uh…whoever she was.

"So she washed up on your shore…" Lila prompted.

"I didna see her wash up. She swam up, I believe. For a dare. And then fell asleep. It's quite a swim. The poor lass was probably tired." Extremely so, he realized. It was summer, but the mornings could be chilly. Regardless, she fell asleep or passed out with exhaustion while soaking wet in the nude. He rubbed his face. "Ah, Christ, I feel bad about waking her up with a foot in her ribs."

"As you should," Annette observed.

"And I didna scream when she opened her eyes. In case you were, ah, wondering."

"No one was wondering that," Oz said.

"Don't feel too bad, Magnus. She could have been carrying a gun." This from Lila, because she was a Stable who had a few guns of her own.

Oz put down his fork. "Where the hell could a naked lady conceal a gun?"

Lila opened her mouth to answer (which was horrifying), and Mama jumped in to cut her off. "What did she look like? Was she pretty?"

"Gorgeous. Deep-red hair. Pale skin."

"Pallor," Annette suggested and snickered. "Possibly from hypothermia."

"Like an Irish milkmaid," he corrected. "Small and slender. And her eyes! One green, one brown. And her pert—"

"That's fine," Mama said hastily. "I don't need all the particulars."

"I still can't get over—she washed up naked?" Oz asked.

"Swam up," he corrected. "Yes. And then she ran—swam off. No doubt to find more trouble."

"Not to sound cavalier," Lila said, and Magnus braced himself for her to sound cavalier. "But why do you care?"

"Don't assume I do, lass."

A silence that could only be described as skeptical followed that remark.

He tried again. "She's just so—"

"Full of life?" From Mama Mac.

"Weird?" From Lila, who would know weird.

"Not a store mannequin?" Oz guessed.

"Yes," Magnus surrendered. "All of those. Yes. All right."

"But isn't it her business?" Mama Mac—Meredith Macropi—had settled back into her seat. She was a short, older woman with a head full of blond-gray curls and the bright-blue eyes of a Kewpie doll. She'd raised Annette and Oz, among many others, nearly always had a house full of kids, and was anywhere from fifty to eighty years old (no one dared ask). "Lord knows I've seen my share of Shifter nonsense from young people—and some not so young!"

"I feel like that was a not-so-direct reference to me," Oz said.

"But don't we all go through it? The predators may be a bit more than, say, marsupials. But at some point, they're driven to test themselves. It comes hand in paw with adolescence. Or late bloomers, like your young lady."

"She's not my young lady." *Prove themselves. Yes, that's what they were doing. But why? And to whom?* "And I don't think this is postadolescent angst." Problematically, he didn't know *what* it was.

"Mama's right. It's her life, Magnus." Annette made a threatening motion with her folk when Oz tried to sneak the last quarter pound of bacon. "Hers to risk or not."

What? "By that logic," Magnus snapped, "you'd never talk a jumper off a bridge."

Annette shook her head. "False equivalence. Someone seeking suicide actually wants to die. This group you're talking about just wants to test themselves, or at least that's what it sounds like. So, going by *your* logic, you have a moral obligation to stop every rock climber, race car driver, Everest seeker, skydiver, BASE jumper, SCUBA diver, and cat wrangler." She paused to sip her tea then continued, "I wouldn't advise that."

"It's not—that's not—" She was wrong, and he knew she was wrong, but damned if he could figure out how, much less put it into words. "I'm wurred if I don't intervene, she won't live out the week."

"That's bad news, since it's already Thursday," Lila observed. "Her days are numbered, depending on if you think Saturday's the last day of the week or Sunday is."

"One of her wet friends already died."

Mama's forehead furrowed. "Oh, dear. What happened?"

"Dunno, the lass freaked out and then raced away. Possibly because of a dare."

"Damn," Lila commented. "Hard-core dares."

"Moot, though, right?" Oz pushed his chair back, inspected his bespoke white shirt for crumbs or (horrors!) bacon grease, then stood. "You don't know her name or where she lives. Where any of them live. And she gave you the slip at the mall, sounds like."

They had. Magnus had sat at the table for thirty seconds or so then made up his mind to go after her (again) but (fucking allergies) couldn't pick up the scent of a Florida black werebear or a red hart in all those people. Only Cinnabon and thwarted frustration.

"I can't believe you're not more concerned," he blurted. "You're IPA! Social workers for child services! Of a sort."

"Technically I'm still an accountant." From Oz. "And the lady in question is an adult."

Magnus ignored the irrelevant interruption. "And Lila, you're a surgeon!"

"Teddy bear surgeon," Lila replied. "I feel like you left that part out on purpose. To try and make your point. Also, I'm not sure what point that is. And to be blunt, *we* can't believe *you're* concerned."

"Maybe she'll come to your island again," Mama Mac suggested, cutting off an argument before it could begin, because she was a clever, clever woman.

He let out a bark of laughter then apologized. "Ah. I don't think so." Life was never so simple. And she'd made her dislike more than plain.

(*So why not let this go?*)

(Because—because what if she ends up dead, too?) He rubbed his forehead and glared at the table. *Lord save me from an acute case of Lancelot syndrome.*

"She doesn't have to come to you." Lila, who was never happier than when looking something up, waved her tablet at him. "You can go to her."

He took the tablet then nearly dropped it (in pancakes!) when he noticed the memorial notice for one Andrew Bray.

Lila pushed her glasses farther up the bridge of her nose and grinned. "This is the point where I say 'ta-da!' and you talk about how terrific I am." Her glasses enhanced her bright gaze, which was in turn enhanced by the mass of curly blond hair that made her look, as the besotted Oz described her, "Like Orphan Annie if she were sexy and packed heat."

"So there you go," Lila finished. "What are the odds that there's more than one Andrew Bray having a memorial tomorrow?"

"Ah. Huh." Magnus cleared his throat. "Well, thank you."

"Your generation will catch on to search engines one of these days," Lila replied. "Classes are available to help you."

"I'm thirty-four!"

"That's the spirit."

"Lass, I'm not sure this is…"

Oz pooh-poohed his (half-hearted) protest. "You already told what's-her-toes you think crashing wedding receptions is fine, so why not a memorial?"

"That isna exactly what I—"

Annette broke in. "Do you want company? I can free up my morning."

"I could, too," Mama Mac put in quickly.

He shook his head so hard, he was momentarily dizzy. "That's not necessary."

"You don't have to go alone," Mama Mac added.

He tried again. "Going alone isn't the—"

"We could all go with you," Lila suggested. "Strength in numbers, once more into the breach, dear friends, et cetera."

"No, no. That's..." He looked around the small group and said with sudden realization, "You *want* me to do this. Verra much."

"Mostly I want you out of my kitchen," Lila replied. "I don't actually care where you go once you've gone."

Oz waved that off. "Ignore her. She doesn't want anyone to know she's secretly sweet and thoughtf—ow!"

"P'rhaps I will, then."

Mama Mac smiled so widely, her eyes were nearly swallowed by her laugh lines. "Good for you!"

"This wouldn't be a date," he reminded them.

"I just like that you're getting out and meeting people," Mama Mac said.

"This. Wouldn't. Be. A. Date."

"Maybe you'll meet someone at the funeral home!" Mama continued brightly.

Ye gods. Her undaunted optimism is terrifying.

They had been treating him like a widower since he confessed his long-time infatuation with the late Sue Smalls, which should teach him to lay off the hard seltzer. (He'd only had seven, and then only because it was bloody hot that morning!)

And it was absurd anyway. He'd moved on over a decade ago; Sue had been happily married longer than that. They'd barely dated in college; he'd never seen her naked. They exchanged Christmas cards and followed each other on social media but hadn't seen each other for years. They hadn't even spoken in the eighteen months before she killed herself to save her family.

But this small group of friends/interested bystanders/what-have-you persisted in mistaking his natural preference to be alone for desolate mourning.

"It's kind of ye to offer to come," he said, "but unnecessary. It won't take long. And I won't need an escort. If she's there, I'll warn her and take my leave."

"Great plan. Women love it when their stalker pops up out of nowhere and warns them of danger," Lila said. "It's a fast track to second base."

"It was your idea!" he cried, pointing at her tablet.

"Yeah, well, again: I want you out of my kitchen. All of you."

"Even me?" Oz asked.

"Especially you," Lila replied but softened it with a smile.

Magnus got to his feet. "Thank you for breakfast, Mama Mac."

"Oh, anytime!"

"You're coming to the wedding, right?" Annette asked. "Whenever it is. And wherever."

"I don't believe you and David are getting married," Oz said. "You're so vague on the details. The whole thing sounds like a gift grab."

"What details? We haven't decided anything yet. Well, we talked about a destination wedding to Cairo, or perhaps the Amalfi Coast, but only to make a point about the selfishness inherent in destination weddings."

"Exactly! You haven't solidified anything. I feel like you're pranking us. Which is a terrible thing to do to Mama," he added then beamed when that earned him an affectionate pat. And a less-than-affectionate poke from Annette.

"Leave your sister be," Mama said. "It takes time to plan it right."

"I'd like to come," Magnus lied, as weddings were the worst, "but I canna commit if I don't know when it is."

"No one will ever know," Oz said. "Because it's a prank. Ow!"

"There's a lot going on," Annette said vaguely. "And a lot to consider. It's not just about David and me."

Oz grinned. "Plus you should give David every chance to back ou—ow!"

"Well, send me an invitation when you have the details," Magnus said.

"You'll just have to stick around to find out what they are," Annette said.

Magnus was struck by a thought… Was Annette keeping the details vague to keep him around?

No. No, that was conceited beyond belief. The lass said it herself: there was a lot to consider. Whatever that meant.

"I'll be heading back," he continued, with no idea of where he actually wanted to go.

"Call us if you need anything," Annette said.

"Or if more dummies wash ashore." Lila glanced around the table. "What? It's weird and only slightly ridiculous. So I'm interested."

"I'm fine," he said.

"Of course you are," Mama Mac replied. "No one's said otherwise."

"I'm fine," he said again, because repetition was the key with this group. "Really."

Chapter 9

HE WASN'T FINE.

Chapter 10

JERRY HART ("OF THE RIVIERA HARTS") LIVED IN A WHITE walkout rambler in Apple Valley's Briar Oaks neighborhood two blocks from the zoo, which Verity found hilarious. "So if the wolves and cheetahs and monk seals make a break for it, you guys are first on the menu."

"Don't be silly," he replied. "The zoo doesn't have any cheetahs."

Jerry always insisted on driving, but on the rare occasions he couldn't, Verity came by to pick him up. He must've been running late, because after five minutes, a bored Verity got out of her car,

Serves me right for not bringing a book.

knocked on the front door, and was invited in by Mama Hart.

Who was a Stable!

"I'm so happy to meet you," she said with a smile. "Jerry just adores you."

"Can you blame him? I ooze adorability." Verity glanced around the living room, decorated with low, comfortable couches, some end tables, and several family photos. "These pics! Debate *and* Speech *and* Mathletes. The sliver of geekiness I detected in Jerry is a full-on nerd stripe."

Mrs. Hart laughed. "Don't talk about his after-school activities. It embarrasses him."

"Shouldn't have given me that ammunition, Mrs. Hart." Verity kept her eyes on the photos so she wouldn't ask the wrong questions. She knew there were interspecies couples in the world—how could it be otherwise?—but probing was rude and roundly discouraged. Once upon a time, Shifters thought that was how squibs were made.

Mrs. Hart's merry blue eyes almost disappeared behind the laugh lines when she smiled. "Wondering how a Stable omnivore with a taste for venison ended up having babies with a Hart?"

"Noooooo. No. No. Yes."

"Would you believe I met him while I was hunting with my folks?"

"I would." Minnesota nice: land of snow and shotguns.

"Tracked him for four miles, and then he turned back into a man, and it was just..." She seemed as enchanted as she had been when she first saw him, which was adorable. "I thought he was magical. Still do. Anytime he wants, he can see the world in an entirely different, wonderful way. Enhanced reflexes and speed, healing—amazing. All of it. And you...um, how do I put this? You turn into a bear, yes? Not that it's my business," she added hastily. "I'm still navigating the protocol, even after almost two decades."

"I hang out with your kid. So it kind of is your business. And no. I don't *turn into* a bear, I *am* a bear. Just. Y'know. A different kind."

"Well, Jerry talks about you all the time, and most of it's positive."

"*Most* is a huge improvement."

"Would you like to stay for din—"

"Aauuggh!"

Verity jumped; she'd heard Jerry coming down the hall, but the anguished yelp took her by surprise.

"Mom! Verity!"

"Yeesh. Calm down. And now that we've taken roll call, are you seriously planning to be seen in public in calf-length, lime-green culottes? Bold choice, Jerry, and if your taste in clothes is crap, I can't fault your courage. And I can't believe we've been friends for months and this is the first time I'm meeting your mom. You—hey!"

Jerry had clamped down on her hand and was dragging her toward the front door. "We're late."

"We aren't, actually. Remember? We were gonna grab a burger before the meetup?" Then, distracted by another picture: "Ha! STEM club!" Verity set her feet to slow their progress to the door. "Look at you in the front row, all cute and smiley. How old's this pic? You look exactly the same. What's your secret? Is it the herbivore diet? Because I would rather age ten years every six months than give up meat."

"Would you really?" Mrs. Hart asked.

"I've stagnated" was Jerry's short reply. "Away with you, Verity. And me, too."

"Home by midnight," Mrs. Hart reminded him.

"Mom! I'm in college now."

"In that case, make it eleven."

"Ha! Nice to meet you, Mrs. Hart. I'll take you up on the dinner thing some other time."

And then Jerry had dragged them out the door and practically shoved her into her own car. "Okay if I drive?" The question was purely for form; he was already buckling his seat belt.

"It's past time for you to admit you've got a hard-on for my baby-blue Prius Prime."

"Gross. I just like being in control."

"Your mom doesn't know where we're going, does she?"

"God, no." Jerry visibly shuddered. "You can't imagine the furor. And how would I explain our clothes? Plus, she'd be like a bloodhound on the scent. Once part of it came out, all of it would come out."

Verity buckled her seat belt. "She seemed nice. Maybe she'd be cool with it."

"Not taking that chance."

"You should be nicer to her."

Jerry snorted. "You should be nicer to yours."

"Well." Verity thought about it for a few seconds. "Yeah."

"—because that's what it all comes down to, Verity."

"Yep."

"Deer are not hot!"

"Yes, you've mentioned this before."

"Deer are never the smoldering bad boys in a paranormal romance!"

So write a paranormal romance where a smoldering deer is a bad boy. JESUS CHRIST, HOW OFTEN ARE WE GOING TO TALK ABOUT THIS?

"Yep," Verity said aloud. "You've told me that."

"I can handle myself in a fight," Jerry continued, because he clearly wanted her to jump out the window. Worse: she was considering it.

"I know. I've seen your savage front-shin kick." Which, it had to be said, was nifty.

He turned to her, which was horrifying since traffic was

whizzing by at 80 miles per hour. "Right? I basically shattered that guy's tibia."

"Yep." Well. *Shattered* was an exaggeration. But the guy probably had a hell of a bruise the next day. Which should teach him to get hopped up on ginger beer and then pick a fight with a mild-mannered, slender geek with a neck beard and a platonic friend who whipped everyone's ass at darts. She had no idea people actually played darts in bars like in the movies. What a delightful evening! Definitely worth being banned for life.

"I'm just saying that the stereotypes *blah-blah-blah* which only makes it more difficult for us to *ramble ramble ramble*, which results in even more *drone drone droooooooone…*"

Verity hit the car window button, stretched her legs, then wiggled her bare feet in the breeze. She smoothed her pale-blue skirt over her knees and listened to Jerry with half an ear while thinking that dangling her feet out a car window wasn't the best idea—Tarantino's *Death Proof* had made that clear.

But movies weren't reality. (Unless they were narrated by Werner Herzog.) Her feet deserved their freedom, dammit! And today of all days, when mortality had to be confronted. Her feet would not live in fear!

"—goddamned infuriating. Verity? You listening?"

"Heard every word, Jerry."

"No, you didn't! You were thinking about your feet again."

"You got me," she admitted. "But in my defense, I've heard this many many many—"

"All right."

"—many many many many—"

"Point made, Verity."

"—many many many many—"

"All *right*." He took the exit, glared at her, looked back at the road. "Got it."

"—many many times. Also, you're being too hard on yourself."

"How so?"

"You're formidable."

"I *know*."

No, Verity thought. *If you knew, if you truly, all-the-way-to-the-bone knew, you wouldn't feel compelled to keep telling everyone. You wouldn't be a Damp Squib. But here we are.* "Besides, some girls like gangly."

That surprised a laugh out of him. "Fuck off, Ver."

"You first, Jer."

Some girls *did* like gangly. Not her. She was more the bulky type. Broad shoulders, long legs, big hands, the kind of feet that—no, she didn't really care about feet. She was more into the type of man who looked great in a bathrobe with mussed hair and a wicked-cool Scottish burr...*oh shit*.

The absolute last thing she should be doing is thinking about Magnus McNosyPants. She should be mourning. Or teasing Jerry some more. Or auditing herself. Or scrubbing out a gas station bathroom. Or anything, anything besides sighing over a Scottish werebear isolating himself on an island in Lake Minnetonka and giving off "I'm so lonely and broody, if only someone understood me" vibes who followed her to a Damp Squib meeting and wanted to ~~go on a date~~ have breakfast with her.

And tell the truth: he was the first man in a while she'd been drawn to. Dating had always been problematic. Mostly she hit the sheets with the Sultan of Suck, her Womanizer Pro. So Magnus's concern (if that's what it was) was, she had to admit, as flattering as it was irritating. But there was no future with a reclusive Scottish werebear who was probably slumming at the moment and homebound any day. And his interest would evaporate like ice on an engine block the moment he realized what she was.

Jerry turned onto Summit Avenue and just in time; now she could think about something besides Magnus Berne. Like how gorgeous the mansions were and how the historic street had two reputations: the Stable and Shifter versions. Stables, who were forever stuck as bipeds and didn't even have the additional strength and speed that squibs like her took for granted, on the right. Shifters, who could show both sides of themselves anytime they liked, and bend metal, and hear pins drop, on the left. Logger barons on the right, Shifter conservationists on the left. Chaplains up street, poachers down street. Empire builders and railroad magnates, politicians and their strange bedfellows, judges and judged, fur traders and fur. If Magnus Berne had been around back then, he would've lived cheek by claw with—

"Dammit!"

"Problem, Ver?"

Yeah. I need to get someone out of my head, but he keeps popping back in. "Just meditating on life and death and—and stuff like that."

"Stuff like that. You're a deep one, Ver," he said and smirked. Before she could retort, or smack him, he had pulled into the Unity Church parking lot. Verity had never been there before; she wasn't entirely sure what a Unitarian *was*

(Are they like Baptists only they're allowed to dance? Or am I thinking of Lutherans?)

but she liked the look of the church as they approached on foot: pale brick, tall windows, and a bank of curving windows that looked almost like an observation deck. And the de rigueur steeple, but this one had such a fat base, it looked like a witch's hat.

And she could smell cookies.

"It's official," she announced. "I'm Unitarian now."

Jer held the door for her, because he was quaint like that. "Your Presbyterian parents aren't going to like that."

"They don't like anything about me." Exaggeration. There was only one thing Ray and Kay Lane didn't like about their daughter, and unlike her religion, there wasn't a thing she could do to change it. But before she could burrow deeper into fret mode, she spotted Maggie and Les loitering near the entrance and started to wave then let her hand fall. It probably wasn't cool to wave at funerals. This was her first.

"Hey," she whispered as they approached. The waiting room or whatever you called it (parlor? narthex? she hadn't been to church since she was a cub) was done in light-blond wood, and the windows let in the summer sunshine. The ceiling was high, making the room feel bigger than it was, and there was a small table to the left of the entrance with pamphlets; she took one.

Maggie, clad neck to ankles in bubblegum pink, greeted them with "I am not looking forward to my funeral."

"Jeez. There really is a *Simpsons* quote for everything. Also, Mags, you should probably watch less television."

"Never!" Maggie glanced around then lowered her voice. "TV gives so much and asks so little."

It wasn't time to go find seats, so they were in a little clump just outside the double doors to the sanctuary. Les stretched out a hand and shook Jerry's while scoping Verity's feet. "You got her to wear shoes. I'm impressed."

Jerry shrugged. "It was all her, man. I barely even had to nag her to put 'em back on before we came in."

"You can both fuck right off," Verity whispered. "Going barefoot is natural to our kind. You're the weirdos for not being into it." Which definitely wasn't fraught with psychological insight, so *that* was all right.

Norm and Darcy showed up at the same time, and after subdued greetings, a short silence fell. Except for Jerry, she didn't have any real friends among the Damp Squibs (the Seventh Squib and last to join, she'd only been one of them for a couple of weeks), so they were reduced to banal chitchat.

"This is a beautiful church," Norm observed.

"A transforming liberal religious experience," Verity read from the pamphlet. "What does that mean?"

"No homophobia?" Jerry suggested. "But loads and loads of cookies?"

"Huh. That *is* transforming."

She cast a nervous eye toward an older couple dressed head to toe in black. They were surrounded by mourners protectively hunched over them, softly sobbing and slumped on the padded bench by the big bank of windows. Presumably Andy's parents. What to say? *Sorry* sounded inadequate. *Inadequate* sounded inadequate.

The doors to the sanctuary opened, thank God, and people began filing in to take their seats. She and the other squibs took seats toward the back, and Verity had a blurred impression of loads of pastels and brights. A couple of weeks ago, Andy had jokingly demanded that if a squib stunt killed him, he wanted bright colors at his funeral. "No black," he insisted. "I look like shit in it." Which was all very amusing at the time because he was only twenty-something and—ha, ha—death wasn't imminent.

All that to say that before today, she'd had no idea you could get a double-breasted suit in banana yellow. And at any other time, Maggie's pink sweatshirt and pink, straight-to-her-ankles nylon skirt might have elicited comment. As would Norm's checked corduroy pants and electric-blue polo shirt. And Darcy's salmon-colored, body-con dress which hugged her from neck to knees. Not this morning; it was a rainbow of weird.

"I definitely want you guys to do this when I die," she whispered to Jerry. "Plus everyone should be chewing gum and constantly popping it. Like, *Chicago* levels of gum popping, the kind that makes people want to kill you. And no flowers! Just bouquets of strawberry Starbursts."

"Noted." Jerry was squinting at the program. "Gah, seven hymns? And they want us to sing all the verses?"

"Surprising number of Stables here," Les commented. "Smells like a fifty-fifty mix."

Maggie leaned forward to scowl at them. "Will you kids shut up?"

They obeyed. And Jerry was wrong. There were nine hymns. It was a wonder the choir didn't have laryngitis when they wrapped up seventy-five minutes later. She'd nearly dozed off—she'd worked late sniffing several brands of almond oil—but Jerry's sharp elbow jerked her back to attention.

Verity stood and waited while other rows filed out. The crowd was understandably subdued, which made her feel guilty. *Should I feel bad about not feeling bad?* Poor Andy's death was a shame. But she'd only met him twice before he went out for his fifth Squib challenge. She had been mildly shocked to hear he'd slipped and died, like she was mildly shocked when the distant cousin she never met died.

And the shameful part: that she felt mild shock but also some vindication. They weren't just blustering, weren't just speculating. Damp Squib shit was dangerous. Andy had proved it, definitively. Which was (argh, so awful to say) a positive. Otherwise, what was the point of any of it?

She closed her eyes and rubbed her temples. *Jesus, I can't believe I thought that. The point of any of it is to prove we're just as formidable. Death is* not *the point.*

And then, before she could block the thought: *I'll bet Andy was asking himself if it was worth it alllllllllll the way down.* If she had time to realize a Damp Squib challenge was going to end her life, would she think it was worth it?

Irrational, she decided. That's what all this was.

"Let's pay our respects to the family," Les began, cutting through her thoughts, and thank God, "and—"

"You." The older woman in black who had sobbed throughout had come right up to them.

"Hi, Mrs. Bray. My name is Les—"

"I know who you are." Then the flat smack of a palm making contact, so hard and fast, it was almost like they heard the slap before her arm moved.

Verity found herself standing in front of a shocked Les, whose cheek was blooming brick red from impact. "Mrs. Bray, this isn't on Les. Andrew made his own...oh hell." Because the grieving mama was winding up again. Worse, Verity would stand still for it. Right? Yes. Hadn't she just been thinking slap-worthy thoughts? That Andy's death validated what the Damp Squibs were about? So she'd stay put for the smack. Unless Andy's mother went for a hammer or something. She drew the line at felony assault.

But before the smack could land, Mrs. Bray's arm stopped like it hit a wall. Which it had.

"I'm verra sorry for your loss, ma'am. But dinna do that."

Chapter 11

"ARE YOU COMPLETELY IRRATIONAL?"

"Verra possibly," Magnus admitted.

Verity fought the urge to rip out her own hair. "What are you even doing here? Did you stalk me again, you bugfuck fruitcake?"

He blinked at *bugfuck*. "Not. Ah. Overtly. An acquaintance helped me deduce where you'd be this morning. So."

"Great. Tell your stalker-enabling pal that I suggested they cordially fuck off."

"We're not exactly pals. More like—"

"Stop trying to make this a conversation! I'm yelling at you!"

"Way to get us thrown out of a funeral, guys." From Jerry, who had ambled out after them. He took out his ubiquitous notebook and crossed something out. "Gotta thank you both. Figured that'd be on my bucket list for at least another decade."

"You're in danger," Magnus said urgently.

Verity felt like she was strangling on the words. "What. Do you think. You're doing?"

"This is just like a romantic comedy," Jerry observed and was treated to twin death glares.

"No, this is a dramedy where I discover I have a stalker and cut his head off, and everyone lives happily ever after except poor Robert," Verity snapped.

"So romantic," Jerry sighed.

"Guys?" From Les. "We're doing this outside a funeral home. And a ton of people are watching from those big windows. And some of the Stables might notice my face doesn't have a handprint anymore."

Verity nodded. "Right, right, say no more." Maggie, she noticed, had no comment. Finally, a situation not covered by decades of *The Simpsons.* "We're out. C'mon, guys. Not *you*, Magnus! Obviously not you!"

"D'you want to die, lass?" He had the goddamned gall to stand there like a handsome, mournful jackass, all tricked out in a sober black suit she just bet was tailor-made. *Guess he didn't get the memo about no black. Ha! He looks like a dork in that gorgeous suit!* "Like your friend? Is that what this is?"

"Oh my God, I'm not having this discussion right here or anywhere else or with you or anyone else. I don't have a death wish, I don't need to be rescued, and not just me, by the way, no squib needs to be rescued, thanks anyway, kindly go straight to hell."

He was blinking faster while Less, Brad, Darcy, and Maggie looked on like tennis spectators and Jerry kept scribbling. "What?"

"I'm not doing the whole speech again, Magnus."

"What's a squib?"

Now it was her turn: "What?"

He doesn't know?

Is it a trick? Or a language barrier?

For half a second, she didn't want to tell him. Which was shameful; the whole point of the Damp Squibs was that there wasn't a goddamned thing wrong with *any* of them. So, of course, she would tell him. And roughly three seconds later, Magnus would lose all interest in her. Which was excellent.

Right? "A squib is—" Mindful of the other mourners who had begun coming out, she took a step closer and lowered her voice. "A squib is a Shifter who can't shift. We're locked into one shape. C'mon, they must have them in Scotland."

Magnus looked shocked. Like, "a grieving mother hauls off and slaps you out of nowhere" shocked. Then he exhaled in relief. "I knew there was something about you!"

"What?" That was, she had to admit, the most unique reaction from anyone who learned about her squib-ish tendencies.

"We're all saying *what* too much," Jerry observed.

"Now my urge to worry about you makes sense!" Magnus cried.

"And the urge to stalk her at funerals, presumably," Les muttered. "Guys. Again. We have to get out of here."

"He's right," Jerry replied. "Mrs. Bray might be ambidextrous, just waiting to wind up with a left hook. In fact, here they come. Mr. Bray looks like he might want a word, too."

"Let's get out of here," Maggie said, so they did.

Chapter 12

"SO WHAT'S THE SCOTTISH WORD FOR *SQUIB*?"

Lesser. Inconsiderable. *Farmadoch*. After a frantic few seconds, Magnus was able to cough up the least-objectionable term: "We call them *misfires*."

"Oooh!"

She rolled her (enchanting!) eyes. "Jerry, why would you *oooh* and write that down?"

The boy with the reddish beard looked up from a battered notebook. "Why would I try to sketch that little black wolf? Not that it let me get close enough for a good look or anything... Why would I write down Les's mom's apple pudding recipe? Some stuff just needs to be scribbled."

"That's not pudding. Pudding is...pudding. That apple pudding thing was an apple crisp. Or a crumble. Maybe a grunt? And are you seriously equating a recipe to a slur?" She turned back to Magnus. "But I have to give it to the Scots. *Misfires* is almost clever, as far as slurs go."

"I'm sorry, lass. I didna know." How could he? They smelled and moved and behaved like Shifters. Which they were! Obviously, they were. Technically. Magnus knew part of the reason for unreasonable prejudice toward the *farmadoch* was that when they found out what they were, some Shifters—not him!—felt...tricked. Like the misfires were Stables in disguise. Which they weren't. Definitely not. Technically.

"Right, right, the scales hath fallen from your big, pretty eyes. So—"

"You think I have big, pretty eyes?" he asked, delighted. Not that he would have described them as pretty. But he was thrilled to hear anything positive from her. And disconcerted. Why should he care about anything she said? Why was he persisting with this woman?

He didn't know. What he did know was that, for whatever reason, he cared very much what she said and did and thought. *Perhaps Mama Mac is right. I should go out more. But that would mean going out more. Ugh.*

"Your eyes are irrelevant!" What's-her-name declared.

"A fair question," Maggie teased.

Magnus looked at the petite brunette with the admirably deep tan (it was barely summer!). "Thank you, lass."

"You're welcome."

"Don't pay any attention to what she says, she bases all her dialogue on a cartoon. We're getting off track. Now that you know our shameful, revolting, disgusting, repellant—"

"Um." From Jerry.

"—secret, you'll be moseying along? Or whatever Scottish people call moseying? Look at my face," she demanded, deep-red hair ruffling in the breeze. Her baby-blue skirt kept trying to billow up, and she knocked it back down again with an exasperated sigh. "Look at how hopeful I am at the prospect of you moseying. Argh, ridiculous skirt!"

By contrast to what was happening at the moment, the walk to Summit Overlook Park had been in near silence. Which suited Magnus well. He was walking abreast with the coyote, Les—

Wait. If they're all misfires, should I think of them as bears and coyotes and deer?

Of course I should. They're Shifters. Even if they don't shift.

—and she'd been in front of him, walking with her friend, Jerry. Every once in a while, she'd turn her head to look back at him then face forward.

Well. She isna frightened. That's something. He'd take anger over fear anytime. He'd seen the damage fear could do. His early twenties were a monument to it. It was part of the reason he'd been a loner for years. He couldn't speak for everyone, but he'd found that putting yourself out there to make friends resulted in a body count.

And then he stopped thinking, because the view from the park rivaled (traitorous thought!) the Highlands. Summit Overlook Park boasted a statue and a bench, which wasn't interesting, and an amazing view of the Mississippi River Valley, which was. The trees boasted their lush summer growth and flanked the river so perfectly, it looked like there were two waterways: one blue, one green. The view must be dazzling when the leaves turned.[2]

"Isn't it great?" Jerry asked, sighing at the view. "I love it here. Great for sketching."

"Among other things, right, Jerry?"

It was quite private this morning, as the park was deserted—doubtless why they'd picked the spot: they could scold him with impunity. Which was fine with him. This was already the most interesting week since... Well, viewing what was left of poor Sue Smalls in the morgue *was* interesting. Technically. As the dictionary defined it.

But this was interesting in a positive way. He had a chance to save What's-her-name. He'd never had a chance with Sue. Of any kind. At all.

"What's the deal?" Maggie demanded.

---

2. It is!

"I'm worried about you." Mostly the foulmouthed enchantress, but this was no time for specifics.

"And we appreciate that," Les put in.

"What? No, we don't."

"Gotta go with Ver on this one," Jerry added.

Ver?

"But we're all consenting adults," Les continued. "If you want to call the cops because of trespassing, that's your prerogative. But it's not gonna stop us." Brave words, which would have made more of an impression if the werecoyote had been able to maintain eye contact. His gaze skittered all over the place. Magnus was used to it. "Though we'll definitely cross your island off the list of places to make mischief."

"And we'll give you one chance to say, 'And let that be a lesson to you crazy kids,'" Darcy said, "and then you've got to be on your way."

"Thank you," Magnus replied, though that wasn't at all what he was after. "But as I told, ah, the young lady..." He flailed for a few seconds, hoping one of them would help him out.

Alas.

"You don't know my name."

He coughed. "Ah, no."

She nodded, not at all put out, thank goodness. "D'you know why you don't know my name? Because we're strangers, fruitcake! Also, it's Verity Lane. Which you should now forget because, again, strangers." Verity Lane, on the other hand, had no trouble maintaining eye contact. If anything, *he* wanted to break *his* gaze. "Once we're done here—"

"How could I forget a name like Verity Lane?"

"*Once we're done here—*"

"We'll have a picnic?" Jerry put in hopefully.

"—we'll go our separate ways, and I'll devoutly hope our paths won't cross ever again, ever."

"Understandable. But as I told you the day we met, Ms. Lane, you're welcome to visit anytime."

"I did forget that part," she admitted. To the others: "He said if we wanted 'room to romp,' which prob'ly isn't a euphemism for something weird, we could come over."

Actually, he'd invited her. *Verity* was welcome anytime. He hadn't mentioned the others. He didn't care what the werecoyote did. Or the deer. Or the little one obsessed with *The Simpsons.* But again: not the time for specifics.

Verity sighed. "Look, I'm sorry I trespassed, okay? Deeply, profoundly, thoroughly, extremely very very very very very sorry."

"I'm not, lass."

"I promise I will never, ever—wait, you're not?"

He chuckled. "It was never about annoyance over a misdemeanor. I found a naked lass in my garden. I worried she was in trouble. As it happens, she is. As are her friends."

"Consenting adults," Les reminded him, while Jerry shrugged.

"I'm aware I've overstepped," Magnus said. "I'll say my piece and be on my way."

"Great! Give us the piece talk already."

He was trying. (Also, failing.) He was also trying not to gape at her like a besotted schoolboy. (Failing.) "I'm glad you like my eyes. Yours are striking. That's not me being a creeper. Objectively, they're striking."

"Objectively, you're skeeving me out. Piece talk, please."

"And what do you even call that?" Les asked, making a

vague gesture toward her eyeballs. "You can't say she's got brown eyes, because she doesn't, any more than she's got—"

Maggie piped up with "Is *beautiful* a color?"

"That one might be a reach, Mags," Verity replied with a grin. "Some things *The Simpsons* are no good for."

Maggie snorted. "I'm going to pretend I didn't hear that."

"Heterochromia," Jerry announced, flipping through his notebook and showing them a sketch of Verity's eyes.

Darcy rolled her eyes. "Don't mind Jerry, he's always got that notebook with him."

"Except when I don't. Look here. This is what we're talking about. The different-colored eyeballs."

"Uh, Jerry, that's a black-and-white sketch."

"I was out of colored pencils that day. Use your imagination. Check it out! Mutant!"

"See, why can't the nickname for who we are be *mutants*?" Les whined. "That'd be cool. Or at least less offensive. Squibs, what the hell even is that? Sounds like we're a pile of cephalopods." Les took Jerry's notebook for a closer look. "On the other page—huh. That's the black wolf you were talking about?"

"Yeah, only a couple of blocks from downtown, can you believe?"

"Pretty blurry," Les said critically. "And little. It's probably a dog."

"Everybody's a fucking critic."

"Or a War Wolf," Darcy teased, then grinned at the groans. "What? They're out there." To Magnus: "Do you have those in Scotland? They're basically foot soldiers for violent reactionary factions. We had a big scandal here a few months ago—"

"The IPA thing," Norm added. "Speaking of reactionary factions."[3]

"—and some of them resurfaced."

"War Wolves?" Magnus shook his head. "Never heard of them."

"Count yourself blessed," Les said. "But you have to admit, we've got at least one thing in common with them."

"Uh, no. We don't."

"Sure we do," he said earnestly. "You have to earn your spot to be a War Wolf. Someone can't just decide if you are. And we have to earn our spots, too."

"That's a reach," Darcy commented.

Jerry cleared his throat. "*Anyway.* It's obviously not a War Wolf, but it *is* probably a Shifter. I was upwind, unfortunately." To Magnus: "Minnesota is lousy with wolves, but even so, you don't normally trip over one in the state capital. But we're getting far afield of Verity's heterochromia."

"Can we all get off my weird freak eyes, please? You! Magnus! Piece talk."

"Eh? Oh. I won't pretend I have any idea what you've faced all your lives with your..." Handicap? Disability? Impairment? "...condition."

"Wow," Jerry said in an admiring tone. "We could actually see your mental flailing."

"...but surely there are better ways to prove yourselves to...to whomever you're trying to prove yourselves to. Ways that won't cost you your lives, which are precious." Like Sue's life was precious. Not that she was killed because she was reckless. Well. Not entirely. *Is there a true parallel? Or am I reaching?*

---

3. Details can be found in *Bears Behaving Badly*.

"We're trying to prove ourselves to ourselves, mostly." Jerry shrugged and put the notebook away. "I mean, it's not like we can talk to our parents about this. They'd collectively shit." Nods all around, and Verity actually shuddered. "Why d'you think we're going out of our way to keep this quiet?"

"The trespassing?" Magnus guessed.

"Well, yeah, a little." Jerry absently patted his beard. "But listen: it's not about what other people think, which is why none of us can take your unsolicited fretting seriously right now. It's about reminding ourselves that the only people who can marginalize us are us. Is us. That's right, right? *Is*, not *are*?"

"Absolutely no one cares, Jerry," Verity said kindly. To Magnus: "That's it? That's your piece?"

"You've already lost one of your number."

"This will sound callous—"

"Oh, jeez," Jerry moaned. "Everybody brace."

"—but accidents happen," she finished.

If it was an accident. He wasn't sure why he had such a bad feeling about…all of it, really, but he wasn't inclined to stifle his unsettled inner voice. The last time he did that, the result had been millions in property damage and a full morgue.

"Magnus? Is that it?"

No. He could have cautioned/scolded for an hour. Half the day. Longer, if she'd let him. But she wouldn't. And it was patently obvious that everything he was saying was met with implacable resistance.

"Yes," he lied. "That's my piece. My best to you all. Good luck. And the offer stands. You're welcome to my island anytime. All of you."

"The way he emphasized *all* makes me think you were the only one welcome before," Jerry faux-whispered to Verity.

"That was earlier in the week," Magnus said. "Now that I've gotten to know all of you so well in these past fifteen minutes, it's an open invitation."

That won him a laugh from Verity. "Nice recovery, Old Man Berne."

"I'm thirty-four!"

"Do not care. Bye."

Nothing for it but to leave, then. Besides, he had a full afternoon of sampling hard cider (today's flavors: 2020 Orchard Reserve and Chestnut Crab, both from Keepsake Cidery).

"Goodbye," he said and turned his back on the glorious view and Verity, too.

Chapter 13

THAT WAS IT, THEN.

Chapter 14

(NOPE.)

Chapter 15

Your timing blows a bit. Dev still isn't home, and Mama Mac is doing that thing where she's pretending everything is all right while simultaneously baking non-stop. Do not go into that kitchen unless you want to be force-fed chocolate pound cake and meringue by the double fistful.

"I'll take my chances, lass." Magnus hesitated then offered the note back to Caro, who took it with the de rigueur eye roll that needed no translation, written or otherwise. All he knew about Caro was 1) the young werewolf had been through some trauma that was none of his business (though he couldn't deny he was curious) and was selectively mute as a result, 2) Mama Mac and Annette were fiercely protective of her, and 3) the lass probably didn't need anyone's protection, as the werewolf tended to bite first and ask questions (so to speak) later. "My own fault for coming by without invitation."

She scribbled something then handed it to him. *DON'T BE DUMB* was slashed across her original note.

"Too late," he muttered, and she laughed at him.

He'd knocked on the front door (this time he'd found himself at the big purple house with the purple birdhouse in the yard, just a block away from Lila's place), and so he now moved through the living room into the big sunny kitchen on the south side of the house.

Why, he wasn't sure. Whenever he "moseyed to Mama's" as Oz put it, the others teased him by implying he wanted a

peer to talk to. Which was ludicrous—he was thirty-four!—
but he couldn't deny he enjoyed the older woman's company. Her efficient, calm, and loving manner, coupled with
her fierce and boundless affection, were obvious reasons
why young ones flocked—

A crash derailed his train of thought. As did the contralto
roar—

"Dammit, dammit, God *damn* it!"

—that followed. He heard Caro making herself scarce
and actually hesitated before stepping into the kitchen. Not
out of fear or even caution. No-no-no-no. It was the simple
hesitation of an uninvited guest pausing before imposing on
a woman who could disembowel a predator with her hind
legs.[4]

Yes, that sounded plausible. He'd run with it: hesitation,
not terror. He cleared his throat as a warning and stepped
into Mama Macropi's normally spotless kitchen. She was
infamous for several things, one of which was that you could
perform surgery on her kitchen floor. And given the shenanigans her foster children got up to, he didn't doubt surgery
had been performed on the floor.

Today would be a bad day for surgery: she'd dropped a
bag of flour and was waving away the cloud with her broom
while kicking the much-deflated bag around. This made
things worse. Which he had to assume was the intent.

"Good morning," she snapped. "Scones will be late."

Noooooooo! Her scones were the definition of divine.
Light, buttery, tender crumb, generously studded with ber-
ries and/or chocolate, not cloying. "Not necessary," he lied.
"I already ate."

---

4. Seriously. Don't mess with kangaroos, Shifter or otherwise.

"They aren't just for you, Magnus!"

Caro had the right idea. "Let me help you," he said, coaxing the broom out of her hands.

Her fury was instantly replaced with chagrin. "No, no. Can't have you do that." She wiped her face, leaving a smear of flour that trailed up into her hairline. "I'm sorry for snapping. It's been a hard day."

"It's not yet ten a.m."

"Exactly."

"Here now," he said, subtly shoving her into a chair. "Let someone else do the work for a bit." He grinned as he swept. "Seeing as how Caro's made herself scarce, it's just me and thee."

"That girl is many things, but naive isn't on that list." She sighed and ran a hand through her close-cropped white curls. The flour blended in perfectly. "She didn't give you a heads-up?"

"She did," he replied. "First thing. But I'm a big strong werebear who fears nothing. And I've taken the precaution of disarming you," he added, brandishing the broom.

She laughed, so he swept, and she seemed content to watch. Her bright kitchen smelled like citrus; the cupboards and pantry bulged with spices, dishes, food. The red tablecloth was faded but clean; the front of the fridge was buried under calendars, pictures (Mama Mac as the Easter Bunny, a young Annette, a younger Oz, and a third child, pale and fair, as eggs), and several of Caro's notes (*"Mama, please consider switching out whole milk for skim, you're killing MEEEEEE! Also we're out of chocolate Malt-O-Meal."*). Smack in the middle was a crayon drawing of Mama, Caro, Dev, and Annette, beneath which was scrawled *I should be insulted that we're only allowed crayons in detention, but I'm not. This looks like a five-year-old's work on purpose, and not because I'm a crap artist*, signed by Dev.

Mama Mac followed his gaze and sighed. "Oh, that kit. Crayons *and* candy in detention now, like that's a deterrent?"

"Sounds pretty sweet," he agreed. "No pun, et cetera."

"The candy machine is right across from the detention room, and Dev hasn't needed money to get a Reese's out of a vending machine since he was nine. I swear, half the time that boy gets in trouble just for the sugar rush."

"A viable theory. Caro said—well, she didna say, exactly, but you understand my meaning—that your boy Dev still isn't home?"

"He's not my boy," she replied. "Which is the problem."

A common one, Magnus thought, given Mama Mac's status as a foster mother to various cubs as assigned her by IPA. "He's run off?"

"Yes. And it's not like him. Not like him now," she amended. "He'd scamper from other foster homes if they weren't to his liking, but not from me."

"It's hard to imagine any cub wanting to leave here," Magnus said. A quick peek in the pantry and he spied the dustpan, thank Christ. How many pounds of flour did the woman spill in her rampage? He found the garbage beneath the sink and dumped the first pan full of flour: *whoosh!*

"Not to be bragging," she replied, "but *I* certainly thought so. After Annette was assigned as Dev's caseworker and she brought him around a few times—I always cook too much anyway, so I'm happy when she brings a cub around—he said he wanted to be *here*." She rapped the table for emphasis. "One time, he ran from his assigned fosters and came here instead. He remembered the route even though he'd only been here once! Of course, I had to tell Annette, but not until I filled him up with chicken and dumplings."

Whoosh! "Would've worked on me. Is that how they met? She was his case manager?"

"They're called caseworkers on this side of the pond, dear. And not exactly."

"Well, don't be coy. Now I'm invested."

"I got the story in bits and pieces over time," Mama said through a cloud of flour. "From both of them. They took to each other right away. Like moths!"

"Moths take to each other right away?"

"Hush."

Chapter 16

A LONG TIME AGO. LIKE, REALLY A VERY LONG TIME AGO. WAY back when.

He hadn't eaten since yesterday's lunch, which was half of a discarded Happy Meal left by a Stable family when they bussed their table and vamoosed. (They also forgot a lone baby shoe.) It was shocking, really. The food waste. If he wasn't picky, he could survive indefinitely. And he wasn't. (Also he ran after them with the shoe and slipped the mom's billfold out of her bulging diaper bag while she thanked him. Then felt bad and put it back. He wasn't *that* low.)

That's right! Because things were okay. Might get tricky this fall—Minnesota got more snow in the fall than lots of places got in the winter—but for now, there were places to kip. Churches were the easiest, and they were always warm. He was making money too—when middle-schoolers were bagging groceries for 4-H or Boy Scouts or whatevs, if he stood close enough, he'd get mistaken for one of them, bag some food, and walk off with cash or food or both. When he got caught, he ran. Nobody could catch him on two legs *or* four. That was just a fact.

But over the past couple of days, that woman kept show-ing up. Never overtly following, never getting too close, but if he stayed in one place longer than half an hour, she'd pop up in his periphery. Not a social worker—clandestine fol-lowing wasn't their style. They tended to suddenly descend with cops and unceremoniously bundle the kid in question into a squad car. A PI? Why? He didn't have anything, didn't see anything, didn't know anything. Was she tracking him to—to do stuff to him? Or hand him over to a pimp? He knew a couple of older kids who earned their meals on their knees. He knew more who pretended to, then kicked ass and snatched wallets. The one time a drunk pedo tried to force him in the park, he shredded him pretty good. Dumbass thought a fox would go easy. So did the dumbass make an official complaint? Was the rando lady a cop? Again: cops didn't do things like that.

A coincidence? She was just bopping around in some of the same places he was? Maaaaaaaybe. But he had to be careful. He could feel how much he wanted it to be a coincidence, that she wasn't stalking him, that he was safe (relatively speaking). But lying to himself was why he was on the streets in the first place. The day he bounced, he swore he was done with that shit.

So here she was again, and discretion was the better part of whatever it was, so he dodged down an ally, snuck through the kitchen door of a sushi place (Minneapolis was lousy with alleys and sushi places), walked through acting cool—if you acted like you belonged, even when you were just a kit, people tended to assume you did—let himself out into another alley, then trotted toward the street. He'd been on his own for almost a year, thanks, and he could handle anything that—

"Ark!" That was all that came out when an arm swooped out of nowhere and caught him by the scruff of his jacket collar, levering him off his feet. And yep. It was her. Worse, she was a meat eater.

No, wait. Not a meat eater. *Holy shit, she's a—*

"Are you lost?" Her bright, brown eyes had friendly crinkles at the corners, and she was almost laughing, like snatching him off the street (literally!) was a pretty good joke.

"No, *non, nyet.*" His legs swung and kicked, not that it mattered. She could have been holding a kitten made of cotton balls for all the strain she was showing. If his feet were on the ground, the top of his head would only hit mid-boob. Usually he delighted in being small; it made the things he liked/had to do so much easier. Not right now. "Are you?"

"No." It was late enough that the sidewalk was nearly deserted, and the few people who were around didn't seem to think anything unusual was going on. Or were too drunk to care. The bars had just closed, and there was money to be made. Friendly drunks were walking, talking ATMs. He made fifty bucks last weekend helping three of them find their cars.

He thought he'd been *très* slick to shake her, but all she had to do to net him was stand downwind just out of sight. It was humiliating but also a tiny bit cool.

Predator.

He snorted. *Predator, jeez, hind brain, is that the best you can do? She's a friggin' bear.* He'd never seen one, never mind been this close to one. Not a meat eater—worse, actually. An omnivore; they were famous for it: they ate *anything.* And, rumor had it, anyone. He had to fight the urge to curl up, knees to belly.

"Dev Devoss?"

"Lady, you got the wrong kit."

"No, I don't," she replied pleasantly.

"If you're going to eat me, could you at least knock me out first?"

"I've already eaten." She set him down and gave him a "don't make me chase you" stare. He was pretty sure he could lose her, but… "Saw me, didn't you?"

"Yeah. Buncha times. You're not slick."

"Caught you, didn't I?"

He refused to concede the point and scowled up at her instead. "You should prob'ly change your hair if you want to blend into a crowd."

Her hand went to her shaggy locks, all reddish brown with white tips. Her eyes were the same reddish brown, big and dark. "Point taken." There was a pause while she looked him up and down, and for a moment, he was embarrassed and wished he smelled better. The jacket he had on wasn't his and hadn't been clean when he'd, um, found it. The sneakers *were* his, and he'd worn holes through the soles. His jeans were stiff with dirt. He washed his hair in various bathroom sinks, and it showed. "You've got people looking for you, Dev."

"Ha!" Did she think that was gonna work? Because it wasn't gonna work. "You mean my mom? Who d'you think sold me in the first place?"

The smile disappeared. "Yes, well. That isn't who I meant."

"Who'd you mean?"

"Me, of course," she replied, like it was obvious. "Also, your mother is an unadulterated menace."

He was so startled, he couldn't say anything for a few seconds. He agreed, but still. "Social workers aren't supposed to say stuff like that."

She shrugged. "It's a simple truth. No one with any sense could ever give you up, regardless of cost, no matter how dire the straits." She rested her hand lightly on the top of his head and smiled down at him, a big, pretty smile that took her from interesting to dazzling in half a tick. "Come along, Dev. We have things to discuss."

Discuss? Like he had some say in what happened next? He liked how she acted like he was a grown-up. Or at least a big kid, a high-schooler. And shouldn't they be halfway to Child Services by now?

"I'll buy you lunch," she wheedled, like she had to persuade him. Like he could choose.

He blinked and thought about it. "It's, um, two a.m. Surely you noticed the free-range drunks."

"I'd be able to notice them with a blindfold on. Fine, I'll buy you supper instead."

In the end, they had supper *and* lunch. After, he even let her put him in her car for the drive to IPA[5]. And stuck around.

He didn't know, then. How it was all an act. How he was just a job to her, another silly kit in over his ears. Even if he'd known, he prob'ly still would've gotten into the car.

That's how dumb *he* was.

5. Interspecies Placement Agency

Chapter 17

"So Annette fixed it. And Dev moved in."

Magnus blinked, still digesting. "That was quite a tale. I have to wonder how you knew the extent of Dev's thought proce—"

"I told you, I got the story out of both of them over time," Mama snapped, ruffling.

"It was almost like you were reading from a boo—"

She threw up her hands. "What, I should tell a boring story? That's what happened. Most likely. The short, dull version is that Annette scooped him off the street and made him safe." She paused, considering. "As safe as a kit like Dev can ever be, I mean." She shook her head. "Foxes."

"Sounds like a lucky break for the lad."

Mama brightened. "I thought so…but I'm not objective. He seemed happy. And he was over the moon when Caro came. They knew each other on the street, y'know. And that's all I'll say about that," she added, as if Magnus had been pumping her for info.

Whoosh! How many pounds of flour had the woman spilled? He stifled a sneeze. "Understood."

"But these past couple of weeks…he's been a different kit." Magnus nodded and pretended none of this was news to him. Poor woman must be deeply aggrieved to open up to a man she'd only known a couple of months. "And she won't show it, but I know Annette's worried. That willful kit won't talk, and we can't get him to try."

"Did something happen? Maybe at school?"

Mama let out a bark of laughter. "Dev runs the school. Well, his grade, at least. And the detention hall. Most of the teachers are mad about him and let him get away with untold nonsense."

"He's very likeable," Magnus said, because Dev Devoss was the poster child for charming troublemakers. He remembered how the fox had stood up for Magnus's goddaughter, Sally, and confronted Magnus when he thought the man was taking her back to Scotland. Dev had offered up Mama Mac's house on the spot, which was in character, without checking with any adult first, which was also in character.

He'd marched up to a full-grown werebear and predicted (wrongly) what Magnus planned to do: take Sally away to his island without any other cubs around, where she wouldn't just be an orphan, she'd be an isolated, lonely orphan.

But the thing is, Mr. Berne, you don't have to even worry.

I don't, eh?

We want her to stay. You don't have to do anything. You can go home. We've got it covered.

And when Annette tried to explain about dreadful things like bureaucracies,

You can't just plunk yourself or someone else into a home and declare it's an IPA-sanctioned foster home, boom, all fixed.

Dev had nothing but confidence in Annette's ability to fix everything.

You could do it, Net. You could push everything through. Everybody follows your lead.

Perhaps that was the problem. Perhaps something had happened that Annette couldn't fix. Dev struck him as a generally upbeat lad, but it was impossible to be in

IPA's system—any such system—without some eventual disillusionment.

Whoosh!

Before he could come up with a platitude, or at least a noncommittal grunt, they heard a car pull into the drive, footsteps pounding up the sidewalk, and then Annette Garsea burst into the kitchen.

She greeted them with "Is he back?" Followed by "Ye gods, what happened in here? Mama, if you've turned to cocaine cookery to make ends meet, I'll be very upset."

"My ends are meeting just fine. We had an accident," she admitted, while Magnus snorted at *we*.

"Clearly. No scones, then." Annette sighed. Even for a werebear, the woman's appetite was prodigious. As her foster brother Oz put it, Annette Garsea was a foodie before *foodie* was code for *pretentious jackoff*. She knew every restaurant in town, memorized every menu, interviewed every chef, intimidated every maître d', grilled every line cook, harangued every sommelier.

"Well, I'm sorry!" Mama Mac threw up her hands in defeat. "All I have is raisin bread, potato bread, English muffins, crumpets, and I think a little rye. Oh, and some flatbread. And *lefse*."[6]

"Ooooooh!"

Before he could ask what *lefse* was, Annette was digging around in the cupboard, found a bag, and extracted something that looked like a flat, naked burrito. She spread room-temperature butter all over it then sprinkled it with brown sugar she scooped out of one of the cannisters beside the microwave. Then she rolled it into a fat cigar shape, cut it

---

6. Norwegian flatbread made with potatoes. Very popular in Minnesota. *Divine*, especially the way Annette eats it.

with a butter knife, and handed half to him. "Prepare to fall in love, Magnus. Or at least like."

He meant to try a polite bite but wolfed it down in three polite bites while letting another flour pile slide into the garbage with his free hand. "Delicious!" he managed, and the inhale brought on a violent coughing fit. Annette whacked him on the back, which was no help at all.

While he got himself under control (and surreptitiously licked butter off his fingers), Mama asked Annette, "How did it go?"

Just like that, Annette's good humor dropped like a switch had been thrown. "As expected."

Mama's lips went thin. "So? Is the one who whelped him causing trouble again?"

Again?

"The opposite," Annette replied. "She doesn't care. Whatever this is, it's not coming from her. At least, not overtly."

Mama Mac shook her head. "That's…good, I guess."

Magnus dumped the last panful into the garbage. "How long has he been—" He cut himself off to listen then added, "Moot, I suppose."

They all heard it: the troublemaker in question had come home. If the kit even considered the big purple house his home; apparently that was now up for debate.

Dev quietly let himself in through the kitchen door and stopped short, staring at all three of them.

Mama Mac greeted him with "Well! I can't wait to hear this one. Lost your books and had to go back and somehow got lost? Flying kites and the day got away from you? You forgot you have a warm bed here waiting for you and slept in an alley instead?"

"Pick the one you like," Dev replied, ducking his head. He was wearing tattered jeans, battered sneakers, and an orange T-shirt. The weather was fair enough that he needed nothing else, but he wasn't carrying a backpack or book bag.

Did the lad really take off with nothing but whatever was in his pockets? And disappear for however long he was gone? That didn't sound right. Dev was impulsive but not entirely reckless. He was pretty sure.

"Dev, why did you run away?" Annette's tone was even, but he could smell the stress coming off her. "I thought we had a deal."

"I didn't run away. I ran out. Now I'm back." Dev swiped his arm across his nose. "I'd like to go to my room now."

"That's nice, but it's also irrelevant," Annette replied. "Where have you been? And why did you go?"

Nothing. The kit just stared at the (newly swept) tile.

"If you won't care about yourself," Annette pointed out quietly, "you might consider Mama's feelings." Magnus found the word choice peculiar. *Won't* instead of *can't* or *don't*. Implying a willful choice. "She's been worrying half to death."

"I don't want to talk about it. And you can't make me talk, either! You can't do anything," he said in a flash of heat, green eyes glittering. "You won't hit me, and you know you can't make me stay. Nobody can. So go plan your wedding or whatever."

"Lad, why in the world d'you want to hurt two women who care about you?" Even as he said it, Magnus knew it was a mistake. Family business, clearly.

Unless, of course, they weren't a family.

Dev leaped at the chance to lash at an all-new target. "What the hell are you even doing here, Berne?"

"Dev!" Mama snapped.

"Actually, I was curious about that myself," Annette admitted. "I was going to work up to it a little more politely, though."

Mama made a tsking sound. "Fine, young man, your wish is granted: go to your room."

"I will!" Then he muttered something that sounded like *snot line.*

Annette accurately read the confusion on Magnus's face. "He said 'it's not mine.'"

"Oh. That makes more sense."

Mama was still focused on Dev. "You can come down for something to eat once you've remembered your manners and your responsibilities as a member of this household and after you apologize. But first, take a shower and get into some clean clothes because, my *God*, boy, you're filthy."

"M'not hungry." Which was alarming to say the least. Dev ate like carbs were going to be outlawed at any moment. Unless he'd spent the past couple of days at a literal feast, he had to be starving. "Need a shower, though," he added, already trudging toward the living room stairs.

"You have to eat some—"

"I'm tired" was the colorless response.

Mama threw up her hands. "Fine! Go!"

He went.

Magnus cleared his throat. "I've imposed on you long enough."

"You didn't impose."

"If anything, the opposite. You swept like a large, hairy Cinderella," Annette observed. "No one would ever know about the flour-geddon that took place here."

"Magnus, you're always welcome," Mama said. Her posture, usually perfect, was less so just now; she looked small and slumped and beaten, which was not how Meredith Macropi should look anywhere, never mind her own kitchen. "On bad days as well as the good."

"He's a good lad. He'll come around." Magnus had no way of knowing if either of those things were true, but what else could one say? *So sorry, can't relate. I never had to run away. There was never anyone to run from.*

"Why *did* you stop by?" And, when Mama sent a glare her way, Annette hastily added, "Not that you need a reason."

I have no idea. "I was in the neighborhood."

His island was an hour away, but the ladies were too polite to point that out. "Did you find out What's-her-name's name?" Annette asked. "When you crashed the memorial?"

"I didn't 'crash.' It was an open invitation. They put the notice in the paper! And her name's Verity. Verity Lane," he said again, savoring it.

"How did it go?" Mama asked, ready to seize on anything positive. "Did you ask her out? Will you see her again?"

"No, and no. But I said my piece." He shrugged. "What else can I do?" Except wonder about Andy's death. His accidental death. Because as Verity reminded him, accidents happened.

His inner voice dissented. Again. But there was nothing to be done. If only he had the means to look into it. *If only I knew a local private investigator...*

"I'm sure she'll be fine," Mama soothed. "Didn't you say she was a bear? Your kind has always been able to take care of themselves. What?" she asked when Annette looked at her askance. "That's not racist, it's just true. Bears can take care of themselves. Have *you* ever had a problem in a fight? Neither has Magnus, I'll bet."

Annette sighed. "Mama…"

"And maybe later she'll—what's her name? Verity? Maybe she'll think of you fondly, and you can go out then."

He cleared his throat. "She's a squib, actually. So a bear, but…not really."

"Ah." Mama sat up straight. "What?"

"A squib? A Shifter who can't shi—"

"The nomenclature isn't the problem. We know what a squib is," Annette said. "I'm sorry to say we've had negative dealings with them. Well. One of them. And he was a doozy. And by *doozy*, I mean pathetic, bullying monster."

"If she can't shift, you *have* to look out for her!" Mama cried. "Poor thing! No wonder she's doing all those silly stunts."

"Uh, yeah. That's…kind of their point. That's *why* they do the stunts." Just thinking about it made him feel confused all over again, and worried, and…a little proud? Not that he had any right to pride. Verity wasn't doing any of those things for *his* sake. "To prove themselves. But not to us," he hastily added. "They were verra clear about that. It's more about proving themselves to themselves. I think."

"How many are there?"

"Half a dozen or so." *Including the dead one.*

"Huh. Well, I don't get it," Annette said. She absently tugged on a hank of her auburn hair. "But then, I've got the luxury of not getting it. I think, at the least, squibs should have an outlet. We've seen what happens when they don't."

"How mysterious," Magnus said. "And why do I have the feeling you're going to decline to elaborate?"

She stopped fiddling with her hair and spread her hands in a partial apology. "Can't. Privacy issues."

Meaning her charge. Dev or Caro. Or both.

"I understand. Thank you for your hospitality."

"It wasn't much," Mama replied. "I just sat here while you did all the work. Are you going to see Sally this week?"

"Saturday." They—the residents of the big purple house as well as Lila's—had all met Sally Smalls, his goddaughter. Lila, in fact, had scooped Sally up out of an alley (mistaking her for a wild bear cub) and spirited her away. Then compounded her protective instinct by risking her own life to keep Sally safe.[7] To say the little girl was a welcome guest was a severe understatement.

All that to say Magnus enjoyed spending time with Sally, if not her father.

"You know you can bring her over anytime you like," Mama added.

He did know and had in the past. His goddaughter was especially fond of Lila and was a frequent visitor. But lately he wondered if dumping her on Mama and/or Lila was taking the easy way out. He knew what Sally liked to eat but not what she wanted to be when she grew up, or her favorite color, or how she was coping with her mother's death. And he had no idea where to begin. Or how.

"You give her a big hug and a kiss from me," Mama ordered.

"Or a firm handshake," Annette added. "Whatever you feel is appropriate."

"Got it." He put the broom and dustpan away, dusted off his hands. "Ladies."

---

7. The sordid, sexy details can be found in *A Wolf After My Own Heart.*

"Come back tomorrow. There'll be scones."

"She can't promise that," Annette put in quickly.

"I'll try," he lied, because he'd imposed enough.

Chapter 18

WHAT WITH ONE THING AND ANOTHER, THE BETTER part of a week passed. Magnus had high tea with Sally, which was gratifying on several levels, not least of which: Who knew you could get a proper tea in Minnesota? The lass had her mother's charm and her father's tendency to whine when sweets weren't forthcoming but was nevertheless a delight to—

No.

No, that wasn't fair. Sam Smalls had suffered; even his worst enemy (Magnus back in the day, his physical therapist now) would have to acknowledge that. Sam had to survive the plane crash that killed his wife then crawl (literally) into hiding while his bones knitted themselves back together, all the while dependent on the kindness of strangers (Stable strangers!) while helpless to protect his daughter. They had never been friends, but Magnus was glad to have been of assistance, glad Sam had survived, glad Sally was safe, and hadn't demurred when his old rival asked him to be Sally's legal guardian (formalizing the "godfather" arrangement) should anything happen to her remaining parent. Magnus had signed the paperwork without a second thought then changed his will.

And to give Sam's mortal enemy (Jonathan Yates, PT, DPT) credit: Sam had gone from despondent in a wheelchair to furious with two canes to grouchy with one in a remarkably short time. He still needed the wheelchair a few hours a day, and he would probably limp for the rest of his life, which was an improvement over a lingering death. Shifters were tough in comparison to their Stable counterparts, but…plane crash.

On a completely unrelated tangent, summer on his island was…nice! He hadn't been back to Minnesota in over a decade and was gratified to find that while the winters were still fierce, summers were lush and pleasant, and when the temp climbed past 32°C, the breeze off the lake kept the heat under control. It was getting so warm, in fact, that a swim in the lake wasn't such a wild idea. Anyone could swim! Sure! Especially in this weather! Right up to him, in fact!

Anyone?

Really?

Fine. He came out into the garden each morning and sipped tea (or coffee, if he'd been up half the night) and watched the water and hoped Verity might swim by for a hello. Which, from what little he knew of her, seemed out of character (much easier to picture her swimming by to yell insults and come ashore to possibly kick him in the shins), but he lived in hope. Pathetic, unrequited hope.

There hadn't been any dummy drop-offs, either, and he had no idea how to feel about that. Relieved? Disappointed? Both? Neither? That was how deeply confusing his life had become: struggling to decide if he would welcome a dummy drop-off. The most interesting things in sight right now were a few far-off sailboats and a small ball bobbing amid wavelets. Someone must have lost their football; it was astonishing, really, the things that ended up in the lake.

But never mind the detritus; spending time with his new ~~friends~~ ~~acquaintances~~ ~~colleagues~~ companions had been agreeable, and he was almost ready to believe them when they claimed he wasn't an imposition. He had a standing invitation to Sunday dinner, courtesy of Mama Macropi, and a verbal invite to Annette's wedding to David Auberon. He was surprised and gratified to realize he felt no hurry to move back to Scotland, and not just because he was curious to see how Dev's situation played out. The original plan had been to ensure Sally's safety, extend condolences to Sam, then retreat to Scotland as soon as he could, preferably for decades, mailing birthday greetings to Sally and politely declining the inevitable invitation to her high school graduation. Assuming he lived so long.

But the Currie estate could run without him, he got regular reports on the same, and Minnesota was (pardon the cliché) nice. Regardless of whether he ever saw Verity again, he'd carved out a small life for himself here, one he was content with for several reasons, and oh, good Lord, that wasn't a soccer ball. It was a head. Even better, a head attached to a body. Verity's body!

Like most bears, Magnus's long vision wasn't great; his greatest asset (aside from strength) was usually (fucking allergies) his sense of smell.

Thank God the wind was blowing the right way; he was picking up lake water, seaweed, dead fish, mud, pine, and, yes, Verity Lane as she swam closer.

All his mental platitudes vanished as he felt a head-to-toe surge of excitement to see her breast-stroking her way back to his ~~heart groin~~ island. To complain? To kill him? To demand food? Who cared?

He ran to open the gate as she staggered out of the water, naked (sensible!), and shoulders bowed with fatigue.

Not fatigue, he realized as she looked up at him. Her deep-red hair was plastered flat to her skull, which only emphasized the dark circles beneath her eyes and the down-turned, trembling bow of her mouth.

"Jerry's dead," she croaked and fell into his arms.

Chapter 19

VERITY SET DOWN HER EMPTY MUG, AND MAGNUS promptly refilled it with tea. Really fucking good tea: strong, black, cut with loads of sugar, and giving off the scent of oranges and cinnamon.

He'd practically carried her into his house, sat her down at the kitchen table, wrapped her in his robe (which she was trying not to sniff, or at least not sniff when he could see), and toweled her stringy, wet hair with the brisk efficiency of a hair stylist. Then he'd started plying her with tea and toast slathered with plum jam and clotted cream. Before today, she'd assumed clotted cream was something terrible that happened to milk left out too long. Now she knew it was something terrific that happened to milk (or cream, or whatever) left out too long.

She was happy to be plied. It had been a shit few days. And she barely remembered what she'd been doing before the urge to swim to Magnus fucking Berne overcame her. Oh, wait—she'd been drinking. Day two of the post-memorial binge. Or was it day three?

It took a lot of booze to shift a Shifter, and she didn't have the wallet for it. So she'd finished the bottle of Grey Goose, wished it were a strawberry daiquiri with extra sugar on the rim (she could've used the vitamin C and potassium), recycled it (the beach was lousy with recycling bins; this week she was a shiftless drunk, but she wasn't a shiftless litterbug drunk), stripped, then hit the lake. She had a bad moment when she got the islands mixed up and started to come ashore at Big Island Nature Park (the early morning hikers were startled but polite) then plowed on.

And, as if she'd wished him into being (which she hadn't, definitely hadn't), he was waiting for her. Right there in his yard, which he persisted in calling a garden, which was dumb because there wasn't a tomato plant or flower in sight, just hostas and maples and ferns. Right there in his not-garden, slack-jawed while she splashed ashore, and it all welled up and she thought she might barf or cry (barfing was preferable) and then she realized anew that she'd never see Jerry's crooked grin again and then she was scared she'd barf *and* cry and wasn't sure of her welcome to the island despite the invitation and then Magnus's arms were around her and everything wasn't okay, nothing was fixed, not a single thing had been made better, but she was a little bit warm, and he didn't ask her for a damn thing.

He took her up the stone steps, shoved open the sliding glass door, walked her past a sitting room that was all bookshelves and windows, past a cold fireplace, through a dining room equally as big as the sitting room (King Arthur and all his knights and his cheating wife and his half sister could've sat for a meal and there'd still be room if Mordred dropped by) that shared the fireplace with the sitting room, and she was pretty sure she caught a glimpse of a living room off the sitting room

(wonder what the difference is?)

and then into a kitchen with red cupboards, warm wooden floors, a marble-topped island that was a third of the size of the kitchen itself, a stainless steel fridge that could've held half a steer, and a cozy table for four in the corner with a view of the dock. Which was where he'd eased her down before fixing her a cup of tea.

When she'd finished her second cup and was halfway through her third, he took the opposite seat and fixed her with his dark gaze. "What happened, Verity darling?"

She loved it. She loved how her name sounded in his rolling baritone. Even now, when she shouldn't care about anything but Jerry. But she was the poster creep for rampant immaturity, so...

"Don't you dare be sweet to me! I've been a complete jerk to you, and now I'm in your face again because I'm on your island again, and yeah, you said I could come anytime but pop-ins aren't cool, and if you're nice about it I'm gonna cry, so do *not* make me cry, Magnus Berne!" She took a gulp of her tea. "Could I have another sugar ball, please?"

Without a word he slid the bowl to her, along with the tongs. She had no idea why Magnus Berne didn't do sugar like anyone else, and she didn't care. For starters, they weren't cubes; they were spheres. And each sweet little sugar sphere had been decorated with a cunning tiny flower with squiggles of pastel frosting: blue, pink, yellow, lavender. Roses, lilacs, pansies. On a cube! (Also on spheres.) Designed to instantly melt! But someone took the time to press them and mold them and paint tiny flowers on them anyway. Astonishing.[8]

All that to say, she kept her head down and took some time deciding because she was mortified that she repaid his kindness with shouting and didn't quite understand why she was mortified. Verity "Take No Shit" Lane didn't take shit. It was in the nickname and everything.

Right. That was why. He hadn't actually given her any

---

8. They're kawaii sugar cubes, and they're spectacular.

94   MARYJANICE DAVIDSON

"I know," she snapped then buried her face in the cup again. "Sorry."

"I only meant…well. What I said, I s'pose. You don't have to talk about it. But I'm sorry your friend is dead. He seemed like a good lad and a good friend t'you."

"He…"—*Say it. Past tense. Time to face it: Jerry is gone*—"…was." Good, I mean. Better than good. And better than me. Didn't have a mean bone in his body, or even a grumpy bone. He always saw the good, and he put up with my shit. And he died alone. And prob'ly scared. That's what I hate the most. And there's no way to fix it. I hate that, too."

Then she did cry, and it was hateful, as bad as she knew it would be; her sinuses filled like a clogged sink and tears poured down her face and dripped on the table and Magnus Berne just sat there and handed her tissue after tissue and didn't say a word, not one word.

shit. Just tea and wordless sympathy. And the most beautiful sugar cubes in the world. She popped one in her mouth
when he wasn't looking and looked around the large kitchen.
Large applied very well to this house; each room she'd seen
had high ceilings, floor-to-ceiling windows, and a view of the
lake. The decorations were sparse; nothing personal was on
display. Just bland paintings and the occasional vase (one big
enough for a garden's worth of flowers), blond wood everywhere, and sunlight splashed in every room. No magazines,
just books. Nothing on the coffee tables, not even coffee
table books. No runners on the tables, just empty bowl cen-
terpieces, no clutter in the corners. This wasn't a home; it
was the model house you showed to clients with deep pockets. And she saw at once why Magnus had rented the place:
every room you were in was like being outside.

She had dithered long enough, so she selected a sugar
sphere with a purple lilac and plopped it in her cup. She
made herself look up, made herself say, "Sorry. Bad week.
And I don't get why you're being so nice, because I've been
a raging asshat. Don't be nice. This is an imposition, and I
expect you to act like it."

He laughed. Laughed! Which was...fine? Probably.
Certainly unexpected. "Forgive me, lass. It's just, I'm constantly telling my fr—uh, some people I know that I'
imposing, and they always deny it. So to hear you say that
know what it's like for them, now. And I'll tell you what
tell me, and I'll mean it, as I suppose they mean it:
not imposing. I'm glad t'see you. Though I wish the
stances were happier."

"Yeah."

"You don't have to tell me anything."

Chapter 20

FOR THE FIFTH TIME IN HALF AN HOUR, MAGNUS RESISTED the urge to peek in on her again. He hadn't wanted to spook her or provoke more shouting (not that he minded, but she certainly seemed to), so he'd saved his questions. It was like trying to coax an angry, dangerous squirrel; you could offer inducements like popcorn or sugar balls, but whatever you did, the squirrel could still bolt at any second. Which was the last thing he wanted. And not just for his own selfish reasons; he honestly believed she shouldn't be alone just now.

Because she clearly was. While he was thrilled to see her, he wasn't oblivious: if she'd had a better option, she would have taken it. There was a reason she came to a near stranger in the midst of her grief, and it wasn't an interest in swimming.

And why did he care? Was it just her looks, which were very fine? The attitude? The sarcastic fearlessness? Or the fearless sarcasm?

He didn't know, which wasn't unusual. And he didn't care, which was. Perhaps this strong attraction to a woman who wanted nothing to do with him was his mind's way of pointing out that he'd been alone too long.

Or maybe it was all bullshit.

After she'd wept, her eyes went to half-mast as she shivered and yawned, and somehow he managed to talk her into lying down in one of the guest rooms. She muttered some half-hearted protests and a few vague threats, but her fatigue and what he was guessing was an astonishing amount of vodka won out. Now it was just past noon, and she was still sleeping deeply. So he paced and guarded her slumber and thought up ways to entice her to remain. Which was why, when she did finally emerge, it was to see him put the finishing touches on the Caesar salad with salmon on the side, which he set beside the bowl of fresh fruit with a lime honey dressing, which was next to a pitcher of virgin Bloody Marys, which was cheek by jowl with a bowl of gazpacho, which was adjacent to cucumber sandwiches with the crusts cut off.

"Whoa. You didn't tell me you were throwing a banquet. Where are the other fifty guests?"

"You're the only guest, which is fortunate since you're a handful all by yourself. Sit," he urged. "Here, try this."

She eyed the glass he offered and held up a hand but not to take it. "Sorry, no. I've never thought the 'hair of the dog' hangover cure was worth shit. Also, I'm not hungover. By some miracle," she muttered.

"There's no alcohol in this. Try," he coaxed. "You need the electrolytes. Tomato juice is loaded with antioxidants, the Worcestershire sauce has B_5 and B_3, and the lemon juice…uh."

"Oh, I can't wait to hear this."

He coughed into his fist. "Lemon juice settles your stomach and is a natural laxative."

She just looked at him, though the corner of her mouth twitched. "Thank you for your efforts to keep me on the regular."

"You're welcome," he replied with equal formality, and she giggled. Even better, she took a sip, and then another.

"Gotta give you props for skipping the celery and going

with a piece of bacon instead." She took a gulp and a bite. "You might have ruined me for celery as a garnish."

"Celery is repulsive, and I'll not have it in this house. Or any house," he declared. "It's flavorless yet stringy and crunchy and somehow meaty at the same time, my God!"

"All right, calm down, no celery for you, noted. Well, you sit down, too. I can't eat all this. Most likely. Damn, Magnus," she added, stabbing a forkful of salmon. "You can *cook*."

He shrugged, ducked his head. "Bachelor. It's learn or starve."

"Naw, there's middle ground there. Somewhere. I'm a spinster *and* a crap cook."

He snorted at *spinster*, and then they ate in companionable silence for a couple of minutes, broken by Verity's "I don't even like Bloody Marys. But this is good. It's almost like a shrimp cocktail."[9]

"Horseradish," he replied.

"Figured you'd be more of a meat guy," she added when he helped himself to more fruit salad.

"Omnivore," he reminded her.

She grinned, showing him her teeth. "Did you just bearsplain to me what bears eat?"

"Noooooo. No. Not at all. That would be absurd. And condescending. And absurd. And so I would never, ever do it."

"Easy, Magnus. Don't trip with all the backpedaling."

"Got it. I'll have my snout buried in this salmon if you need me."

She laughed again and helped herself to some more of the salmon. They finished their meal companionably enough, the silence broken only by requests for seconds and pepper.

---

9. The best Bloody Marys, which are almost like shrimp cocktails, can be found at the Scargo Cafe in Dennis, Massachusetts.

It should have been uncomfortable, especially given why she'd swum all this way, but wasn't.

"I appreciate it," she said out of nowhere.

He almost jumped. "Eh? You're welcome."

"Not just the food."

"All right."

"You're not gonna ask?"

He couldn't tell if she was disappointed or genuinely curious or just making conversation. "No."

"You don't want the details?"

"In your own time."

She blinked, took another bite of fish, swallowed. "Thanks."

He inclined his head, and they finished in silence. But the moment her plate was clean, she all but jumped to her feet.

"Welp, my belly's full, and my grieving is all done..." She trailed off and her face contorted, like she was swallowing sorrow. A half second later, she managed a smile so small, it was more like a grimace. "So I'll be on my way."

"Let me take you in the boat. I know..." He held up a hand to forestall her inevitable protest. "You don't need a boat. You don't need me. Or anyone. You can get back with zero assistance from any and all parties. And zero clothes. But if you allow me to take you—"

"Magnus..."

"—you'll make it to shore bone-dry and fully clothed."

"Magnus..."

"Try it! You might like it."

"Hilarious." Another few seconds ticked by as she mulled and determinedly did not speak of Jerry. Then: "Fully clothed how? I'm not taking your robe, Magnus."

Chapter 21

WHICH WAS HOW SHE FOUND HERSELF IN MAGNUS Berne's navy-blue FIFA Futsal World Cup sweatshirt, whatever the hell that was, and a pair of gray, fleece-lined sweatpants that were so long she had to roll them three or four times to get them above her ankle. They were well-worn and sinfully soft.

She'd refused the shoes. Even the man's flip-flops would be like clown shoes on her small, shapely, delicate feet, and yeah, she was vain about her feet, so fucking what? Besides, she liked how the ground/sidewalk/planks/shingles felt under her tootsies.

"I'll get these back to you." *Maybe. Pretty comfy, TBH. It all feels like it's lined in velvet!*

He shrugged. "Not necessary."

"After I wash them, naturally, since I'm... How do the Stables put it?" She had to laugh; leave it to Stables to think up a phrase to explain simple nudity, because the phrase *simple nudity* didn't quite get the job done, apparently. "Going commando?"

"Not necessary." He ducked his head and added, "Truly, you don't need to go to the trouble. Unless you really want to."

"Magnus Berne, is that a blush?" she asked, delighted.

"It's warm in here," he muttered.

Then they just stood in his huge dining room, looking out the floor-to-ceiling windows at the lake, shoulder to shoulder.

Not *quite* touching.

In companionable silence.

Companionable silence with Magnus Berne made her nervous. She gave him a side-eye glance, only to see he was doing the same. She also felt an annoying urge to run her finger along his stubble, and squashed the feeling. "So! It was super-duper decent of you to put me up…"

"No, it wasn't," he replied seriously. "It was common courtesy."

"…but I'll be on my way. Well. We'll be on my way. Where's this so-called boat?"

He pointed to the obvious, and she cursed herself for being so distracted by his proximity she failed to notice the seventy-foot white sport yacht tied up at the dock. Now that she was properly paying attention, she couldn't wait to board. She loved boats, if not boaters.

"Oooh, excellent. Did you bring that all the way from Scotland? Never mind, I don't actually care. Let's jet. Or boat, I guess."

Still he hesitated. He was practically dithering. *What the hell is—oh.*

"You have to shift!" she said and couldn't keep the accusatory tone out of her voice.

He flinched like she'd struck him, and just like that, the old frustrated rage swept through her. Here was another one who needed to give in to a biological imperative but wouldn't because they didn't want to hurt her *feelings.*

"So. Do it."

"What?"

"Shift." She tapped her bare foot. "Don't mind me."

He just looked at her. "Why are you angry?"

How much time you got? "Because you have to and you won't!"

"But I don't 'have to.'"

"Of course you do!" Wait. Was that unique to her parents? When she was little, they were always explaining that bears *had* to shift, or they'd go wild. Then they'd leave her and disappear into Florida swamps for days on end. Did... did that not apply to all werebears?

She shook off the new thought. Time enough later to figure that out. "Even if you don't have to—which I haven't decided is true—"

"Wait. What?"

"—you won't! Because I'm here! Which is ridiculous! You want to shift, go ahead and shift. Don't hold back your beast just because I'm here."

He shook his head like he was trying to dodge a bee. "I'm confused."

"You think you're being nice—"

"I don't think I'm being nice. I'm being...confused, I guess, if I had to put a name to it."

"—but you're really just—just talking down to me. You think it's good manners, not shifting because you don't want to offend someone who can't. Well, it's not nice. It's just condescending."

"Verity..."

"You know what? Fuck it. I'm out. And I'm keeping the clothes!" She was into the windup, poised for the storm-off. "And also I'd like to know what you use for fabric softener. But later! Since I'm leaving now. So leave your big, ridiculous, beautiful sport yacht with its twin turbo diesel engines tied up because I definitely wasn't dying to go for a ride in it!"

Swimming in overly large clothing would be difficult but ultimately worth it because she could gloat over her stolen treasures in the weeks, nay, months and years to come. *That'll teach him to treat me like I can't shift, even though I can't—uh, what?*

There was a low rumble behind her, and then a gigantic, dark blur shot past her. Then the blur stopped, becoming much less blur-ish, and plopped down on the gravel path in front of her.

"Touché," she admitted. She'd all but dared him to shift in front of her, and he took her up on it. She took a step toward the bear, the really very enormous bear, and then another step, suddenly off-balance and nervous, and irritated with herself as a result. Her tiny, mincing steps transformed to stomps, and she was beside him in a couple of seconds, and Jesus Christ, Magnus Berne was huuuuuge. "Jeez, you got out of your clothes and shifted in, what? Two and a half seconds? Which I probably should have picked up on, but I was well into storm-off mode." She turned to look behind her, saw his clothes flung everywhere. "Ha! Your shirt's in a tree."

All the babble of bravado was, of course, to cover up how thoroughly unnerved she was. She was no stranger to bears. Hell, she *was* a bear, even if she only felt it in her hidden heart. But her parents had always been hypersensitive to her, um, condition, and as an annoying result, she almost never saw their other selves. Instead, Ray and Kay Lane would head off for "bear time," and she would be left with a succession of deeply sympathetic Shifter sitters who treated her like a defective bomb. Though she reminded herself it hadn't been entirely awful. She'd been able to play on their sympathy for hot fudge sundae dividends.

A gentle *whuff*—the bear equivalent of throat-clearing—brought her back to the present, and she took her time, giving him a long, greedy look. Magnus wasn't just enormous—almost three yards long, for God's sake; he'd be almost nine feet tall on his hind legs, and she just bet he went sixteen hundred pounds, easy. But there was more to him than sheer size: he was striking. His dark, chocolate-brown fur had a sort of violet tint, and his eyes were a deep, penetrating brown; his skull was as broad as a basketball. She knew if she picked up one of his paws for a look, the claws would go five inches. She also knew he would let her, and wasn't *that* interesting?

What the fuck did he say he was? Kamchatka? Note to me: look that shit up.

She plopped down beside him on the path, looking out at the lake, enjoying the sun on her shoulders, secretly glad she didn't have another long swim ahead of her. And Magnus, bless him, seemed content to just sit there and enjoy the sun with her.

She had no idea what to say to him. Or if she should say anything at all. She opened her mouth, more than a little curious about what might come out.

Chapter 22

"THE THING ABOUT JERRY IS, HE DIDN'T MIND BEING A squib nearly as much as he minded being a deer. Like that *Simpsons* episode Maggie made us watch—I'd better narrow that down a little, she's made us watch so many—anyway, it's the Halloween episode where they make fun of *Twilight*[10]. You guys had *Twilight* in Scotland, right? Yeah, probably. International bestseller and all… Anyway, in this particular weird-ass episode, Milhouse is a Shifter, and he gets all worked up and jealous and turns into…a poodle. A little white poodle all coifed and clipped, wearing a pink ruffled collar and carrying a pink ruffled parasol. Not even a proper umbrella—a parasol! Anyway, Jerry said that's what being a red hart was like: total anticlimax. Complete letdown. It didn't provoke fear or even awe. Just giggles."

She well remembered Jerry's deer-based grievances. Now she wished she'd dished out fewer eye rolls and more empathy.

At her silence, Magnus made an inquiring huff.

"Right, right…bottom line, Jerry was so annoyed by that, he barely cared about being a squib. His attitude was all 'Why would I *want* to shift into a deer?' His sister's the same way. I guess she goes to school with a bunch of wolves—you might not have tumbled to this because you don't live here, Magnus, but Minnesota's lousy with werewolves. And oh, my God, she's so cute…anyway, her

10. "Treehouse of Horror XXI": Tweenlight.

attitude is 'If I shift during recess, it's snack time!' Hard to argue that point, right?

"So when he told me about the Damp Squibs, I was really surprised. He didn't care that he couldn't shift, but suddenly he joined a club of people who did care? He knew people didn't expect feats of strength and cunning from a deer but wanted to do dangerous stunts to prove he could also be dangerous. I might have this wrong, but I think, for him, it was more about trying to be badass. Or at least be seen as one. But I couldn't be sure, and it's not giving him much credit, so at first it was more about trying to solve the mystery of Jerry than proving myself. Though of course that part would come, too. The thing is, he talked about the Damp Squibs all the time. So finally, I was all 'You gotta introduce me.'"

Magnus yawned, but she didn't take it as a critique of her exposition. The sun was climbing high; even on the lake, it was warm.

"And he did. And I liked it. I liked them a lot. I'd never met a coyote before Les. And Maggie—she only speaks *Simpsons*. What's up with that? Did she lose a bet? Gotta get to the bottom of that one. And Darcy, and Norm…everyone was nice. They called me the Seventh Squib. Except…I'm not anymore, am I?

"We all wanted the same thing: to be treated like 'real' Shifters. And I loved the challenges. I mean—you saw the aftermath. I got a fucking gold star! And even though it's silly, I loved it all the same. We all loved 'em—every time we came back from one, it was like being high for a week. Often after literally being high—Les really likes having us scale heights, for some reason. And the gold stars were icing on the Cinnabon." She wiggled her bare toes in the gravel.

"Which I also loved. Climbing. But also Cinnabon. The first time my folks found me in a tree, I was two. Not that I remember. But they were terrified and made a point of bringing it up as exhibit A for why I had to be scrupulously careful and avoid trees, among other things...

"But we were talking about Jerry." *We* being a generous interpretation, but never mind. "For one of his challenges, he had to dodge traffic on the 494 at midnight, just before the bars closed. And Jerry was all 'Observe, a deer who doesn't end up as roadkill,' and he didn't." She paused, took a second to swallow the sudden lump in her throat. "That time."

She sighed. "But I guess he didn't get lucky twice. And now for the 'I've learned something today' part of my monologue: as much as we want to be in charge of our own fates, and even better our own endings, sometimes it's out of our hands. Lots of times, actually. And that's part of it, too. Acknowledging that—that essential helplessness. Whether you can shift or whether you're stuck with one form. Eventually, it's gonna be your turn. And so, I guess it was Jerry's. I'll never see him again. He's going in the ground. And it's times like this I wish I were religious. An afterlife...that'd be great. But it's just another lie to make us less scared of the dark. Or the drop."

She'd been looking down, hands in her lap, and saw tears splashing her hands and realized she was crying again. She was grateful Magnus had showed her his other self, because it was the easiest thing in the world to bury her face in warm fur that smelled like pine and sunshine and weep for all the things Jerry had been cheated out of.

She wasn't crying for herself. She had nothing to complain about, relatively speaking.

Oh, but it hurt anyway.

Chapter 23

"GET LOST, YOU SADIST."

"C'mon, man. Three more."

"You're exacerbating my internal injuries, for fuck's sake!"

"Except I'm not, since they're all healed up."

"Don't say *healed up*, it's redundant. Just say *healed*."

"Three more, Sam."

A long, drawn-out groan. "Go fuck yourself, you're killing me. I can actually feel my lungs inflating with blood and angst."

"Again, no internal injuries at this point. As you well know. I get cc'ed on everything in your chart, Sam."

"Remind me to get an entirely new medical team."

"Sure, I'll definitely do that. It'll go to the top of my to-do list. Why, I'll cut this session short and leave right now to expedite that request! Three more, Sam."

Magnus hesitated in the entryway of the small white-with-green-shutters Cape Cod as he held Sally's hand. She looked up at him and put a finger to her lips. "We're not s'posed to interrupt," and she may have thought she was whispering, but she wasn't. "Daddy doesn't like me seeing him all hurt and sweaty, and Jonathan says Daddy tries to use the interruptions to quit early."

"So, then, Sally darling, we'll keep out of the way."

"Let's go to the kitchen."

"Sally, you just had breakfast."

"Maybe there's cookies!"

There were cookies. It was only 9:30 a.m. and the cub had had scrambled eggs, ham, and two glasses of chocolate milk, but what the hell. He poured her a glass of white milk, and they both munched contentedly for a bit while Sam yelled and complained and threatened and groaned his way through three more whatever-they-were.

And then: "Thanks, man. Don't know what I'd do without you helping me get back to myself. Besides sleep later in the mornings. And not do leg lifts until I barf. And not be a man-sized pile of sweat. And enjoy a relatively pain-free morning."

"Happy to help, Sam. I think I heard your daughter come in."

"Of course you did. You also heard her godfather come in, because Magnus never misses a chance to see me humiliated."

"Untrue," Magnus called.

"Yeah, that's fair," Sam admitted. They could hear the wheelchair coming down the hall. "He's missed one or two chances. By accident, mostly."

"Hi, Daddy! Hi, Jonathan!"

Sam beamed and hugged her from the chair. "Hi, sweet cub. Did Magnus fill you full of processed garbage?"

"No, just eggs and Oreos."

"*Your* Oreos," Magnus couldn't help pointing out. He held out a hand to Jonathan, PT, DPT. "I've seen you, lad, but I don't think we've officially met. I'm Magnus Berne."

"Jonathan Yates." The towering—nearly two meters tall!—Shifter shook his hand. Magnus rarely had to look up at a male and, even more interesting, he wasn't sure what kind of male he was looking up at. Sometimes you instinctively knew a Shifter was a wolf or a bear or what have you, but all Magnus was getting off Jonathan was *herbivore*. Going by the man's lanky build and long, slender limbs...one of the ungulates, maybe? Antelope? Giraffe? "Sam's told me about you."

Magnus chuckled. "No doubt."

"Mostly the good stuff," Sam whined. "I swear!" Then, in a more serious tone, "Thanks for taking Sally out again. I'm still waiting for them to deliver the automatic." And when Magnus opened his mouth, Sam added, "And don't offer to pay for one of those cars with hand controls for paraplegics again. Bad enough I had to give up my four by four, but now I've got even more incentive to get out of this chair and back into the world. Hey, cub, next month I'll be the one ruining your appetite for lunch by taking you out for ice cream and pie."

"Yay!"

"Thanks again, Magnus."

Magnus shrugged it off. "She's a delight. I should thank you."

"Yes." Sam nodded and stroked an imaginary goatee. "Yes, you should."

"I'm happy to get a chance to get to know her."

"Oh, is that what you're doing?"

Magnus blinked. "Pardon?"

"Pardon me, gentlemen, but I've got another patient at the top of the hour." Jonathan's hair was so thick it nearly stood up on its own, and he had the pale complexion of a natural redhead. His green eyes were calm and watchful. *Definitely an ungulate. Tapir? Camel?* "Sam, if you'll sign off on my time sheet, I'll be on my way."

"Never," Sam replied, taking Jonathan's pad and swiping.

"I'll never be complicit in my own torture by paying you. Okay, here you go."

"Keep up the hand exercises," Jonathan warned. "It's not just about getting out of that chair."

"Yes, it's also about being able to hop in my automatic, drive to your apartment, and kill you in your sleep."

The redhead laughed. "If you can make it all the way to my building and then haul your carcass up to the fourteenth floor—"

"Don't say *up to the fourteenth floor*, it's redundant. Just say *to the fourteenth floor*."

"—I'll happily sit still for my murder."

"Witness!" Sam replied gleefully. "You heard him, Magnus. He as good as invited me to kill him. Your days are numbered, Yates!"

"Big talk, Wheels. See ya. Bye, Sally. Nice to meet you, Magnus."

Amused, Magnus watched him leave. The hospital had chosen wisely; there went someone Sam couldn't intimidate or drive away. Then he turned to Sam. "I'll be leaving, then."

"Aw, c'mon. You always drop and run. Stick around, have a cup of tea."

Magnus shuddered. "I've had your tea, Sam. Never again."

"The microwave is perfectly adequate for heating water for tea!"

"Sam, y'daft bugger, are you *trying* to make my gorge rise?"

Sam shrugged off Magnus's gorge. "So have you seen any of your new friends? Mama Mac and Annette, and David? Oh, and how could I forget Oz and Lila. I never thought I'd owe so much to a goddamned Stable, of all people. Normally the thought of one of their kind finding my cub would make me feel like shattering my legs all over again, but we lucked out with this one. And Sally loves going over there almost as much as she loves going to Mama Mac's. Christ, I'll be in their debt the rest of my life."

"Swear jar, Daddy."

"Yeah, yeah, put it on my tab. What? You know I'm good for it. Now scoot while I finish talking to your godfather." And, as Sally ran off to her room, to Magnus: "And don't tell me they're not your friends. Not after what they did for us."

Magnus gave up the idea of an early getaway. "Yes, I…I met someone, and I talked to them about it."

"Hey, all right! Tell me about her."

"It's not like that. We just met. The dictionary definition of *met*, not the *meet someone* in the—what d'ye call it? Modern vernacular. It's nae a romantic entanglement of any sort."

"Do you know why you never get laid? Because you throw around phrases like *romantic entanglement*."

"You have no way of telling when I last had sex, Sam, so don't pretend otherwise." Over Sam's chortling, he added, "Anyway. I needed to track her down, and they were quite helpful. And they, like you, misinterpreted the nature of my interest."

"And then, like *you*, you went the *Hamlet* route and protested too much about how you weren't interested in a 'romantic entanglement.'"

Magnus nearly growled. "Do you lot do this with every unattached person in your lives, or just me?"

"Speaking for myself, I only do that with you. Look, Magnus, this isn't about Sue—"

"Best not to bring her into it, then," he warned.

"—it's about you."

"I never thought otherwise."

"I'm just saying, you've closed yourself off for so damned long. And for what?"

He kept quiet.

"That wasn't rhetorical," Sam added. And when Magnus still had nothing to say: "Is it because the last time you opened yourself up to new experiences and set out to make friends, you unwittingly joined a terrorist cell, which resulted in long-term repercussions including the eventual violent death of your dearest friend?"

Magnus rubbed his forehead. "That might have something to do with it."

"And now that you've let the past go—"

Wrong. Nobody ever just "let the past go." "Now you're just pulling observations out of your arse."

"*Accurate* observations. Look, I'm glad, okay? This is great for both of us. All three, actually. I'm not busting your balls for the sheer spiteful pleasure of it. Y'know, this time. And I'm grateful that you decided to stick around for a couple more months. But this is a fresh start for you. All kinds of fresh starts, to be honest. And you'd be a fool not to take advantage."

"I'm just trying to deal with one thing at a time, Sam."

"Yeah. I get it, man, but take it from me. If you have a shot at a 'romantic entanglement,' go for it. Life's too damned short. Take it from the guy who nearly died a few weeks ago."

Chapter 24

VERITY KNOCKED ON THE DOOR IN THE MOST WISHY-washy of ways, hesitated, then knocked again like there was a serial killer on her tail. Then wondered why the hell she couldn't have found middle ground. The door opened, and thank goodness, because apparently she had no idea how to properly knock at the door of a house in mourning.

In her defense, it was her first. She'd never known her grandparents. She was an only child. Her parents were alive and well, or at least they had been when she'd last called home. She'd never had a friend up and die on her before Jerry.

Jerry's little sister, Penny Hart, stood in the doorway, blinking red-rimmed eyes. "I'm trying to help with the coffee maker and Mom won't let me, so I'm stuck on door duty but I know how to make coffee because I'm not a fawn anymore!"

I'm no child psychologist, so I could be waaaay off base here, but I'm not sure the coffee maker is the issue. "Of course you aren't. And even if you were, you'd be a badass fawn. You have lunch with wolves, for God's sake."

Penny beamed, then frowned, then burst into tears. "Jerry loved that story."

"It was the first thing he told me about you." Verity leaned forward and scooped the little girl up. "Crappy, crappy day," she said into Penny's pale-gold hair.

"Uh-huh."

"Just all-around sucky."

Penny sniffed. "Yeah."

"Inside or out?"

A long pause while Penny thought it over. "In. I guess."

So Verity carried her in and put the girl down in the entryway by unspoken agreement. They'd only met a handful of times, but Penny was an exuberant, affectionate fawn who immediately latched on to Verity. Verity found a clingy younger sibling charming, possibly because she didn't have any. Penny was a smaller, female version of Jerry: slender, long-limbed, loads of freckles, big bright eyes. Fast, unbelievably fast; Verity deeply pitied whoever went up against her in track. Her parents referred to the child as *Delightful Surprise*, which, given the age disparity between siblings, seemed perfect.

Penny scampered off somewhere, possibly to sabotage the coffee maker, as Verity walked through the living room, smiling at the familiar pics of Jerry and the debate team— she wondered if any of his old high school pals knew about the memorial—and poked her head into the kitchen, where several people were gathered around the table. "Hi, Mrs. Hart. Mr. Hart."

Mrs. Hart was dry-eyed, while chopping onions, no less, which was quite a trick. Most likely channeling her sorrow into hors d'oeuvre prep and the minutiae of hosting the memorial, due to start in another half hour or so. "Hello, Verity. Thank you so much for coming."

"Of course. I'm so sorry about Jerry." She eyed the two others at the table, more than a little curious. They were a striking couple, the woman with shaggy dark hair and incongruously white tips, the man a casting agent's dream for "private investigator for low-budget Netflix series." Right down to the rumpled suit, trench, and major stubble. Verity half expected him to greet her with "The dame had gams all the way up to her chin."

And they were bears! Verity had only lived in Minnesota for a year but was starting to suspect that whole "werebears are rare bears" thing was garbage. There were at least three of them in Apple Valley right this minute. And plenty in Florida, which was part of the reason she'd left.

"Um, hi there," she said, because greeting strangers in her dead friend's kitchen while his mother pulverized onions and his father stared blankly into space wasn't awkward or sad in any way.

Mr. Hart seemed to rouse himself, making a half-hearted gesture toward the guy with stubble like steel wool. "This is David Auberon, a private investigator—"

Ah-ha!

"—and Annette Garsea, from IPA."

"IPA?"

"David, Annette, this is Jerry's friend, Verity Lane."

The woman, who had extended a hand with knee-jerk courtesy, cocked her head to the side like that dog from *His Master's Voice*. "Verity Lane? That's…"

"Huh." From David Auberon, whose gaze had sharpened.

"That's a…that's an unusual name."

Why do I get the feeling she wasn't going to say unusual name? *And why is the guy staring? I'm cute but not "gape at just before a memorial" cute.* It was one of the reasons she was somewhat suspicious of Magnus's motives. A guy like that could get laid with minimal effort, probably *no* effort, so why bother with the rando who washed up, so to speak, on his shore?

Meanwhile, the two of them were waiting for her response. "Thanks. My parents were hippies. Just kidding, they're cutthroat corporate suits. Just kidding, they're between jobs." That last actually being true. Ma and Pa Lane had retired from their respective jobs (managing various tanning salons and parking ramps) and were thinking about taking up antiquing. Possibly on a dare. Possibly because Verity had dared them.

Tanning salons! In Florida! Verity wouldn't have believed it if she hadn't seen it for herself, but Stables pay good money to expose themselves to concentrated, cancer-causing rays. Even Stables who lived in the Sunshine State. She had never been able to decide if it was obtuse or courageous. Stables took forever to heal, but you'd never know it from the way they hurled headfirst into danger. It was as cool as it was self-destructive.

None of which was suitable memorial chitchat, not least because Mrs. Hart was a Stable. Thus, what followed was small talk so awkward, it was physically painful. Verity explained that Les wouldn't be there as he was under the weather (though perhaps the thought of another Damp Squib funeral so soon after the last was too much to bear), but it was obvious neither Mr. nor Mrs. Hart cared about who would be in attendance.

After five minutes, Verity had to flee, so she offered to take out the garbage, which was full of onion skins. *What the hell is she making?* She had a moment where she wondered if Mrs. Hart was trying to hide the fact she was a Stable by filling the room with syn-Propanethial-S-oxide. (It was crazy the stuff you remembered from high school science projects.)

But that was an unworthy thought. Surely anyone who

knew them well enough to come to the memorial knew Mrs. Hart's secret. Or was it her son and daughter's secret? And if anyone didn't know, it's not like they'd make a scene at a memorial. Like, "Hey, the dead guy's mom is a Stable! Should we, I dunno, do something?"

Unfortunately, while she pondered and lugged garbage, the two bears followed her out.

Jerks. Could've at least offered to help instead of sniffing up my back trail.

"Well!" Verity dumped the garbage, clapped on the lid, then turned back to the bears who were staring at her. "At least this isn't off-putting."

"Sorry," David said, which was bullshit. He didn't sound even a bit sorry.

"We have a mutual acquaintance, Ms. Lane," Annette added.

Verity sighed. "Let me guess. Magnus Berne." He was the only other bear in the territory. That she knew of… Seemed like you couldn't walk a city block without tripping over half a dozen werebears in the Twin Cities metro area.

"He told us about your little club," Annette added. On closer inspection, the woman's brown eyes were more of a reddish brown. Bet they glowed like coals when she shifted. If ever a Shifter needed contact lenses, it was this one.

"Because of course he did. Also, phrases like 'little club' are exactly why we have that little club. I hope you caught that I dropped the quotes the second time I used that phrase. Also, this is why we have the Fight Club rule! So randos don't tell other randos about our personal business."

"Except, given recent events," David said, "it's our business, too."

"Look, I don't know how you know Jerry—knew Jerry—but you should understand, oh, now, what the shit?"

That last because Magnus fucking Berne had pulled into the driveway.

"I'm in a loop," Verity observed. "I'm caught in a temporal loop. Watch him get out and offer me a robe."

Annette laughed at that, so Verity decided she might not be completely terrible.

Then she realized the only reason Annette had gotten the joke was because Magnus had been telling her about their island meetups and decided they were all terrible.

Magnus Berne got out of what she assumed was a rental car, a purple Ford Mustang convertible, which was just ridiculous; the thing was a metal eggplant on wheels. Flashy and not the type of get-around-town vehicle she would have thought he'd want. Were they out of SUVs? Or whatever Scots preferred to drive? Where did he even keep it? Had to be a garage on the mainland. Or he had his own private ferry she had somehow failed to notice.

As he approached, she was annoyed to see he looked great in another dark suit (navy blue this time, with a crisp white shirt, and shiny, pointy black shoes that made her toes hurt just to look at them). His hands were empty; no robe. So, progress.

"Newspaper notice," he said before she could begin to harangue. Verity had an evil thought

(*maybe the obit section should give the Damp Squibs a discount*)

that she banished almost immediately.

"I don't even know where to start with you," she began, then fell silent because she didn't even know where to start with him. She was embarrassed to see him because the last time they'd been together, she'd been getting tears and mucous all over his fur. And she was (a little, a very, very little) glad to see him because the last time they'd been together, she'd been getting…well.

"David. Annette." They shook hands all around. Which made Annette look amused for some reason. Not that Verity cared; she wanted them all gone. Or she wanted to be gone. A combo of both wishes granted would also be good. "Thank you for the call."

Oh, goody, the stalker had henchmen. Verity revised her opinion of Annette sharply down. So they called *and* Magnus saw the notice in the paper? How fortuitous.

"It's not what you think," Magnus told her, because he thought he was a fucking telepath. "You need to—I would like it if you—" Then he cut himself off, took Verity by the elbow (gently, she'd give him that), and pulled her off to the side.

"I'm trying to decide if I should stab you in the eyes or the balls," she informed him, and behind them, David laughed.

"I don't blame ye, lass, but there are things going on y'might not know." He'd lowered his voice and bent toward her, which was alarming and exciting and alarming. "I reached out to David because—"

She leaned away from him. "Why do people always do the thing where they move three feet to have a private conversation? Despite the fact the people they're talking about can hear every word? David just laughed because *he could hear us*. Just have the chat, Magnus! Don't bother moving us seventy-two inches first!"

"I think there might be a chance Jerry's death wasn't an accident."

She blinked. "That's a little out of nowhere." That might—*might*—reflect well on Magnus. That he didn't immediately assume squibs were clumsy and inadvertently caused their own deaths. That he thought squibs would have needed a push, so to speak. "Why would you think that?"

"I can't really explain."

"Oh. That clears everything right up."

"I just know that it never sat right, ever since Jerry talked about Andrew Bray's memorial the day we met. And the feeling's only gotten stronger. I wish I could be more definitive, but…" He shrugged. "I have hunches. Bad things happen when I ignore them."

Is he serious? Hunches? "Okay, that's—that's a lot to unpack."

"And Jerry was underage."

She blinked faster. The word *underage* rolled through her brain. *Impossible.* They'd met on campus. The only reason he was living at home was to save money while he finished his degree. In fact, he was embarrassed to be living at home, which was why he never talked about it and hustled her out each time she went

to

his

house.

"I don't…think that's right," she began, but a horrid suspicion was growing. "Because—well, the neck beard, for starters."

Magnus cleared his throat. "I had a full beard at sixteen."

"Huh. Bet you got alllllll the girls." To David and Annette: "I think you have it wrong. We met on the U of M campus. He's a junior, and I'm a dropout who pops in for the occasional keg party or to sniff out semidecent hard cider."

"He was a junior, yes," Annette said carefully. "Because he graduated high school early."

Don't talk about his after-school activities. It embarrasses him.

Jerry's horror at finding her in his living room eyeballing pictures of STEM pals took on an entirely new meaning.

How old's this pic? You look exactly the same.

As did the presence of IPA at the memorial. And she remembered how Jerry never wanted to talk to his parents. About anything. And never wanted any of the Damp Squibs to come over. For any reason.

I mean, it's not like we can talk to our parents about this. They'd collectively shit. Why d'you think we're going out of our way to keep this quiet?

An underage Shifter would have even more reason not to talk about Damp Squids. That was why he had a curfew and always wanted to drive, she realized. And when he couldn't drive, it was because his mom wouldn't let him have the car.

And the age gap between him and his sister. It wasn't so much of a gap if he was—

"How old?"

"Sixteen." This from Mrs. Hart, who was on the porch and who had heard everything because the porch was only seven feet away. "He graduated high school two years ago. He was so excited about getting into the U's chemical engineering program."

"I'm—I'm so sorry, Mrs. Hart. I didn't know." Worse: Why hadn't she? Once she thought about it for longer than ten seconds, it was obvious. "Jerry probably cherished my vast reserves of self-absorption."

A ghost of a smile. "He especially didn't want you to know, Verity. He liked you so much."

"I liked him a lot, too." To put it mildly. Jerry's reluctance to introduce her to his family, despite the fact he and Verity had been hanging out for months, made new, awful sense. No matter how brief the visit, there was a chance his parents and/or sister would have unwittingly given him away.

"He loved having 'a cool grown-up' friend," Mrs. Hart continued. "That's why—" Her jaw worked, and then she abruptly turned and went back into the house.

"You need to come with us, lass." Magnus's voice was low and urgent. "With me and my…ah…my—Annette and David are verra good at their jobs. They want t'help. We look after each other and help each other as the occasion demands. Because we're…ah…"

"Are you trying to spit out the word *friends*?" Verity asked, incredulous.

"It's as painful to watch as it is to listen to," Annette remarked.

Magnus glanced over his shoulder at Annette and David then turned back. "Well, I dinna know if they consider themselves—they helped me a couple of months ago and—listen, lass, they're good people. You should go with them. If you'd rather I didna accompany you, that's fine, but…you should hear them out."

"The fact that you're going out of your way to describe them as 'good people' is making me leerier and leerier. That's a word, right? *Leerier*? Probably." She threw up her hands. "I'm in a temporal loop in a box, looks like. My options are go back into that house or take off with strangers."

"Or you could stab Magnus in the balls," David pointed out.

"Let's see how the rest of the day goes."

Chapter 25

ON THE WAY OVER, SHE HAD TUNED OUT WHATEVER MAGNUS was saying, slipped off her flats, and stretched until her feet could feel the breeze. If her toes could talk, they'd be praising her to the skies. And maybe Magnus, for renting a vibrant-plum vehicle.

"You look lovely, lass."

"Really? Because you look like hot garbage."

"I do?"

She sighed. "No, you don't. Lukewarm garbage at worst. So where are we headed? The island? IPA? Somewhere new and dreadful?"

"The latter, and I hope you're only half right."

"Yeah, but which half?" She let another minute go by and then came out with it: "So is it a rich guy thing or a gearhead thing or a toy thing or a combo?"

"Lass, I dinna—"

"The car. The sport yacht. The ginormous house you live alone in."

"Ah. Rich guy thing. I don't know anything about gears. But I like what I like. And what I really like is space." He shrugged. "And so."

"Great, super forthcoming as usual." Though she had to give him credit, he always answered her questions. She just didn't necessarily like the answers.

She wiggled her toes in the breeze, thought for a few seconds, and then said, "So are you and Annette and that other guy, Don—"

"David."

"Yeah, him… Is it a bear club? And note how I didn't make that sound condescending in any way."

"No, it's pure coincidence. Though my goddaughter and her father are also bears."

Goddaughter? "I lived in Florida my whole life and never met more than a dozen. I move up here—I had to, I lost a bet—and I meet half that many in just a couple of months. Weird."

"And dangerous, some might say."

Well, yeah.

"Not for you, though," he continued. "I know you laugh in the face of danger."

"Annnnnd you ruined it." But the guy had a point. (Two points!) Too many predators in the area = competing for food = slaughtering the competition. Maybe not so much these days, with a McDonald's, a Whole Foods, and a snack-stocked gas station on every block, but old habits didn't die easily. Bears needed and defended their critical space. Six hundred years ago, that meant a full-on war in the forest. These days, it meant cutting in line at Red Lobster.

"So tell me about your goddaughter. Specifically, why you even have one."

"She's a wonderful cub. Her name is Sally. But I canna go into much more detail."

Pounce! "Oh-ho. You get to shove your nose straight up my ass, but I can't know anything about you?"

"I. Um. My nose isn't—uh." Magnus was so rattled, he nearly clipped the truck he was passing.

"If you kill us in a hideous accident, my feet will never forgive you."

"It's just that she and her father have been through a rough time, quite a dangerous time, and she's lost her mother, and I dinna think he'd like me talking about her to strangers."

"Yes, discussing someone who merits privacy with pure strangers can be off-putting." Verity decided to ease up but only a smidge. "That's awful about her mom, though."

"Yes, and we knew each other back in the day, but it never really went anywhere, and no matter what anyone says, I was glad she was able to have a family with someone she loved, so you might say it worked out in the end except for how she's dead now."

Verity took a second to digest that. "First, wow. Second, you should have stopped after *yes.*" She held up her hand when he opened his mouth. "No, that's fine, let's just drop it. Okay? This is called *minding your own business.* I know it's new and scary to you, but if you see others practice it, perhaps it will become habit."

His knuckles were white on the wheel as he stared through the windshield. "I have no idea why I just told you all that."

"It's fine." *Fine* didn't cut it. Weird. Weird was what it was. And interesting. But mostly weird. He just…blarped all that up. And his outburst provoked soooo many questions. Like, how did the goddaughter's mother die, exactly? And what was she to Magnus? Still, if she squashed the queries, she could have the moral high ground. Which she normally didn't have. And so: "Let's drop it."

Long pause, broken by "Did you say you lost a bet?"

"Yep. I bet the next national headline that showcased someone doing something asinine would *not* be preceded by 'Florida man' or 'Florida woman' or 'Florida preschool class.'

In retrospect, a terrible bet. Which I lost in about eight minutes. Not even a full news cycle!"

She was leaving out some of the details. Like how she
wanted to see snow. And didn't want to see her parents. Ray
and Kay Lane meant well, which was as damning an accusa-
tion as she could make. They loved her, despite everything.
And she loved them the same way. And they worried about
her. Constantly. The pop-in visits in particular were irritating. "Oh, we just stopped by to make sure someone who *can*
shift hasn't taken advantage of you. And you know this milk
is expired, right, dear?"

Half an hour after she lost the bet, she'd rented a U-Haul
and was looking for an apartment. God *damn*, she loved the
internet.

"And so, you moved north?" he asked. "Just like that? No
family up here? No job waiting for you?"

"Nope."

"That took courage, lass."

"No, it didn't." Irritation, yes. Courage, not so much. "My
folks are only cubs, just like me." That was the norm with
werebears, probably one of the reasons the 'werebears are
rare bears but not really' thing caught on. She'd never met a
bear who had a sibling. "And I love it up here. It all worked
out great. Mostly," she added, giving him a side-eye glare.
Which was surprisingly painful. Instant headache. "The cost
of living is cheaper up here, for one thing. A lot cheaper. My
apartment would've run three times as much in Tallahassee.
And there's plenty of work up here, too. Before you butt in
yet again, I'm a freelance odor tester."

"What?"

"Which word are you having trouble with? Is it *freelance*?

No? Basically, I'm paid to smell things in a professional capacity."

"That's amazing!"

Hmm. That was a nice reaction. Usually people just went into gales of derisive laughter then demanded to know how they could land such a job.

"Well, I like it. Like any job, there are good days and bad. I mean, there are days when I get to smell fried chicken when it comes right out of the deep fryer because the restaurant owners want to find out which oil made it smell better. Lard, by the way. But then there are days when I have to smell different kinds of charcoal shoe inserts. So anyway, cheap, nice weather—look at this! We're in a convertible on a gorgeous sunny day, but it's not so hot you feel like an ambulatory puddle. Plenty of work, great schools—I met Jerry at the U the first week I...I moved here."

Jerry had made such a great impression, she mentioned him in the first of her pseudo-obligatory weekly phone calls home. Ray and Kay loved that she'd made friends with another squib, and so quickly, too. What were the odds? Because only a tiny, deeply unfortunate percentage of Shifters couldn't shift. God knew, in all their lives, they'd never met one. That they knew of. And not that there's anything wrong with being a squib. But it was great that she made a friend! And so quickly! Someone who could understand her. Someone she had something in common with.

And maybe now she wouldn't be such a loner. And maybe she would want to bring her new friend to Tallahassee for Thanksgiving, if they were home in November, but they might not be because they were taking advantage of their sudden empty-nester status to travel. Before, they never felt comfortable leaving her on her own for very long. Sure, she'd had her own place for the past couple of years, but that could be dangerous. What if someone broke in? What if she drank expired milk? Anyway, now they were traveling! But they would see her soon. Almost certainly for Christmas. Or perhaps Easter.

"Me making a friend right away—they were relieved, you know? Because that wasn't my style at all. They could stop with all the fretting."

Her mother's fear for her, her father's defensive pride. Their smiles too wide and bright at family reunions. Jerry sympathized and shared his own troubles: His father didn't mind having a squib son, but his Stable mother didn't get it. Couldn't get it. Impossible to make her see the stigma. So he stopped trying. And then he joined the Damp Squibs.

She decided she wasn't crying again. It was the wind. Ridiculous big purple eggplant convertible. Should've made him put the top up.

Chapter 26

NOT LONG AFTER, THEY PULLED INTO THE DRIVEWAY OF a neat two-story in Lilydale, a small 'burb about ten minutes from Saint Paul. The house was gray with brown trim, with a postage-stamp lawn and a front porch so big, Scarlett O'Hara could have a seat with all her beaus and all her dresses and would have room to spare. The sunny day and the welcoming porch brought on an absurd urge for an ice-cold glass of lemonade garnished with little paper umbrellas. Annette and David's car was already parked in the driveway, but they weren't on the porch drinking lemonade because they were silly.

"If I didn't know better," Verity commented, following Magnus up the walk, "I'd think you took the long way on purpose."

"It's these twisty Midwestern highways. There's no logic to them, lass!"

"Highway 94 is literally a straight line from Apple Valley to Lilydale."

"I dinna know anything about that," he replied as he knocked. "This is locked, but don't fret. Lila will unlock it for a friend."

"That's a weird thing to go out of your way to mention."

Then the hollering started.

"I've had just about enough of your nonsense, young man!"

"Lila said I could have the last of the turkey!"

"Not *you*, Oz."

Oh, goody. More ridiculousness. But what else could I expect after ditching Jerry's memorial for a ride in a gigantic eggplant?

The door opened, and behold, a Stable! One with a headful of blond curls, blue eyes, and the expression of the long-suffering and/or reluctant hostess.

"Hello, Lila."

"The fight started at Mama Mac's," Lila replied as if Magnus had said something besides hello. "It was then relocated to my house. I'm still trying to figure out why."

"This is Verity Lane," he continued. "Verity, this is Lila Kai."

"I don't understand," the blond continued, "why the fight had to migrate like an autumn goose. Hi, Magnus. Nice to meet you, Verily."

"Verity."

"Yeah, okay. Come in, I guess."

She'd had warmer invitations, but whatever. Magnus courteously stepped back so Verity could precede him into Fight Night (Fight Day, technically), giving her a triumphant smile as she did. She could almost read his mind. *See? It was locked, but she unlocked it for me!*

Ye gods, did everyone in Scotland lock their doors twenty-four seven? Or just Magnus Berne's neighbors?

There were two kids in the living room, a willowy teenager with dark hair and another brunette, a little girl—six? seven?—scraping the last drops from her cereal bowl and watching television. *Teen Titans*, from the looks of it. *Argh, they never get Koriand'r right. Not even in the comics.*

"Maggie!" the little one squealed, jumping up, upending her (fortunately empty) bowl, and arrowing toward them.

A delighted Magnus caught her on the fly. "Why, lass, what're ye doing here?"

"Daddy's physical therapy changed, so Mama Mac said I could come here today instead of Monday."

"She said you could come to *her* house." To Magnus: "She followed the fight." Lila sighed. "And the cereal. Who has a house full of kids and runs out of cereal?"

From what Verity assumed was the kitchen, a strident "I heard that, young lady!"

Lila rubbed her eyes. "Oh, Christ, I've awakened the beast."

The teenager gracefully uncoiled from her position on the floor and ambled over, head cocked to one side in clear inquiry.

"And this is Caro," Lila said, indicating the werewolf. "She's mute."

"Oh." Verity called on her rusty ASL. *Hello*, she signed. *My name is Verity Lane. It's nice to meet you.*

Caro's dark brows arched. "Appreciate the effort," she said hoarsely.

"Sometimes mute," Lila amended as Caro laughed. "C'mon in the kitchen and meet the others and maybe get them to leave, if you can manage it. Or just meet them."

Magnus, who'd been holding the cub the whole time, set her back on her feet. "Sally, darling, this is my...my..."

Oh, this should be good.

"...my Verity."

Annnnnnnnd a swing and a miss.

"Verity," the admirably undaunted Magnus continued, "this is my goddaughter, Sally."

Verity squatted to get to eye level. The child was striking, with short, wavy dark hair and tip-tilted dark eyes. Her fair skin had faint gold undertones; she would be breathtaking in a few years. *If I were Sally's dad, screw teeth and claws, I'd also start stocking up on shotguns.*

"I'm happy to meet you," Verity said, extending a hand, which the cub shook after a moment's hesitation. "And I was sorry to hear about your mother."

"She jumped out of a plane to save my dad," Sally said.

"Oh."

"And then it got worse."

"Okay."

"But my dad is getting better, and he hates his physical therapist, but only because he's really good at his job and he's a giraffe, so *that's* all right."

"Ah."

"It's okay to have bad days," the fascinating blabbermouth continued. "Even a bunch of them in a row."

"You know, I've thought that exact thing, and more than once, too."

"C'mon," Lila said, herding the two of them toward the kitchen. "Quickest in, quickest out."

Annette and David were at the table, and a short, older woman with a head full of white waves was scolding a fox and a werewolf.

"Again," the werewolf said, "Lila said I could have the last of the turkey."

"And *I* said that obviously you weren't the target of my wrath!" Then she turned to Verity, and her tone changed. "I'm Mama Mac, dear. it's nice to meet you. Magnus has told us so many lovely things about you."

"Disconcerting," Verity commented.

Caro came in just then, found the cereal, and dumped a third of the bag into her bowl, smirking at Lila's groan.

"Don't you dare take the last of the Frosted Mini-Wheats!"

"They're actually crunchy oat squares with frosting," the werewolf pointed out helpfully. "Because Lila's a fool for generic cereal. And everything."

"It's the same exact product!" the Stable screeched. "They even make it in the same factory! It's just, the boxes going out the left side have the brand name, and the boxes out the right side don't. It's beyond ludicrous to pay extra for the same thing just because it's in a different box!"

"This is Dev," Mama Mac continued, admirably undaunted, "and the big lug who now has his head in the fridge—"

"What, I have to eat this turkey dry?" The big lug/werewolf straightened, holding a jug of OJ and a bottle of mayo. He was almost as tall as Magnus, with only two-thirds of the body mass but at least as much money, going by the fancy wardrobe. A bespoke suit on a Saturday for breakfast? Must be nice. "I can't have anything to wash it down with?" Friendly green eyes sized her up. "Hi, nice to meet you."

"—is my son, Oz. We were sorry to hear about your friends, the ones—"

Please don't say "in your little club."

"—who passed on. Such a shame." Mama Mac shook her head and let out a noise between a cluck and a sigh. "And so young, too."

At least this isn't weird and getting weirder. "Thank you, that's very kind."

"Friends?" This from the fox, a blond boy who was not quite a teenager. Eleven? Twelve? He was small and compact, with a pointed chin and gleaming green eyes. "Wait, you're talking about the squib club, right? And you're one, too?"

Before Verity could answer, there was the crash of shattering crockery as Caro dropped her bowl, and then Verity was face-to-face with an enraged werewolf. Whose eyes Verity was only just noticing were a baleful yellow.

No. Wait. She wasn't enraged.

"Uh," Verity began, because she had no idea what to say or do.

Then the floor jumped up and smacked her in the back of the head, or at least that's how her poor, confused brain interpreted Caro's speed when she rushed past Verity and burst through the kitchen screen door. Literally burst; the thing was barely hanging by one hinge.

Not rage.

Terror.

Chapter 27

"Okay, ow." Verity blinked up at the ring of concerned faces. "Just really very *ow*. Girl's got some speed when she wants it."

Magnus had gone as white as Oz's crisp shirt. "Lass, are you all right?"

"Don't worry. I'll feel better once I get off my feet. Just kidding, I know I'm lying down. Just kidding, I can't actually feel my feet—*whoooof*!" Magnus had levered her off the floor like he was her own personal elevator. "Whoa! Head rush."

Mama Mac's hands were fluttering like she didn't know what to do with them: in her pockets, running through her hair, reaching out to Verity, changing her mind, cupping her elbows as if she were cold. "Maybe you should lie down, dear."

"I just got *up*." She looked around the ring of anxious faces and added, "You guys, relax. I'm fine. And apropos of nothing, Caro doesn't care for squibs, does she? Guess she's a dog person."

"Agh!"

Lila looked; Dev, the werefox, was trying to remove his ear from Annette's pincer grip. Given that he was halfway through the doorway, the woman must have grabbed him in mid-getaway.

"You did that on purpose," Annette said. Her tone was calm, but her eyes were red-red-red. Verity had to make a conscious effort to squash the urge to back up. "And I'll want to know why…later. Apologize to Verity. And then excuse yourself to your room."

"It's *not* my room. And I didn't do anything wrong! I'm not in charge of what Caro does! Maybe Magnus's girlfriend should be more careful around Shifters owwwwwww!"

"Up. Stairs. Room. Now." Her teeth were clenched so hard, Verity could actually see a muscle tic in one of Annette's cheeks.

Dev fled.

"Not his girlfriend!" Verity called after him. "Just… y'know! To set the record straight! Also, I'm a Shifter! Just like you! Only taller!"

Annette faced Verity. "I'm so sorry. There's quite a bit of foolishness going on right now. My wedding, and…" Annette gestured vaguely in Oz and Lila's direction. "Whatever *that* is."

"Prenegotiated cohabitation." From Oz.

"Jesus Christ, I rescind the invitation. I'm gonna rescind a few other things, too," Lila threatened. "Never refer to our shacking up like that again."

Oz turned to Verity. "So we're moving in together—"

"Okay," Verity replied, bemused.

"—but Lila doesn't want to give up her first house just yet," he continued, because he thought all this personal stuff was her business for some reason. "So we're still negotiating."

"Except we aren't," Lila interjected. "My terms are fixed. If you don't like them, go ruin some other woman's life." But she took his hand as she said it and smiled at him.

"So it's been more chaotic than usual," Annette continued. "And Dev is feeling the effects."

Verity rubbed her own ear in sympathy. "That's not all

he's feeling." Then she waved it away. All of it: Caro's stampede, Dev's thoughtless comment, Mama Mac's fretful hands, prenegotiated cohabitation, Oz's unnecessary explanation, Magnus Berne's presence in her life. "I've heard worse." Occasionally from family members.

"No excuse," Mama Mac said. "And certainly not why you came over."

"Uh-huh. Speaking of coming, I've got to be going." Not really. But lingering wasn't something she especially wanted to do, either. What did they even need her for? She hadn't known about Jerry's age. Now she was up to speed. She held up a hand to forestall protests: "Annette, David, I get why you wanted to talk to me. I didn't know Jerry was underage. None of the Damp Squibs did. Obviously, that's gonna be a concern for IPA. You'd be pretty crappy at your jobs if it weren't."

"Don't be so quick to discount their crappiness," Lila put in. And damn if the Stable wasn't starting to grow on her. She was moving in with a werewolf, and lived in the midst of werebears, and seemed to run things, at least from where Verity was standing. That was...kind of cool, actually. If they had kids, would they be Stables or Shifters? You never knew what you were gonna get with interspecies marriage.

Same with squibs. Nobody knew until they tried to shift and couldn't.

She shook all that off and tried to stay in the now. "But we didn't push him into anything," Verity continued. "The opposite, in fact. Jerry was an active recruiter. He recruited me, Darcy, and Norm."

"And now he's dead." From David.

"Yes, thanks, I remember," Verity snapped.

"You guys are dropping like flies." Also from David. Then: "Ow!" Mama Mac had produced a wooden spoon from nowhere and given him a sharp rap on the elbow. Verity decided to take his rueful expression as an apology.

"If it's not dangerous, what's the point? And that's not me saying that, by the way. Well, it is, but it's also a direct quote from Jerry." That said, now that two of the Damp Squibs were down, it was time to have a chat with Les. And the others. Scale back their dares, maybe. Or even quit? Or take a leave of absence? If that's what you did with death-defying clubs. If they were, say, a jump club, and two of their members died when their chutes didn't open, did the jump club disband? Or resolve to take more precautions?

She'd have to think about it, all of it—what Jerry would want, what she wanted, what she should do going forward. If anything.

She fished a card out of her wallet, handed it to Annette. "If you have any questions, I'm glad to answer them."

Annette put the card on the table, dug out her own billfold to reciprocate. "Thank you. It was good of you to cut short your time at the memorial to indulge us."

Oh, indulging? Is that what I'm doing?

Yeah, probably, she decided. They hadn't grilled her. They'd been sympathetic and attentive (mostly). TBH, she owed Dev a thank-you. They were so mortified on her behalf, no one could blame her for leaving after only ten minutes. Whatever they'd had in mind had been shelved. Probably only temporarily, but she'd take it.

"I'll be glad t'give you a ride back to your car."

"My car's in my driveway, Magnus. I Ubered to Jerry's house. Do you mind giving me a ride home?"

Chapter 28

HALF AN HOUR LATER, THEY WERE IN MINNEAPOLIS'S North Loop, and Magnus was pulling up to her apartment building, a refurbished warehouse that looked better every week. If the landlord kept updating—and he showed no signs of slowing down—he'd price her right out of the building.

"Talking about Minnesota versus Florida," Verity said, though they weren't, but she was getting nervous, so fuck it. "This would cost me three grand a month down there."

"It's charming," Magnus replied, though how he could tell from the warehouse-y exterior was a mystery.

A short silence fell. Verity took another breath (Magnus, cotton, cereal, leather seats, half-and-half) and jumped. "Aren't you going to walk me to—whoa." Because he'd all but leapt out of the driver's seat, circled the car, and had her door open in half a blink. And bowed!

"This means nothing," she warned him, getting out.

"Understood."

"It's just, although you're a creep, you've been a decent creep."

"Oh, aye."

"I keep showing up without an invite, but you seem cool with it."

"Indeed."

"Just so we're on the same page."

"Yes, lass."

He smiled so wide and so happy, she was mome
disarmed. "You don't mind me knowing where you liv

Verity pointed to the fridge, where Mama Mac had
her business card like it was a finger painting. "The e
house knows where I live. Also don't press your luck, Bei

"Mama, that's not even *your* fridge," Lila said irritably
didn't move to take the card down.

"This way it won't get lost," Mama Mac replied.

"You can't argue with common sense like that," Verit
teased, and Lila snickered in response.

"Aside from the color, y'seemed to like the car." Magnus
held out the keys. "Would ye like to drive?"

"Of course not. If I drive, I can't put my feet out the
window. Learned that one about a month after I got my
license." To the others: "I'm from Florida."

As always, that was all the explanation required.

"I like that. *Lass.* I shouldn't, but I do."

"Noted."

"I'm the only one on this floor so far," she continued, leading him down the corridor through the lobby, which currently boasted an empty desk for a future concierge or security guard or ice cream vendor, and a lone chair because the landlord assumed only one person at a time would ever have to wait in the lobby to be buzzed in. They walked past the mailboxes and the enormous rust-colored pillars, and while the lighting was industrial, when paired with warm prints on the wall and comfortable furniture, it was homier than not. "When the landlord's done, there'll still only be three apartments per floor. Y'know, if you get tired of your island."

"Are you inviting me to move into your building?"

"God, no." She got her keys out, faced him. "No, definitely not. No. No, no, no. Didn't mean to lead you on, but no. Unequivocally no. All the way around no. Could not be more of a no. Thanks for the ride."

He smiled at her, dark eyes crinkling at the corners. He wasn't wearing aftershave, which she liked. The fluorescents brought out the violet tinge to his hair. She'd looked up the Kamchatka brown bear the night before. *Ursus arctos beringianus.* Largest bear in Eurasia. Dark-brown fur with a violet tint. Yum. Oh, his yummy lips were moving. Time to tune back in.

"…you're quite welcome, lass."

In response, she stood there and stared at him. Gotta hand it to him: Magnus Berne knew how to dress for funerals. If another Damp Squib dropped dead tomorrow, his wardrobe had it covered.

"It occurs to me that I've only seen you in a robe or suits."

"If you come back to my island, Verity darling, I'll wear whatever you like."

"Careful," she teased. "I can think of some truly freaky things you could wear."

"My invitation stands."

She dragged her gaze up from his bod and settled on staring at his mouth, which was probably worse, and not subtle, but Jesus, the guy's lips looked designed for sin.

What? Designed? By whom? That doesn't even make sense!

It doesn't have to. Shut up, brain! Nobody invited you!

She decided to take a tiny step forward then realized she already had. "Magnus…"

"Yes, lass?"

"You, um…do you…" His mouth was the moon, taking up her sky.

That makes even less sense than designer lips! Will you for Christ's sake GET A GRIP?

"Did you…"

"Yes?"

"Did you have a thing for Sally's mother?"

Magnus blinked, and his hot mouth tightened as he nodded. "Yes. Years ago."

"Did you get a chance to say goodbye?"

He was silent for a long moment then shook his head. "No. By the time IPA reached me…she was gone."

Jumped out of a plane. About as gone as it was possible to be. Ohhhhh, so many questions. Which I won't ask. Dammit.

"Yeah. I didn't say goodbye to Jerry, either. It wasn't the same thing," she rushed to assure. "We were only friends. But the last thing I said to him was 'If you ever take the last pudding cup again, I'll kill you.' I have to live with that, Magnus! To the end of my days."

There. That squashed the mood, the odd "Should I kiss him and is this wise?" energy. Whew! Right? Right. Total relief at the mood squashing.

"Well, bye!" she said brightly, and fumbled with her keys, and let herself in, and didn't peek through the peephole to see if he lingered. Because why the hell would he?

Chapter 29

She was close now, so so close and that other that
(squib)
wouldn't be allowed to hurt anyone not Caro and not
(Dev)
her foxfriend her best and greatest brother she would see to
it she would she would see blood on the ground and they would
be safe and the other would be meat so she had to be sly she had
to be a shadow with teeth and so she was quiet now, so so quiet,
the other mustn't see mustn't hear mustn't smell until it was too
late until the other was in the ground and she was she was almost
there and it was easy! The other was careless just like the other
other was careless and it would cost them both the same it would
cost them everything and that was all right that was

"Caro, will you quit skulking around and get your furry
butt in here?"

eep

Chapter 30

THE PATIO, IT HAD TO BE SAID, WAS A HUGE SELLING POINT. Several of her kind tried to be near woods or water, even in cities. It's why Central Park was still Central Park. (The best thing about Central Park? It was only the *fifth* largest park in New York City.) It's why state and national parks were sacrosanct. *Thank you, President Wilson and the Organic Act of 1916!*

And while she might not be able to shift, who wouldn't appreciate a walk-out patio that led straight to the Mississippi?

"This chick," Verity announced to no one, "that's who. Wait, that means I don't appreciate—ugh, finally." This, as Caro finally stopped farting around in the dark and arrowed straight at her, golden eyes like baleful lamps, teeth like… teeth? She wasn't quite sure, things were happening kind of fast. Verity slid the patio door open farther and stepped back. "*Mi* warehouse, *su* warehouse. That's how the saying goes, right? Just kidding, I know that's not exactly how the saying…um…watch out, I guess?"

That last because a fox kit had come rocketing out of nowhere to latch on to Caro's tail. Though *rocketing out of nowhere* was an exaggeration. And it was a silly one, since nothing came from nowhere. Everything came from somewhere. The fox actually came from the north side of the warehouse, probably caught the scents he was looking for (so to speak), and slipped around to the back in time to intercept the black wolf (currently yelping and trying to shake a fox off her tail) but not in time to get in front of her.

Verity sighed and pinched the bridge of her nose. "Very clandestine, you guys. You're like furry ghosts, if ghosts yowled and snapped and rolled around behind my apartment building in full view of anyone who might be out for a walk. Thank God the sun's down. That was a hint, by the way. For you to stop already? And come inside? It's a quiet neighborhood, but let's not push it. Okay? Cubs?"

Another selling point: access to a hose hookup, which necessitated buying a hose. Her first hose! When she'd bought the thing, she had no idea what she would use it for—watering a garden? No, then she'd have to plant a garden. A Slip 'N Slide? Maybe, but only if she waited half an hour after eating before slipping *or* sliding. Seeing how many hoses she'd need to go from her place to the river and then filling up the Mississippi with more water for some reason?

"Fuck's sake," she said and blasted the wolf and fox, full force. The howls were music to her ears, which was ironic given that she wanted them to just knock off the racket already. "That's the Jet setting, if you're wondering. I know, I know, it's overkill. You're wondering why I didn't go for something subtler, like Shower, or Mist. But the thing is, I don't do subtle. And neither do you. And when did a mist ever prevent anyone from doing anything?"

The surprise had jolted Dev back to his other self. He knelt in the wet grass, naked and shivering, one arm slung around Caro's neck, green eyes bright in the patio light. "I'm sorry," he said. "I'm so, so sorry."

And burst into tears.

Ten minutes later, Dev was wearing a pair of Verity's shorts and her purple "I like to party, and by party, I mean take naps" T-shirt. His wet hair was sticking up in unruly spikes, and he was sucking down the last packet of Little Debbie Swiss Rolls. She wondered when he had shifted and where his clothes were. How'd he even get here? Caro's appearance was to be expected. Dev's, not so much. He must have hitched a ride from someone, and who'd let a fox into their car? Besides a rogue animal activist?

Caro wouldn't come in.

Verity left the patio door temptingly ajar. Then she set up a snack plate of cookies beside the door left temptingly ajar. Then she ate the cookies and replaced them with a tuna sandwich beside the door left temptingly ajar. Then she went to the other side of the living room and stayed there, far away from the snack plate beside the door left temptingly ajar. But the cub wasn't having it, and now Verity was craving tuna.

Not that Caro looked much like a cuddly cub. She was all lean limbs and black, bristling fur and glaring eyes and low, ripping growls. She was a good size too—big as a black Lab and a hundred times more dangerous. Labs were only dangerous to snacks and ducks.

"So, just ballparking some theories here…well, one theory." Verity refilled Dev's glass with milk. "Caro's met a squib before tonight?"

Dev nodded. She hadn't been able to get much out of him since his sobbed apology. She'd brought him inside, found clean towels and clothes, and fixed him a snack because she was a terrific person who rose to every occasion, no matter how sudden or weird, but other than another apology and a muttered thanks, Dev had nothing to say.

"It's fine, you know. About what you said at Lila's house. There were three bears and a wolf in the room. And whatever Mama Mac is." Capybara? Porcupine? Some kind of herbivore... "I was always going to be fine."

"It's not fine. It was mean and thoughtless."

"Also, I can take care of myself. I probably should've said that part first."

"Still not fine."

Verity shrugged then rooted around in her pantry until—success! "Hellooooo, lovers," she told the Ding Dongs. "Where've you been all my life?" There was a snort behind her, but by the time she turned, the kit was poker-faced.

"So. Um." Dev looked around the kitchen and living room. Everything was minimalist, because Verity was cheap and didn't want loads of furniture. "Are you rich?"

She saw the place through his eyes: exposed brick and pillars flanked by sleek, modern appliances (which came with the apartment). Industrial tile but loads of soft, fluffy throw rugs (carpet remnants). Industrial shelving lined with bright colors, holding books and knickknacks (contact paper and her egg cup collection, because every cup in the world should be an egg cup).[11] Visible pipes and the ventilation system in her ceiling, prints on the wall (Target). Not many windows and little to no natural light, but colorful curtains (also Target). Concrete ceiling, but track lighting and lots of pendant lights (Home Depot).

"I'm not rich. Middle class all the way. I got a deal on the rent because all day long there's construction. But my sleep apnea machine drowns out the noise. Just kidding, I don't have sleep apnea. Just kidding, I do, but nothing drowns out the noise."

---

11. Truth!

"I wanted to see what you would do," Dev added, because they were apparently having two different conversations. "I didn't think about what Caro would do. That was dumb, *estupido, blöd*."

"Sure, okay. All those things."

He gulped more milk. "How come you weren't scared?"

"How'd you know I wasn't?"

"You didn't smell scared. You were giving off that smell like when an engine starts to overheat." Dev mimed billowing smoke, and she nearly choked on her Ding Dong. "You know—exasperation. Testiness." When she didn't immediately reply, he added, "*Ärgerlich*. And…um…"

"It's fine, you don't have to wrack your brain for the Portuguese or Mandarin word for *exasperation*. I was just digesting what you said. Why would I be scared? You're a kit and a cub."

"Caro was scared."

"I know." Terror smelled like a five-alarm fire. Once you scented it, you never forgot. "But she wasn't trying to hurt me. She was just trying to get away."

"Want to know why?"

She regarded Dev for a long, unblinking moment. He broke first, his green-eyed gaze dropping to the floor. "I think that's Caro's story to tell. When she's up to it, I mean. She doesn't owe me an explanation. We only just met."

"I'm sorry," he said again.

"Oh, enough with the mea culpas."

"Wouldn't it be meas culpa?"

"What, like I know? Finish your snack. It's fine, I told you."

"I'm leaving soon, is all. I won't be around later to apologize. So."

Leaving? As in going to a new foster home? Or back with his parents, whoever and wherever they are? Or running away? Does Mama Mac know? Or is she kicking him out?

Not my business.

"And," Dev continued, "I needed to talk to you about something."

"Well." She sat across from him at the small table. "Now would be the time, then."

Dev looked over at the patio doors, where Caro was still prowling. "Caro? Can I?"

The werewolf crept closer, reaching the concrete patio but stopping just short of coming inside. She sat, got up to take a few more steps, sat again, and let out a low whine. Verity tried not to think about the hundreds of mosquitos soaring inside and starting families while Caro made up her mind.

"C'mon, it's okay," Dev coaxed. "We'll leave right after. Promise. I've got money. I'll get you a Filet-O-Fish." To Verity: "Her favorite."

"Because she's a woman of fine culinary taste." Dammit! Now she wanted a Filet-O-Fish. And how? How would they leave right after? Would he call Mama Mac? Or Annette? *Not my business. Except it is, because they're kids. Like Jerry...was.*

Dev got to his feet as Caro crept across the threshold, then he crossed the room and slid the screen door shut. Caro didn't come any closer, just lay down right by the door, gaze fixed on Verity. *Gah, she isn't blinking! How does she pull that off?*

"I've got lunch meat," Verity volunteered. "And some leftover rotisserie chicken. I bought three of the things." *Oh, rotisserie chicken, is there anything you can't do?*

"Naw, she can't eat when she's nervous."

"I'm the same way. Just kidding, I actually eat twice my body weight when I'm nervous."

"Great. So, a few years ago…"

Chapter 31

A FEW YEARS AGO, A TERRIBLE GROUP OF STABLES AND Shifters got together to form a vile club that trafficked Shifter juveniles. A Shifter werewolf (or werebear, or weretiger, or werecoyote) was, in some dark circles, that year's version of a potbellied pig. Shifter juveniles made excellent guard animals, too, and others could be used for breeding.

The man in charge of the caged weres was a squib. He couldn't shift, but he had power over so many who could. He helped the club figure out which juveniles to steal—runaways and fosters were easiest—and what to do with them once they were in custody. His job was to watch them and break them and, after the breaking, arrange transport to their new owners.

Despite the inherent risks and the very real likelihood of getting caught, he was devoted to his terrible tasks and vowed to prove to the club that even though he couldn't shift, he had value.

The squib kept them in cages and kept the warehouse very, very cold then punished anyone who grew fur without permission. He gave them dog food, because it wasn't for them to decide what they would eat. He brought in a vet who would fix the broken ones who could still be salvaged. He forced the addicts to dry out. He proved, over and over, that no one was coming for them. That no one cared about their disappearances or even noticed they were gone. They ate, and slept, and shat only when given permission. Shifters who were good pets got to eat good food, and be warm, and eventually leave the warehouse to live with their new owners, too shattered by the experience to ever cry for help.

Caro was never a good pet. When he starved her, she growled and glared. When he shocked her, she yelped and glared. The thinner she got, the angrier she got. The angrier she got, the more she reminded herself that he would slip. One day, even if only for a moment, he would make a mistake. And she would be ready.

This squib was good at his job until he wasn't, and Caro escaped. Then she met Dev, who was also living on the streets. And then they met Annette Garsea.

Chapter 32

"BUT THAT'S NOT IMPORTANT TO THE STORY," DEV finished.

Really? Seems kind of significant. That last sentence, you dropped it like a little bomb. "Okay," Verity said, because what the hell *else* could she say? *Should I have made popcorn before you got started?* Or, *You guys sure are up late for a school night!* Or, *Tell you what, I'm giving that story an eight for the ick factor and a six for the tear-jerking factor.* "That's an awful story. Hair-raising and horrifying. I'm gonna be thinking about that a *lot* in the days and nights to come. Thanks so much for telling me!"

Dev smiled a little and shrugged.

"I can't imagine what you guys endured." To Caro: "I'm so sorry for everything those fu—those shi—those jerks forced you to endure. I know you don't know me, but I'd never hurt a cub. Not even if a Stable stuck a gun in my ear." Because that was what a lot of them liked to do, apparently. Stables, in particular American Stables, loooooooved their guns and stuck them everywhere: ears, foreheads, kidneys…

On the other hand, you had to give them credit for thinking up guns in the first place. Amazing how they ably—more than ably!—compensated over the millennia for their lack of claws, fur, and tails. And she'd always thought there was something to the Shifter theory about how Stables held on to their guns with such ferocity because their subconscious perceived Shifters, even if they consciously couldn't tell the difference between both species.

And why was she even thinking about guns right now? Or theories? Oh. Right. Because she didn't want to think about why Caro was selectively mute. It made awful sense if you thought it over. Her voice was one of the things entirely under her control. Once upon a time, maybe the only thing.

"But see, the worst part—" Dev began.

"Oh, God." Verity squashed the urge to cover her eyes. "There's a worst part?"

"—is that it all happened down here. In the Minneapolis warehouse district by the river. Like, two blocks from your apartment. So you can see why Caro—"

Verity was on her feet before she knew she would move. "It was the low rents!" she practically shouted. "How could I have known? It's not like the lease spelled out 'one indoor parking space plus free membership into our Shifter trafficking club,' for God's sake!"

You're shrieking. Get a grip.

"Sorry. Sorry about that." She slumped back into her chair. "That is to say, I am shocked and appalled and had nothing to do with any of it, though I cannot blame you for wondering otherwise, and in your place I would have done the same and perhaps even more, and worse, and eventually set fires." Then, in a mutter, "None of this came up during the tour, that's for sure."

"No, it wouldn't have," Dev replied, not at all fazed by her screaming. "Annette and Judge Gomph—he's one of the juvie court judges—cleaned it up and kept it quiet."

Because of course they had. And she'd just bet they did a

great job. A perfect job. *Everything in service of keeping Shifters out of the public eye.*

Even good things, like wiping out child traffickers, had to be covered up.

Verity straightened in her seat. "Gomph? As in *gomphothere*? You know, a were-elephant? I've never seen one. Not a lot of elephants in Florida. Y'know, anymore."

"Well, he's big and black and wrinkled, and he loves salad, so."

"Wonderful!" Verity put aside the elephant in the room to get back on track. "And this trafficking pack of shit stains, they were Shifters *and* Stables?" Because that raised all sorts of troubling, terrifying questions. Shifters were massively, laughably outnumbered by Stables: Verity and her kind were…what? Less than 2 percent of the population? Something like that. So, while it was perhaps inevitable that your average Shifter would have relationships of all sorts with Stables, they didn't go out of their way to flaunt their dual natures. Imagine: "Hey, great job on the pipes, thanks for coming over so quickly. Did you know I'm a wolf with a bite force of six hundred pounds?"

Just…so awkward.

Not to mention dangerous. And that wasn't even going into the SAS movement and their random bullshit.

Verity had to move, so she paced while keeping her distance from Caro. "So you're telling me there are Stables out in the world who know all about us…"

"Well, there always have been. It's why there are all those stories about werewolves and monsters in the dark across every culture. Except in our version, Little Red Riding Hood had a crossbow and took the wolf down with, like, *no* trouble.

I'm sure your folks did the 'watch out or Stables will get you' thing."

"No, my parents did the 'you can't shift so watch out for real Shifters' thing, and they made sure to put the emphasis on *real*."

Dev's brow furrowed. "Oh. Sorry."

She waved her annoying parents away. "Nothing compared to what you guys endured… So some Stables know about us *and* worked with Shifters so they could have…" Verity had to swallow the urge to spit. "…pets? Because that's fucking horrifying. Uh. Sorry."

"Don't apologize. It *is* fucking horrifying."

"So are you and Caro sc—" No, that wouldn't do. *Never tell a kit you think they're scared. Overcompensation inevitably ensues.* "Are you guys worried they're still down here? The trafficking numbnuts? Because I'll walk down there right now and check the place out if you want. Actually, I'm gonna want to have a look-see regardless of what we decide to do tonight." This, even as her brain blared that was a *terrible* idea. But how could she ever sleep here again, knowing what happened just down the street? She needed to see for herself.

"You won't find anything. Annette fixed all that."

"How?"

"Who cares?"

"Oooookay. What happened to the bad guys?"

"Annette gobbled 'em up," he replied matter-of-factly. Then he grinned, showing small, sharp teeth. "Fee-faw-fum and all that."

"She also ground their bones to make their bread?"

"What? No. Gross."

The mild-mannered IPA bureaucrat devoured evil? She of the frosted hair and reddish-brown eyes? Huh. Bears were opportunistic omnivores, but that was ridiculous. "And the squib in charge of it all?"

Dev let out a snort. "He was never in charge. His family hated his squibness and he did all that shit, *merde, mierda,* to try and show them he could be useful. Puh-*thet*-ic."

"Pathetic and in the ground, right?"

"Yup. Caro got a piece of him. His 'partners' finished the job. That's how Annette and David got involved. Back when they—" He cut himself off and picked up his now-empty milk glass then set it back down. "Anyway."

"Excellent. Very happy to hear that particular squib is deceased." Caro, Verity noticed, had been creeping closer until she was sitting very close to Dev but not looking at Verity. Progress? "Listen, I appreciate you taking the time to explain all this—"

"You do? Because you smell sort of horrified."

"Prob'ly because I'm sort of horrified. And I appreciate the apology and all, but I'm still not sure what—"

"Your friend. The one who died. The one in your club. The club that lost two members in one month?"

"Uh, yes, I remember. Also, thanks for not prefacing *club* with *little*."

"What if they didn't die by accident? What if it's a mean way to target squibs, like the traffickers found ways to target vulnerable Shifters?"

Before she could begin to digest the utter revulsion that idea conjured, there was a sudden, booming knock at her front door. They all jumped, and Caro went from aloof and looking away to bristling and snarling in half a tic.

"Lass?" *Wham-wham-wham!* "Let me in, you're in danger!"

"Oh, fuck me," she groaned, and for the first time, Dev giggled.

Chapter 33

MAGNUS DIDN'T HAVE WORDS FOR HOW RELIEVED HE was to see Verity hale and healthy and—

"Jesus Christ, you'll wake the neighbors. Just kidding, I don't have any. Get your ass in here."

—aggrieved.

He repressed the urge to take her by the shoulders and scrutinize her for injuries. "Lass, I have good reason to believe that—oh." He took in a damp, bizarrely dressed, milk-mustached Dev and Caro in her other form, looking remarkably calm under the circumstances. "And here you both are."

"Hi, Magnus."

"Lad. Caro." To Verity: "Forgive me, but I wurred you were in danger."

"You're having déjà vu also, right? It's not just me? We're fine," Verity added. "Dev had the last Little Debbie and I'm full of Ding Dongs."

"What?"

"Caro won't eat, though. Not that I blame her. Actually, I do blame her. I've offered an array of delectable treats. And rotisserie chicken!" To Caro: "Those don't grow on trees, young lady! Though they might as well, they're pretty cheap."

Magnus was having a hard time parsing…well, every-thing. "It's just—forgive me, Caro—it's just that th'lass has attacked squibs before."

"Squib, singular. And he had it coming. If I'd caught him, I'd have cut his throat and taken about a week to do it. But yeah, Caro showed up ready to rock. Isn't it cool?" At their expressions, she added, "Sorry, it's just—Shifters are never scared of me. So I'm a little giddy." This earned her a snort from Caro, which was an improvement over a chomp on the ankle.

"So you're all right," Magnus said, because the relief was crushing. And *confusing*. What was it about this particular woman?

Maybe nothing.

Or maybe you're tired of being alone, and your last excuse to keep hiding jumped out an airplane a few months ago.

"Sound as a pound, except not really, according to the BBC. Relax. I knew Caro was with us all the way."

"You—what?"

"There was no other reason why your trunk would smell like cereal and half-and-half," Verity said.

"It's so gross that you put half-and-half in your cereal," Dev told Caro.

"Yeah, but that's a different issue. Obviously she was back there," Verity continued. "Prob'ly ran outside—well, ran me over, then ran outside, stayed close to listen, realized I'd be getting in your big ridiculous purple car, and stowed away."

Fucking allergies.

"Why do you think I let you walk me in?" Verity continued, equal parts dazzling and annoying. It had to be said: the woman did love the sound of her own voice. He loved it, too. "I know how to walk to my own apartment, Magnus."

"I never said otherwise!"

"You didn't really think I believed the banal bullshit I was sputtering, did you? With the tour? I was giving Caro time to get out and set up her ambush."

"Wait," Dev said. "You were? So you're saying my beautifully timed entrance was totally unnecessary?"

"Entirely, completely, no-doubt-about-it unnecessary."

"I'm glad you're safe," Magnus said, because he'd take the embarrassment of misinterpreting Verity's motives over finding her like he found the dummies. Worse than the dummies, in fact—Caro could have ripped her up. He wasn't sure why the lass had stayed her teeth, but he was ferociously glad.

"And I'm glad you're here, which is something I didn't think I'd say tonight. Or any night. You can give these two a ride back." At Caro's rumbling, she added, "Oh, knock it off. There's nothing to see here, and you damned well know it. It's like you—well, Dev—said: Annette made it all go away, evil was punished, case closed. So go home."

"Okay, but—"

"You play your cards right, Mama Mac will never know you were gone. Magnus takes you back, I eat more Ding Dongs, you guys do the 'you know, I learned something today' speech, and everyone goes to bed except me, because I had a Frappuccino after supper."

"Boring," Dev announced. "But good. Y'know, for now."

"One thing I don't get, Magnus," Verity said. "How'd you figure out that Caro had stowed away? Did you mainline Benadryl to get your schnoz working?"

Mainline? Argh, American slang. "One of my tires is a little low. I checked the boot to make sure I had a proper spare. And I did, plus an ungodly amount of wolf fur."

Verity laughed.

"But how did *you* get all the way out here, lad?"

Dev rolled his eyes with the patented scorn of the preteen. "I lived on the streets, Magnus. You think I don't know how to cadge a ride? Besides, it's good to keep the skill set sharp. You never know when you have to bolt."

"Lad, it's none of my business—"

"Ha! Dev, I promise you, that won't stop him."

"—but it sounds like you're planning to run."

"No, it sounds like I know how to take care of myself, and everybody keeps forgetting that. Not you, Caro." Caro had used the distraction of Magnus's arrival to creep ever closer, and now Dev raised a hand to rub behind her ears. "Just... I'm not a kit anymore. I've been on my own for a while. I could do it again. I wouldn't be scared this time."

"I don't think it's a matter of people thinking you can't take care of yourself," Verity said tentatively. "I think it's more like they don't want you thinking you have to. But I could be wrong. I'm oblivious and had no idea my best friend was underage."

"Yeah, and that reminds me, you should know that Annette and David are going to be all over that. They're gonna want to track all the others to make sure none of them knew Jerry was a kid, because then you're looking at reckless endangerment of a minor. That's a felony in Minnesota. They'll have to make sure the rest of you are old enough to risk your lives doing dangerous stuff."

"Annnnnnd you've officially worn out your welcome. But thanks for the heads-up on felony endangerment, Dev."

"Lass—"

"You, too, Magnus. And I think they got everything they need, you guys. They were both at Jerry's memorial—it's how I ended up at Lila's house—and they let me leave, no problem."

"Because they knew they couldn't make you stay," Dev said simply. "Which is why they kept it friendly. Trust me, they're not done with any of you."

"You probably didn't mean to make that sound ominous," Verity began.

"I did, though."

"Oh. Good job. And thanks for the warning. But as much as I don't like people up in my business, I can't fault them for wanting to make sure there aren't any other li'l squibs in the Damp Squibs." And, in response to Dev's giggle, "Look, I didn't think up the name, okay? It was like that when I got there."

"How *did* you get there?"

"My teenage pal recruited me and then died."

Magnus cleared his throat. "All right, lad. Let's get going, then. The lady would like to see us out."

"Yup," the lady replied. "Out, out, all the way out."

Dev plucked at the T-shirt. "I'll get these back to you before...before too long."

"No rush."

"Wrong, *incorrecto, falsch*."

"I feel like one *wrong* would've been sufficient," Verity said with a smile.

Caro padded right on Dev's heels while giving Verity an understandably wide berth.

"Sorry t'barge in on you, lass."

"Again."

"Again," he admitted.

"Though to be fair, I've barged in on you, too."

"So ye have."

"At least when you barge, you're fully clothed."

Magnus laughed, and Dev started to turn back, only to be propelled by a gentle shove as Magnus opened the door and let the cubs precede him, when Verity cleared her throat and said the most wonderful thing.

"Wait." She paused a long moment then went on, "I should go see the other Damp Squibs. I was thinking that earlier, at the memorial. That it's overdue and we have to figure out where to go from here. And I was thinking. Um. That you might. That you might want to come with?"

Warmth bloomed in his chest even as he reminded himself to keep it together. "I would. Verra much. Not just for the pleasure of your company—"

"Barf." From Dev, loitering in the hallway.

"—but I'm wonderin' how the club came to be. And a few other things."

"Me, too," she admitted. "I'm embarrassed to say I really don't know much about them, since I signed on in midstream, so to speak. And I'm more embarrassed to say it took *two* deaths to get me wondering. Why did Les think it up? What's the endgame? I couldn't ask him about that stuff at the memorial, he wasn't able to come. Even if he had, we left early. It's okay," she added, as if Magnus had protested. "Jerry always told me that if he had a memorial, I should either be a no-show or desecrate the funeral home with random sex."

"Random sex? So, er, nothing planned? Or is it the partner who is the random element?"

"Who cares? Obviously only one of those was an option. And a chat with Les is loooong overdue. I'm embarrassingly late to the party on this one."

He dug for his keys. "Let's go have a chat with him."

"Yeah, but simmer. Not right this minute, obviously. It's ten o'clock."

"Oh. Yes." *Stop staring. Walk out the door. Try to escape with a semblance of dignity.* "Verra well. See you tomorrow, Verity." Magnus turned away, when she did it again.

"Wait."

"Oh, Jesus Christ," Dev said and began stomping down the hall toward the parking lot.

"How would you even get back to the island at night? Boat, right? I mean, is it even legal to be on the lake after dark?"

"Well…" *Magnus, you utter dolt, don't do it.*

"Yeah, that's what I thought," she replied, because she hadn't lived in Minnesota very long. "It's too dangerous. Okay. So. You could—and don't read into this—but you could stay here. Don't read into this, but I've got a guest room with a horribly uncomfortable futon. Don't read into it. But that futon *will* wrench your spine, and you'll wake up wondering who tried to beat you to death while you were sleeping."

"All right."

"Don't read into it!"

"I'm not, I swear." This was nothing but the truth. And speaking of the truth, when Verity found out what he'd done, she'd stab him in the face.

Worth it.

"All right, so, ditch the cubs—"

From the hallway: "Hey!"

"—and then get back here," Verity said. "And we'll go see Les first thing in the morning."

"As you wish."

She cocked her head to one side. "Did you ever see *The Princess Bride*?"

"No," he admitted.

"Oh." This seemed to disappoint her, and he made a mental note to watch the movie ASAP. "Okay. So. See you."

"Soon," he promised, and left, and definitely didn't dance his way out the door. On the outside, at least.

Chapter 34

THE EXPECTED RAP AT THE DOOR WAS LATE BY A GOOD half hour. Her pulse jumped, and she had to force herself not to scamper across the room like she was anxious to see him. She opened the door to see Magnus Berne holding a small grocery bag. Vodka? Underwear? Both?

"If that's full of condoms and Benadryl, I'm gonna be upset."

"No need." He tipped the bag so she could see inside: Ding Dongs, Little Debbie Swiss Rolls, and chocolate Zingers.

"All right, I might have a tiny weakness for chocolate snack cakes in all shapes and sizes that can be stored for years and still enjoyed. Sue me. But come in first."

Magnus complied, because he was like a vampire that way: he'd only come in if invited, and sometimes not even then. Conversely, he would come when no invitation had been tendered, because the guy lived for memorials, apparently. And she hadn't forgotten how he couldn't refer to Annette and Lila as friends. Their fond exasperation when he did it (or, rather, didn't) was telling.

"Zinger?"

"No. I dinna understand, you've got this gourmet sniffer—"

"I've got a what?"

He made a vague gesture toward her face. "You sniff things for a living. But you eat junk."

"Both those things can be true without it being weird."

He grinned. "Disagree."

"Well. For example, I can tell you the difference between Gorgonzola and Stilton, and whether the blue veins are caused by *Penicillium roqueforti* or *Penicillium glaucum*, but guess what? I fucking hate blue cheese. I dunno who in history said, 'You know what would be delish? Moldy cheese,' but they were unhinged, Magnus, deeply, *thoroughly* unhinged."

"Ah."

"And don't get me started on pâté. Just because I appreciate the difference between liverwurst and foie gras doesn't mean I want to chow down on either. Again: Who woke up one day and said, 'We should grind up the organ that filters urine and spread it on crackers'? And why weren't they driven out of their village? My point being, hit me with some Zingers, baby! What? Stop laughing, I'm being serious."

"I know. That's why it's funny."

"I'm already regretting my impromptu invitation. Now I'm going to give you an unnecessary tour, because this apartment is the 'open floor plan' plan and what you see is what you get. My duties as hostess are limited, but I'm bound to them, so. Kitchen with weirdly deep cupboards so I never know what I have because my arm isn't long enough to hit the back of the cupboard. So I only go elbow-deep, except sometimes when I'm putting away the Cocoa Pebbles other stuff gets shoved to the back, and that's why I need a chair and a flashlight to make my grocery list, which is why I never make a grocery list."

"That seems t'be the best way to handle the problem."

"Hold all questions and comments to the end of the tour,

please. Dining room, which is just an open room with a table smack in the middle and no walls, so is it even a room? And is a card table I got at a garage sale even a table? Yes. Living room, which is what happens when you take four steps away from the dining 'room', tiny bathroom, which is basically a toilet and a sink the size and height of an elementary school water fountain…that's half of it." She led him down the hall.

"Bedroom with blinding white walls, bathroom with same, plus shiny chrome faucets so it's not unlike peeing on a brightly lit film set while all the spotlights are trained on you, closet space behind frosted sliding doors for some reason so it always looks like someone's lurking in there, chilly floors because, again, warehouse, guest room in blinding white except for one wall that is the original brick, furnished with hideous instrument of torture disguised as futon, and another creepy frosted closet…"

"You should run your own B&B," he commented. "Ye have a way of making everything seem so homey and welcoming."

"What did I say about comments? And now we're back in the living 'room,' and the kitchen closes at midnight. Just kidding, it never closes. Just kidding, it never closes except to you. But you may have a Zinger. Well. Half a Zinger. You shouldn't eat Zingers. Your Scottish blood won't know what to make of it."

"My Scottish blood survived the rigors of haggis and Irn-Bru. Your Zinger holds no terrors for me," he proclaimed, and she had to laugh. "I can't tell if you love it or hate it here."

"It's love." She went to the sliding doors, checked that they were locked, and looked out into the night. She couldn't see the river in the dark, but she could hear and smell it. "But

I can't have the landlord getting a big head and charging me twice as much rent, which even then would only be a third of what it's worth. The construction's annoying, but when it's over, I'll be looking for new digs."

"Perhaps your job—"

"Sniffing stuff for a living pays well, but not 'luxury apartment in large metro area with water view' well. So I run down the place while the landlord does the literal opposite. But the nice thing—"

She cut herself off when she heard the most nightmarish of all sounds: her laptop chiming to let her know the 'rents wanted a chat.

"Oh, *shit*," she breathed.

"Verity?"

They never did this. Never called so late. Their next semiobligatory Zoom chat was four days away and took place at suppertime. What in the name of fuck could they possibly want? And did she want to find out?

"Lass?"

Ignore it? No, then they'd worry. Plus she'd lie awake half the night wondering what was so urgent they had to call this late. And they were in Florida. For them, it was approaching midnight. Were they hurt? Had one of them died? Were they, perish the thought, planning to visit her on their way to Sitka?

"Verity, d'you know you're grinding your teeth?"

"Don't bother me with petty dental details when there's a disaster in the making." She nodded toward her laptop. "My folks are on the other end of that call."

He raised his eyebrows. "Ah. Perhaps they would worra if they saw you had a strange man over so late?"

"A very strange man, but that's not the issue." Worry? They'd be thrilled. They'd hand her over in marriage if they could. Right then and there. On Zoom. Magnus in his mourning suit and her in her Pavlov's cat T-shirt. The wedding of her dreams!

"It's not?" Magnus asked, and he wasn't nearly panicked enough considering what was about to go down. "Well, I'm happy t'step outside…"

"You'd literally have to go all the way outside—open floor plan, remember? Not much privacy. You could be hiding upstairs in my closet with the cloudy doors closed tight and you'd still be able to hear my dad fart. And I won't have you lurking in the dark like some weirdo who lurks in the dark."

"Then where d'ye want me?"

A complicated question. "Just…have a seat in the living 'room.'"

"The living area?" he suggested.

"Yes, adjacent to the dining area adjacent to the bathroom area. I'll be in the kitchen."

"Area."

"Well, yeah." She grinned at the absurdity of…all of it, really. Then hurried to the kitchen where her laptop was, flipped it open,

"God help me."

and answered.

And there they were, Ray and Kay Lane, sitting shoulder to shoulder, dark heads bent together so they could talk at her at the same time. Her father was in one of his checkered flannel shirts, which was absurd for Florida in summer. Her mother was in a tube top, also absurd.

"Verity?" they said in disconcerting unison. More than

once, she'd wondered if her parents were siblings. "Are you okay?"

Normally, she would put that abrupt, fretful question down to whatever urgent reason necessitated the phone call, except they opened every conversation the same way. Worried, ready to panic, slightly shrill. "Of course I'm okay. Are *you* okay? What's up that you want to talk so late?"

"We just got your message about your friend, that Jerry?"

She gritted her teeth over the upward inflection that was her parents' preferred mode to communicate—they made questions out of so many things—and stifled the urge to reply, "What Jerry?" Instead, she said, "Yes?"

"He's dead?"

"Yes." She had left them a voicemail with the sad news a few days ago, as they were on one of their "hooray, we're free from the shackle that was Verity Lane!" trips. "How was Qinghai?"

"A *shame* is what it was. It's beautiful, but the Stables have wiped out so many bears, it's awful."

"They won't be happy until they've killed and eaten everything." Her father shook his head. "And then where will we be?"

"In a bearless world," her mother replied dolefully.

"Careful, guys. You're giving off SAS vibes."

"Oh, Verity, we are not," her mother snapped. "You can acknowledge the Stables are destroying everything they touch without being speciesist."

Verity smirked. "Whatever you say."

"But at least we had the chance to go. That's something."

"You've had a chance to go for the last few years, Mom."

"Oh, well, yes, but…not really?"

"Right. What with me cramping your style by being born. Rest assured it was always part of my sinister plan." What was worse, enduring the conversation, or knowing Magnus Berne could hear every word? Was there a third option?

"Oh, just stop it," her father said. "Okay? We love you just the way you are."

That might be true. But it never stopped them from wishing she could shift.

"I'm glad you went, too," Verity said, because a truer thing had never been said in this warehouse. "And don't worry about me. I'm sad about Jerry, but…" *Let's see, what would be an appropriate platitude?* "…life goes on." Insipid but factual. Perfect.

"Well." Her father cleared his throat then followed it up with…nothing. Her mother also cleared her throat. Then they stared at each other for long moments, first Mom tilting her head toward the screen ("No, you go.") at the same time Dad tipped his head the other way ("No, I insist, *you* go."). Then they both stared at Verity. Then looked at each other again. The silence got heavier as neither of them wanted to make the leap, and Verity was frazzled enough, a mere thirty seconds in, to rip every lock of hair out of her head. So far, the typical semiobligatory Zoom chat.

After 1,265 years, her father said, "Well."

"Yes?"

"Well. Maybe you? Should. Come home?"

Oh, here we go. "I *am* home, Dad."

"No. I mean—"

"To Florida," her mother added.

"Ahhhhh…" Verity pretended to think. "No."

"But now you're alone again! It's just so sad!"

"Thanks for that, Mom, but I will somehow find the strength to go on. Jerry wouldn't want me to scurry back to Florida with my tail between my legs."

"Oh, but Verity? You don't have a tail, sweetie."

"That's the whole problem right there," Dad added with a definitive nod.

"It's just a figure of speech." *But only for Stables.* "Jerry wouldn't want that for me and, more importantly, I don't want that for me. I appreciate your concern," she continued, because she decided to go all-in on lying through her teeth, "and I miss you both, but I'll be fine. Plus I'd be a third wheel on your trip to Nunavut."

"Well, about that? Obviously we'd cancel. Because we'd—I mean, you'd be there. Home again. With us?"

"Obviously." Verity sighed. "Say, apropos of nothing we're talking about, when are you going to stop treating me like I'm in a coma in the ICU?"

"Don't be silly, you're not in a coma, you're just..." Mom trailed off.

"There's no shame in admitting you need help," Dad added.

Disagree. "I. Don't. Need. Help."

"Well, not *all* the time, obviously—"

"Is it, Mom? Obvious?"

"—but sometimes you do, sometimes everyone does. It's only that while you were with Jerry?"

"I was never 'with' Jerry." And thank God. On top of everything else, she didn't want to be pinched for statutory rape.

Her dad picked up the narrative. "When you had Jerry, we knew you had someone to look after you? So we didn't worry?"

"First, Jerry never looked after me. Not his job. Second, if anything, *I* should have looked out for *him*. Turns out he was only sixteen."

"Oh *dear*."

"Yeah, that's one way of putting it."

"But you're alone now!" her mom pointed out in a near wail. "And your only friend was a child!"

"For God's sake, Mom, please get a grip. I'm fine. I have been fine, am fine, will be fine. Seriously, just…just go off to Likhvin or wherever."

"It's Chekalin, actually," her dad said brightly. "They changed the name."

"Right. Well, as they say in Russia, *bon voyage*. I'll be fine. Life goes on. Cherish the little things. Or the big things, like world travel."

"What time is it? Where you are?" Dad asked.

Wait, now they don't understand Central Standard Time? "Well, figure out what time it is where you are, then subtract an hour."

"See? This is a perfect example."

Verity blinked. "Of a real-life math problem?"

"It's a Saturday night," Mom pointed out, because she thought Verity didn't understand calendars. "You should be running around partying. Or running around on a date. You shouldn't be home is my point?"

"Jesus, Mom, I have to eat and sleep occasionally."

"My point? You've made a nice den for yourself and you just want to hole up."

"That's right," Dad chimed in on cue.

"When you should be out meeting people. Safe to be in groups, right?"

Depends on the group. "Say, this has been just terrific, but I think my amoebic dysentery is coming back, so I've gotta run."

"You always use that as an excuse."

"Yeah, well. It's a pretty good excuse, you've got to admit."

"Or you pretend the pizza man is at the door."

"Often the pizza man *is* at the door." Mmm, Pizzeria Lola and their Korean BBQ pizza with short ribs. Or the Sunnyside with pecorino, cream, leeks, and two eggs. She'd have to bring Maggie sometime, just to hear her patented Homer Simpson drool: "Augglllgggllggllaggllaa..."

"Or that you smell smoke," Dad added, wrenching her away from pleasant thoughts of drool. "And you don't know where it's coming from."

"That was true!" Once. Spoiler: it had been coming from the broiler.

"At least come down for a visit?" Mom asked.

And let them go to work on her in person, where the amoebic dysentery lie wouldn't be as effective? And the Sunnyside pizza would be harder to come by? Hard pass, if for no other reason than she owed it to Jerry to cooperate with the MN IPA. Which was tough to do from Tallahassee.

"Maybe for Christmas," Verity suggested. "I don't have any seniority at work, so I have to save up some vacation time."

"But that's months and months away! You could be dead by then!"

"And thank you, as always, for the vote of confidence."

"I'm sure, under the circumstances, your boss would give you time off."

"What circumstances, Dad?"

Her parents fell silent, neither willing to put it out there: *You being a squib. Those circumstances. Surely that's worth some vacation time. Maybe even a paid leave!* Pointless to remind them that she worked with a Stable.

Verity sighed. "Well, this has been a treat as always. To reiterate, I'm fine, you're fine, everyone but Jerry is fine, I'm staying, you're leaving."

Her mother's dark-brown eyes, which had narrowed at Verity's recalcitrance, now widened. "But—"

"You two crazy kids go have fun in Russia."

"Oh, now you're just being stubborn."

"Yes, Dad. You could say it's my defining trait."

"Why won't you at least go out to meet—"

"Verity? Darling?"

Everything in her froze. From eyebrows to ankles, she couldn't move. She knew Magnus had come into the room, but she was so busy trying not to grind her teeth to nubs, she hadn't realized he was now standing at her shoulder.

"Terribly sorry tae interrupt, but the others will be here soon, and you wanted me to make more appetizers." Magnus smiled as he bent down and peered at the screen. "Hello, Mr. and Mrs. Lane."

Ray and Kay: "Oh!"

"Uh. Thanks for the reminder, Magnus. You're right, I did want you to make more appetizers. So it's weird that you're not churning out more shrimp puffs."

"I live to serve," he said with a chuckle.

Ray and Kay: "Who's this?"

"This is my, um, Magnus. Berne. Magnus Berne. I met Magnus—" Was she saying his name too much? It felt like she was saying his name too much. "We met at one of the memorials." Technically true, though it wasn't their first meeting. Also, how sad and awful was the phrase *one of the memorials*? "He's, um, we're just hanging out. Here. Together. In my apartment."

"Charmed." His hand was resting on her shoulder, and it was probably her fevered imagination but she could almost feel his velvety baritone through his hand all the way down to her bones. "I hope you don't mind. Verity has exacting standards for all her get-togethers. It's why invitations are in such demand in our crowd. But I'm sure you knew that."

Given their instant, giddy grins, his baritone was working on Ray and Kay Lane as well. *Jesus fuck. I have no idea how to feel about any of this.*

"It's so nice to meet you!" they gushed in unison.

"I hope you're not thinking of taking our darling away from here," Magnus continued. "We'd be quite lost without her."

"First," Verity began, "I'm pushing thirty. They can't 'take' me away from anywhere. Second—"

"Oh, no, we wouldn't dream of it," Dad replied, because he was clueless, and she was in the third circle of Hell.

"Social responsibilities are *so* important," her mother added. "Which is what we've always said. Right, Verity? We always say that? About the importance of social responsibilities?"

"This is literally the first time you've said it."

For that, Verity earned a scowl. "Well, I'm sure we've talked about it before," Mom grumbled.

"Quite sure," Dad piped up.

"Well, not to intrude on a private family call…more than

I already have," Magnus said with another warm chuckle. He had that whole self-deprecating thing down pat.

Ray and Kay: "Oh, not at all!"

Verity: "Jesus Christ."

"But we've got to run. Lovely to meet you both," Magnus added.

"Oh, it was," her mother replied. In her rapture, she hadn't noticed she'd just given herself a compliment. "It truly was!"

"Yes, we hope to talk to you again, Mr. Berne," Dad added.

"Magnus. Please."

"Magnus, yes, of course. As my wife said, so nice to meet you. Verity, you take care. And thank you for calling!"

"You guys called me, though, so—"

"Can we reschedule next week's call? We'll be in Nunavut."

Because of course they would. The trip they would have cancelled because they'd expected she would move back home was revived the second they laid eyes on Magnus. The reason for the call had been eliminated. The reason for their concern, also eliminated. Exit Jerry, enter Magnus, and all was well in Ray and Kay Land.

"Yeah, we can reschedule next week's call." And the week after. And the month after. They could pick them back up around Verity's fiftieth birthday. And even that might be too soon. "No problem. Bye."

"*Bi turas math*," Magnus said, and Verity snorted to see *both* parents practically swoon.

"Goodbye, Magnus!" they chorused.

Verity slammed the laptop shut, slumped back in her chair, and let out a long breath. Then she looked up at an amused bear.

"Dunno about you, Magnus, but I could use a drink or three."

"Of course, darling."

"Oh, God, stop it."

Chapter 35

"I HAVE JOHNNIE WALKER AND GLENFIDDICH." MAGNUS stepped back as Verity hopped down from the counter, holding two bottles of amber liquid. She probably shouldn't keep booze over the stove—heat issues—but she wasn't much of a drinker. Normally. Plus she'd polished off the vodka and bourbon after hearing about Jerry's death. "So, whiskey or whiskey?"

Magnus's face creased into a grin. "Lass, are ye *trying* to make me fall in love?"

"Not even a little. I also have crème de menthe. But I'd have to climb back up."

"Not even on my deathbed."

"Spoken like a man who's never had a grasshopper. You need Breyers or Häagen-Dazs for it to be peak grasshopper, though. None of that Kemps garbage. Unless it's toasted almond fudge. Then it's Kemps or nothing." She poured each of them a healthy splash of Glenfiddich, neat, then raised her glass to click his. "To anyone but my parents. *Salud.*" She gulped it down, relishing the sudden explosion of warmth and the resulting honey-smoke aftertaste. For literal poison, it was fiiiiiiine. Magnus knocked his back as well then let out a satisfied sigh. "We probably shouldn't be slugging these down like tequila shots."

"Agreed."

"Another slug?"

He wordlessly pushed his empty glass over. While pouring, she said, "So! My parents in a nutshell."

"I dinna know where to start with…with all that just happened."

"I'm beyond mortified you heard all that. Cursed open floor plan!" She shook her fist at the living room area. "And thanks for swooping in. Not that I needed the rescue," she added, because she was occasionally a broken record. "But… like I said. Thanks. It was thoughtful."

"Happy t'help."

She sipped her drink. "But some clarification is called for. In this fantasy world you created on the spot, I regularly order you to make hors d'oeuvres?"

Magnus smiled and shrugged.

"And I'm a demanding hostess in demand because I'm demanding about the great parties I throw, which are in demand? This on-the-fly dreamworld you conjured up has given me an extra-special glimpse into your odd noggin."

"And your parents gave me one into yours."

"Touché."

"I wasna trying to score points, lass," he said earnestly. "It was an honest observation. If ye don't want tae talk about them, we can talk about anything else."

"Too late. You saw the dynamic in all its glorious horror. No point pretending otherwise. They mean well. I mean, they love me, they're not abusive, I always had a roof over my head, and I never missed a meal, and Christmases were always great, and they let me sleep in on weekends—they just…worry. All the time. It's why my curfew at age seventeen was the same as when I was ten. They're afraid a Shifter will kill me out of prejudice. Or by accident. One of those 'they didn't know their own strength, how could they have known she couldn't shift?' situations. Or a Stable will kill me because I'm too weak and un-Shifty to defend myself. My plan is to die slowly of cancer just to spite them."

Magnus had chosen the wrong time to take another sip, because he choked on his drink. She gave him a couple of whacks on the back until his color started to return. "That's one way to deal with the problem. Your parents, they like to travel? I've never heard of one of the places you mentioned."

"They like to go where the bears are. Werebears as well as plain old garden-variety bears. They're convinced the Stables are going to blow us all up any minute now, and they want to get in as much sightseeing as possible before we all die."

"Christ."

"Yeah, it's an interesting mindset. Brave and scared at the same time." Privately, she had long thought *brave and scared* should be the family motto. "I didn't really notice until I hit high school. Y'know, when you get a glimpse into other people's lives and you realize how deeply screwed your family dynamic is."

A vigorous nod from Magnus. "Aye."

"Anyway, now that I'm off their hands, they're making real progress on their travel bucket lists. They've also started making their own sourdough loaves, God knows why. And I get the feeling that if the Stables don't finish destroying the planet and kill us all, Ray and Kay Lane are gonna feel a little let down. Like, 'What was all the prep for? If nothing was gonna happen, we should've watched more TV instead of spending all that time in airports.'"

He didn't crack a smile. "You mentioned SAS."

"Yeah. But I hope you didn't get the wrong idea. It's not like they're card-carrying members of the Shifter version of the KKK. I'm pretty sure. Well, if they have cards, I've never seen them. My folks don't think Shifters should wipe out every Stable in a position of authority and start over. Though it *is* an interesting idea," she added, just to see what Magnus's reaction would be.

Nothing. That was his reaction.

Huh.

"But they're pretty open about how they think Stables have ruined quite a bit of the world," she continued. "All the places you can't swim, all the cities where you can't breathe, all the forests paved to make parking lots, the farmland razed for golf courses, every sea animal in the world choking on microbeads and straws…like that."

"I only ask," Magnus said, so quietly she had to bend forward a bit to hear him though he was only three feet away, "because I was one. Years ago."

For a moment she didn't understand. He'd been a Stable in charge? He razed a golf course? And choked on microbeads? "One what?"

"A card-carrying member of SAS. Not that they had cards. But I checked out a few meetings. I didn't mind what I heard. I was…on board. For some of their agenda. And I took too long to quit."

"Oh."

"It's how I knew Sue Smalls."

"Ah. The one who got away."

"Literally," he said gloomily. "And not just from me."

She sized him up. Sober, standing perfectly still in front of her, solemn expression, shoulders squared against whatever her reaction was going to be. Anticipating the worst. "Why are you telling me this?"

"I dinna know."

"Oh." She poured them another drink, picked up her glass, thought. And finally went to the core of what interested her most: "So, past tense? You *were* a member?"

"Yes. I was a fool for too long. I didn't get out until the blood started flowing. And then only because Sam Smalls helped me. A man I resented and didn't respect saved my reputation and possibly my life."

"Bastard."

She thought he would smile then, but nope. Instead, he settled in and told her. The whole sad story.

Chapter 36

ONCE UPON A TIME, MAGNUS BERNE WAS A LONELY FOR-
eign exchange student who decided to put himself out there
and make friends.

Chapter 37

"Wow."

"Aye."

"Just…so much to unpack."

He nodded.

"We need more booze for this."

He looked so relieved, she wanted to hug him. Had he thought she'd banish him into oblivion? "More whiskey would be good," he replied.

"I was thinking about making a blender full of grasshoppers."

He didn't flinch. "Whatever you like."

"All right, unclench. I'm not gonna scream at you and kick you out and make yours the name I never speak after I set your big ridiculous purple car on fire." She pulled the kitchen chair over, stepped on the seat, opened the cupboard over the stove, pulled out the booze.

A small twitch at the corner of his mouth. "But you'll force grasshoppers on me."

She hopped down. "Well, there have to be some repercussions."

Over the roar of the Blender of Punishment, she hollered, "I'm glad you told me! I didn't have even a glimmer of your sordid past! Don't get me wrong, it's problematic! But I'm glad you didn't get blown up in the Kiyuska disaster!"[12]

The nutshell version of the Kiyuska disaster: SAS

---

12. Check out *A Wolf After My Own Heart* for the horrifying details.

(Shifters Above Stables) was formed ostensibly to answer the question: How much more of the planet are we going to let them ruin before we take back what's ours?

SAS maintained that the 1 percent was never about privately held wealth. It was always about biology, evolution, and how Stables didn't deserve their planetwide dominance, which they'd enjoyed for…forever, really. And topping the list of things SAS hated about Stables: how they classified themselves as apex predators. Which Verity had always thought was missing the point.

So, years ago, they attempted a bloody takeover in Shakopee, Minnesota, the kickoff point for a worldwide coup. It failed, thanks to the intervention of Stables disinclined to genocide.

But there were also SAS members like Magnus: men and women who knew they were biologically superior and were tired of hiding it. Because every Shifter had to decide what to do about the exposure question: Hide? Hang out with, work with, and marry only Shifters? Reveal your dual nature to a few Stables you trusted? Intermarry and hope for the best?

SAS didn't want it to be an individual choice. They wanted the world to know about Shifters. And they wanted acknowledgment of their inherent superiority. And so, SAS was all-in for exposing themselves[13] to the wider world. But *their* idea of "coming out" was radically different than Magnus Berne's. SAS didn't just want to come out. They wanted to replace every Stable in any position of authority. If that meant violence, no problem. If that meant killing them, okey dokey. And step one was Shakopee.

Like many violent coups plotted by a fringe group, it was

---

13. Heh. (I'll see myself out.)

poorly planned and executed, needlessly bloody, and ultimately a waste of time, resources, money, lives.

"It was good that it failed."

"Yeah, Magnus, obviously."

"But in the years since, the Stables have only made the
planet worse. Most of them still don't take climate change
seriously. They'll still raze a meadow to build a Walmart.
SAS wasn't what I thought it was—that's one thing. But they
weren't wrong about everything. And when I began to suspect their true goals, I should have trusted my instincts and
acted right then: denounced them. Fought them. Instead, I
ignored my internal warning system and hoped our other
selves would reveal our *better* selves."

Mistake. People died. SAS was wiped out...but like
any radical cell of malcontents, it was hard to squash each
individual.

"Terrorists," Verity said.

"Yes, to call them what they were. Absolutely. And I have
no excuse for my complicity."

"So you licked your metaphorical and actual wounds
and...what? Slunk back to Scotland where you pined for a
decade?"

"Essentially."

"Times were different all the way back then." Verity shut
off the blender and poured them each a glass of minty-green
goodness.

"Again, I'm only thirty-four."

"Not that it's ever okay to be speciocust." When he opened
his mouth to correct her, she added, "*Speciesist* is too clumsy.
Specious with a *t* on the end makes more sense. So shall it
be, says me. Anyway, it was never okay to be...uh, like that.

But the other part of it…the part that interested you in the first place. Acknowledging that we're stronger and faster and far more resilient than Stables is just, what? Biology? Paraphysiology?"

Magnus winced, but it could have been the grasshopper.

"Okay, I know how it sounds," Verity said, "but hear me out. Like that tired stereotype about how Black people aren't strong swimmers. Nobody ever set out and, y'know, scientifically proved that. It was always an assumption based on a slur. But the average Shifter is, objectively speaking, stronger and faster than the average Stable. That *has* been scientifically proven. None of which makes it okay to kill them and take over the world," she added.

"Glad we're on the same page, lass."

"We were talking about this very thing before you crashed the Radisson. About how it can be easy to cross the line between 'genetically superior' and 'violently speciesist malcontent.' Plus, aren't War Wolves still a thing? A pathetic thing? Their propaganda was always 'we're soldiers, we're not actually affiliated with SAS,' except I'm pretty sure they only ever did jobs for SAS. Are they even recruiting anymore? And yeah, big groups of SAS got stomped, but they're like the KKK…there's always a few around. And now I'm off on another tangent."

"I like your tangents."

"Hmmm. Anyway. Gross murderous intentions aside, I don't think a small group of pissed-off would-be autocrats should get to decide that *all* Shifters should out themselves."

"Yes, I see that. Now."

"So you signed up with SAS in the hopes of getting lucky with Sue Smalls—"

"That isna true! At least not entirely."

"And her then-boyfriend future husband got you out of there just when buildings started blowing up."

"Yes."

"Well, yay Sam Smalls."

"Yes," he admitted. "I owe him more than I can repay. It's why I came to Minnesota, to help what remained of his family. To ensure the safety of his daughter."

"Who is now your goddaughter."

"Yes."

Verity wondered if Magnus knew he'd actually squared his shoulders and straightened proudly. The guy might resent Sam Smalls, but he sure took pride in how the man trusted him with his only cub's well-being.

"So all's well that ends well, if you overlook the whole 'Sue Smalls jumping out of a plane' thing." Also? *Badass. Reason #262 why you didn't fuck with mama bears.*

"Yes."

"So." She topped off his grasshopper. "To Sue Smalls, who went out on her own terms and in so doing complicated the lives of a ton of bad guys."

He smiled, clinked her glass.

They toasted the dead, and then Verity smiled, moved closer to Magnus, and used her sleeve to dab away his grass-hopper moustache. "Whew! Thank God I did that. You were barely gorgeous there for a moment." Magnus ducked his head and blushed. "Oh, man, that's so cute! I've never seen a grown man blush the way you do. Wait. I want to try something."

And she leaned in and kissed him on the lips with a hearty smack. "Whoa! Okay, you should calm down. I'm actually a little worried you might stroke out. I've seen tomatoes that were less red than you are right now."

"I'm thirty-four!"

"And I'm fresh out of Ensure," she teased and was still giggling when he kissed her back. The giggles turned into full-blown guffaws when he moved in and started planting raspberries on the side of her throat. "Gaaaaaaah! No one's more ticklish than I am in that spot. If that sounds like a brag, it's not, it's my greatest weakness, aagghh!" She gave him a gentle shove. "Good Lord, your five o'clock shadow probably shows up at noon."

"On occasion," he admitted with a smile. "Forgive me. You were entirely too irresistible."

"I know you're kidding, but for the record, I really *am* irresistible. You, though, you're eminently resistible."

(This was a rather large lie.)

Chapter 38

"ARGH, MY HEAD. JUST KIDDING, I DIDN'T DRINK ENOUGH to end up hungover. My headache is unrelated to whiskey." Most likely low blood sugar, since she and Magnus were up until 3:00 a.m. talking, and in all that time she didn't eat or drink. Just stared at his mouth while he stared at hers. Which should have been weird. And was.

Verity poured herself a tumbler of orange juice and drained it in three gulps, then grinned to see Magnus limp into the kitchen area.

"That futon," he moaned. "My God."

"Thought I was exaggerating, didn't you?"

"My. *God.* Stuffing the mattress with ground glass was the perfect sadistic touch."

"Not glass. Razor blades. Just kidding, it's mostly synthetic latex. Which is almost as bad for you as ground glass." She pushed a glass of juice over to him. "I can't help but notice you're not wearing yesterday's suit." Dark jeans, a sky-blue button-down, clean socks. "Nor are you sporting anything from my closet."

"I stopped at the Target on my way back to your place last night. It's why I was late."

"Just Target, Magnus. Not 'the Target.' Like how you guys say *to hospital* or *to university*. That's wrong, by the way. You're all doing it wrong and have been for years. You okay to drive?"

"No." He set the glass down.

"Okay. The meetup isn't far from here, so just follow my car."

"One moment." Magnus tossed a dozen Advil down his gullet and chased them with more O.J. "All right. Shall we?"

Twenty minutes later, she was pulling into the parking lot adjacent to the Graduate Minneapolis hotel, which was enough time for her to stop crying and get a grip already. She'd no sooner buckled her seat belt and checked the glove compartment for an errant Ding Dong when three of Jerry's Blow Pops (he favored black cherry) fell onto the floor mat. She'd stared at them for a good thirty seconds, remembering Jerry rhapsodizing about how it was a lollipop *and* gum

("Two tooth-rotting snacks in one! A bargain, Ver!")

before she realized tears were running down her face.

She dashed them away then rubbed her eyes, hard. *This is mourning. You think you're finally getting used to the idea and then WHAM! A Blow Pop leaps out and kicks you in the face all over again.*

She stuffed the ridiculous fucking Blow Pops back into her ridiculous fucking glove compartment and slammed it shut. *I should toss them. I'm gonna forget all about them until the next time I open the glove compartment. Then: WHAM. Blow Pop in the face again.*

Yeah, probably.

Traffic was light, so she was five minutes early, Magnus on her ass (so to speak) the whole way. She locked her car and practically ran to where he was parking then seized him by the arm—

"Well! This is a nice—hey!"

—and hauled him across the street and into the lobby.

"Your eyes are red. Are you all right?"

"Shut up, Magnus." Despite the circumstances, she smirked at the wood stacked behind the reception desk (the Graduate Minneapolis was always ready for a bonfire) and the blue neon slogan (*We are all students*) in the lobby. What did that mean? That everyone was always learning all the time? Or that she forgot about a term paper that was due a decade ago?

She hauled Magnus through the lobby, giving the air hockey tables a wide berth

(remember how Jerry always whipped your ass at that game?)

(nope, if I remember, the waterworks will start up again)

and led him up the stairs and down the hall to the Focus Room, a twenty- by thirty-foot conference room with a long, dark wood table which seated sixteen and had been polished to a glossy gleam, and sixteen black leather chairs to match. As usual, Maggie had arranged snacks at the front of the room: bagels, cream cheese, muffin assortment, juice assortment, coffee, hot water for tea. No one had touched anything but the coffee.

"Magnus, you remember—um, I actually have no idea who you remember." Verity flapped a hand toward the group. "These are the Damp Squibs. Y'know, again."

"What's left of them," Les said glumly.

"Which brings us to the agenda," Norm said. "What now?"

"Let's start again," Maggie suggested.

"Are you nuts?" Verity asked. "Or are you shoehorning

Simpsons dialogue to try and come up with something closer to your agenda?"

"Yes, that's the one."

"Maggie! We don't have time for this," Verity said and nearly stomped her foot for emphasis.

"We don't?" Norm looked around the room. "Why? Anyone have to be anywhere else right now? I don't. I mean, this is pretty important. I cleared my whole day."

"I cleared my morning, but I'm not rescheduling my root canal again," Darcy said. "That has to count for something."

"Did any of you know?" Verity asked.

"About…" Maggie prompted.

Darcy snorted. "Really, Maggie?" To Verity: "About how Jerry was a secret prodigy who wasn't old enough to vote and who we, in our clueless arrogance, might have gotten killed?"

Verity snapped her fingers and pointed at Darcy. "That's it, that's the one."

"Jeez, no," Les said, appalled. "No idea. *No* idea. Verity, you were pretty good friends with him. How come you didn't know?"

"Whoa! I didn't show up for a witch hunt. I showed up for free bagels and to throw around wild accusations. Look, in retrospect, I can see the signs. He never wanted me to come over to his house—"

"Neither does Les," Norm observed.

"Is that why you all meet in hotels?" Magnus asked. He'd been so quiet, Verity had almost (almost—the guy filled up every room he was in) forgotten he was there. "I was wondering. There aren't so many of you that you need a hotel for your meetings."

"No, there aren't. Why? Do you think he's underage too?"

Verity turned to Les. "Tell the truth: Are you sixteen? We won't be mad, I promise. Just kidding, we'll be horrified and furious."

"I'm thirty-four!" Les cried.

"Careful, lad. Verity considers that nursing home age."

"Is it a privacy issue, Les?" Verity pressed. "Or is it just that you don't want us knowing where you live? Because it would be hard not to take that personally."

"No!"

"What part are you saying no to?" Darcy asked.

"I'm not sixteen, and it's not a privacy issue! It's just my dad—"

In near unison: "Ah-ha!"

"*He* lives with *me*." Les crossed his bony arms over his narrow chest and glared. "And why is Magnus Berne even here? This is a private meeting."

"In a hotel," Magnus pointed out.

Whoa, déjà vu. "What happened to all that 'Magnus could be an asset to our message, better tell him all about us' plan, Les? What, now that dead bodies are piling up, suddenly you want to keep everything among the Damp Squibs? Actually, that's pretty sensible," Verity admitted. "Especially if one of us knew. Or more of us. Because then the police will get involved. Or worse, IPA."

"But we *didn't* know," Norm protested. "Honest to God, I didn't find out until the memorial! I was looking at his glee club photo—"

Oh my God. Debate and Speech and Mathletes and STEM and glee club. I didn't even know glee clubs were still a thing! Jerry, you glorious, breathtaking nerd.

"Like I said, there were clues, but only in retrospect. He

never wanted us to see his house—his parents and sister
would have given him away." Penny might have kept his
secret, but his parents? Nope. The Harts loved Jerry and
wanted him to be safe; they would have made damned sure
his friends knew he was underage. It just never occurred to
them that he might be passing. "His number one concern
about being a Damp Squib was that his parents would find
out."

Maggie and Darcy were nodding. "And he always had
to be back home by ten p.m.," Darcy added. "He said it was
because he had to get up early for a special class, so. Probably
a curfew."

Verity nodded, and fixed herself a cup of coffee, and saw
Magnus visibly shudder when she dumped four sugar pack-
ets into the cup.[14] "Okay, so. In hindsight, we're all blind and
should have tumbled to this conclusion months ago and
should spend the rest of the month kicking ourselves. But
where does that leave us right now? Other than showing
each other's licenses to prove we're legal and making fun of
Les for living with his dad—"

"He lives with *me*!"

"—where do we go from here?"

"Disband?" Norm suggested. "Immediately?"

Les let out a snort. "How courageous."

"Yes, it's almost as brave as a man in his thirties living
with his father," Darcy snapped back, and Les blushed to his
hairline. "But I don't know about just up and quitting. Wasn't
the point to prove we're just as good as quote real Shifters
unquote?"

"So we ease off the challenges," Norm suggested.

---

14. Coffee is undrinkable unless heavily creamed and sugared. Fight me.

"Again: missing the point."

"So we come up with newer and more dangerous stunts that will probably kill us." Verity took a sip, added more sugar. "Problem solved."

"No need to be so pissy," Norm sniffed.

"Disagree. Because the point—at least, this was how Jerry explained it when he recruited me, that deceptive juvenile delinquent—was to feel better about ourselves in a world of Stables who have no idea we exist and Shifters who do know we exist but wish we didn't. Except for SAS jerks. They want us to be cannon fodder." Verity looked around at the small group, all of whom were still too sickened by current events to eat. "Anybody feeling better about themselves right now?"

Silence.

Les cleared his throat. "You all raise good points. Obviously, we need to decide where to go from here—"

Maggie sighed. "What are you, the narrator?"

"—but what's more important is that we need to keep IPA off us. Once they start crawling up our asses—"

From Maggie: "Eww."

"—they won't stop until they're satisfied."

Verity waited for the inevitable "that's what she said," but since it wasn't 2005, it didn't happen. She took another sip. *Mmmm...sugar, with cream that tastes faintly of coffee...* "It almost sounds like you're suggesting we obstruct justice. But *that* can't be right."

"No, Verity, that's not what I'm saying. But we have to deal with IPA, and the main reason we're meeting right now is because we need to—"

"Get our stories straight? Again, I'm getting a strong obstruction vibe from this."

"We haven't done anything wrong," Darcy protested. "At worst, we trespassed. And either people don't notice…" She waved an arm in Magnus's direction. "Or they don't care!"

"Lass, I wouldna say I didn't care, exactly—"

"So we don't need to worry about IPA."

"You do, though, Darcy. They're coming for all of us." Verity paused. "Sorry to make that sound sinister. What I meant was, they want to talk to us, make sure we're not recklessly endangering minors in our downtime. But since none of us knew, we'll probably get a lecture and be sent on our way. An annoying, condescending lecture to which we should listen politely—I'm picturing gratuitous use of *there, there, you silly things* and lots of pats on the head—before we go back to our lives."

"I prefer prison," Darcy said, appalled.

"I don't!" Norm cried. "Bring on the pats on the head. If we have to choose, I mean. How foolish *are* you?"

Verity threw up her hands. "Look, I get it. I don't like being patronized, either—Magnus can attest to that—"

"That's not true!" Magnus protested. "Wait. What I mean t'say is that I don't patron—"

"So we're all agreed: we tell IPA the reality, the whole reality, and nothing but the reality. They go their way, we go ours. But we should let them come to us," Les added. "If we go to them, it might look like we're hiding things."

"How does *that* make any sense?" Maggie asked.

"I've got to side with Maggie on that one," Darcy added. "Seeking them out is the opposite of hiding things."

"We *have* been hiding things. Just not things IPA cares about. So we're agreed?" Verity asked. "The truth shall set us free and also get IPA off our backs?"

"But that still leaves the question of where we go from here."

It did. And Verity didn't have any clearer thoughts on the issue than she had when she walked into the hotel. Too soon?

Or something worse, something she wasn't quite ready to look in the face and call the truth?

Before anyone could answer, there was a sharp rap at the door, and then Magnus—of all people—crossed the room to open it.

There stood David what's-his-name, the guy from the memorial. Correction: the guy who was at the memorial with an IPA caseworker.

Oh, shit, Magnus, what did you dooooo?

Chapter 39

"Good morning." To Magnus: "Sorry to be late."

"*You* called this guy?" Norm asked.

He sure did, Verity realized. *Called him, reached out, whatever you call it. He thought something was fishy and hired a PI. He even tried to tell me about it at Jerry's house, and I cut him off.*

"Who is he?" Darcy asked.

Verity sighed. "This is David Applebee—"

"Auberon. Applebee's is a restaurant."

"—right, sorry, David Auberon, not affiliated with the Applebee's chain in any way."

"Then what *is* he affiliated—"

Best to rip off the Band-Aid. Well, best for other people. Verity personally preferred to ease it off a millimeter at a time. "He's an investigator with IPA. Magnus hired him to look into Andy and Jerry's deaths."

Two seconds of silence, followed by thirty of uproar. And Verity had to give the guy credit, David was utterly unruffled. Just stood there in dark slacks, a red T-shirt, a casual navy-blue blazer, battered-but-clean loafers. His stubble looked like it could shred cheese. His brown-eyed gaze was direct. He gave them a few more seconds to rabble-rabble then stuck two fingers in his mouth and let out a shrill whistle that sounded like someone set fire to an ostrich.

Damn. He keeps doing that, the hospitality guy is gonna be in here in half a tick.

"Point of order," David said into the startled silence. "I don't work for IPA. I'm an independent contractor."

"Not better," Darcy insisted.

"Are you an investigator?" Norm asked.

"Yep."

"Who reports to the police?"

"When necessary."

"Then Darcy's right. It's not better."

"Only if you've got something to hide," David replied mildly. "Though maybe your very nature—the Damp Squibs' nature—makes that inevitable. It's not like you advertise in the paper or anything."

"Nobody reads the paper anymore, David," Verity pointed out.

"I do. You don't advertise anywhere," he amended. "You get new people by word of mouth, right? And the only people who can join are brought in by existing members?"

"Yeah," Verity replied, nodding. "That's how we do it. This is going to sound stupid given that we've lost two members in four weeks, but it seemed the safest way to do things."

"Did you know about this, Verity?" Les demanded. "That IPA was coming to our private, *closed* meeting?"

"In a public hotel," Magnus pointed out.

"No, I had no idea David would be here. But I'm not sure—"

"Great! Just bring out the handcuffs, then," Darcy snapped. "We didn't know about Jerry, but IPA loooooooves their scapegoats. Remember the uproar when you guys busted the weretraffickers?"

"It was less than a year ago, and my fiancée and I were nearly killed," David replied calmly. "Of course I remember."

Darcy had the grace to flush but plowed ahead. "Then you remember that one of IPA's own was one of the traffickers![15] Which blew up any credibility they ever had, so they've been overcompensating ever since. They got caught sleeping at the switch, and now every other Shifter has to pay for it."

"Darcy, do you hear yourself?" Verity asked. "IPA being ever more vigilant about protecting cubs is not a bad thing, and it's amazing that I have to explain this."

"Oh, c'mon," Norm replied. His face was calm, but the hand he ran through his thinning hair was trembling. "You said it yourself, we didn't do anything wrong. Because we haven't. At worst, we—"

"*Please* don't finish that sentence in front of the IPA investigator," Darcy begged.

"Again, not with IPA," David said amiably. He gestured to the bagels. "Are these for anyone?"

"Sure," Norm sighed. "Help yourself before you sic *les flics* on us."

Darcy rolled her eyes. "*Les* what?"

"Uh, guys?" Verity set her coffee down in case they rushed her. "While we're on the subject of bad things that aren't bad, Magnus reaching out to a PI to make sure nothing falls through the cracks is also a good thing. A ham-handed good thing that he did without bothering to check with any of us, but still."

"So you did know!" From Les, stabbing a finger in her direction.

"First, don't point that thing at me. Second, Magnus tried to tell me, but I cut him off. I didn't think anything of it until I saw this guy in the doorway."

---

15. The blood-soaked details can be found in *Bears Behaving Badly*.

"That's right," Magnus cut in. "Verity didn't have a clue. She was utterly ignorant. I made sure to keep her out of the whole...ah, let me rephrase..."

She tried to glare at David and smile encouragingly at Les at the same time, which sparked a pinprick headache between her eyes. "But, again, guys: this is a good thing!" To David: "That's why you're here, right? To find out exactly what happened, regardless of IPA taking an interest? So we know the truth about Jerry? No matter who the culprit is, no matter who they're affiliated with? If IPA wants to sweep it under the rug, you'll yank said rug?"

Chomp. "Yep."

"You're a man of few words, Auberon." Verity decided not to tell him he had cream cheese on his nose. "I like that in a man, except when I don't."

"But if IPA clears us, and of course they will because none of us have done anything wrong so there's nothing to worry about, then there's no point in investigating," Darcy said.

"Of course there's a point, lass," Magnus said. "Isna it obvious?"

Given the short silence that fell, it wasn't.

Maggie, of all people, spoke up. "It wasn't an accident?"

Darcy blinked. "Uh, what?"

"Wait, we're talking about murder now?" Verity was very glad she'd been leaning against the snack table to listen to the uproar, because she might have fallen. "You think someone set out to kill Jerry?"

"That's way worse than reckless endangerment of a minor," Norm observed.

"No shit, Norm!" Verity clutched her temples. "Murder? You think someone planned to kill a perfectly sweet guy who wouldn't hurt a fucking fly?"

"And Andrew Bray," David said, scanning his notebook while chomping on a bagel.

Verity was horrified and...a little, a very little...unsurprised? There'd been an odd silence surrounding Jerry's death, and coming so quickly on the heels of Andy's death... had part of her been waiting for the other shoe to drop? *Speak up a little louder next time, subconscious. And don't give me that 'but I'm your subconscious, by definition you don't know I'm there' excuse again.*

Verity shook her head. "That's—that's—that's—"

"Bizarre," Darcy finished.

"Is it?" Norm asked quietly. "What are the odds, after all?"

"That people would die doing death-defying stunts? Not as low as you'd think," Darcy shot back.

"But—why?" Verity asked, clutching her temples. Her head felt like an electrical storm was raging all through her neurons. "Who'd want Andy and Jerry dead? They were completely different guys. Andy just finished his degree in—what was it again? Veterinary science?"

"Animal osteopathy," Darcy replied.

"That's a thing?"

"That's a thing."

"Huh." Verity made a mental note to look it up when she got home. "I only talked to him a couple of times, and when I did, all he wanted to talk about was opening his own clinic."

"And?" From Maggie.

"And he was a grown man who was focused and had a plan is my point. Jerry wasn't even old enough to vote, still lived at home, and had zero plans. He switched majors twice and was thinking about dropping out but he knew his folks would flip."

"So?" Norm asked.

"So, if you think about it, the only thing they had in common—" Verity cut herself off, finished the sentence in her head. "Oh."

"Yeah." From David.

"*Oh.*"

"Yeah. And it gets worse."

"Nobody ask him how!" Darcy cried. "Mr. Auberon, you don't have to finish that thought."

"Find your metaphorical balls, Darcy," Verity said. "I expect more from the woman who picked a fight with a werecougar and won."

"It was a bobcat," she snapped, "and I needed stitches after."

David (wisely) ignored the interruptions. "Andrew Bray's degree wasn't in animal osteopathy. And he wasn't opening a clinic. His degree was in criminal justice, and he was a cop."

Uproar. For considerably longer than twenty seconds this time.

Chapter 40

MAGNUS STEPPED OUTSIDE TO SEE AN AMAZING SIGHT, even by Shifter standards. A sleek red kite with a two-meter wingspan soared in on lake downdrafts, clutching a large cream-colored envelope in her talons. Her feathers were a deep reddish brown, except for her wings which were black with white tips. The raptor circled, dropped her cargo, then settled on one of the dock posts and preened while Magnus caught the envelope.

"Good morning, Nadia." He put his cider on one of the dock posts (Cherry Rhubarb Scrumpy), slit open the heavy envelope, and read the contents with—yes, no mistaking it—a warm feeling of inclusion. "Tea?"

In the time it took him to put the invitation back in the envelope, the elegant kite had transformed into a petite—about a meter and a half tall—pale woman in her midthirties with ice-blue eyes and a cut-glass accent.

"Of course, *tea*, darling, don't be ridiculous."

Fifty minutes later

("I'll need just a moment to freshen up, Magnus, do go back to whatever delectable thing you were preparing when I popped by.")

they were sipping tea on the deck. Black jasmine for him, Buddha's Blend for her, with Nadia all but drowning in one of his button-downs and a pair of sweatpants. For mid-June, it was going to be quite warm; 23°C already, and not yet noon.

Drinking tea did not slow Nadia's litany of complaints by so much as half a second.

"—imagine? I am shocked, *shocked*, at how little Annette has prepared for this, the grandest and most exciting day of her life. She is going to pledge herself for all eternity and perhaps longer to David Auberon. And thank God. Frankly, I despaired that she would ever find a mate, so naturally I took a hand."

"Naturally." Magnus had heard about that and hid a smile. Nadia had apparently started rumors that Annette and David were dating long before they were actually dating. Magnus suspected they held off getting together more to thwart Nadia's plans than any reticence about exploring a romantic relationship.

"And see? Not quite a year later, she has pledged her troth to someone almost suitable. Which must be celebrated! And in the grandest, most elegant way possible whilst staying under budget. Which she does not understand in any way, despite all my lectures and memos. When I think of the time I put in trying to make that stubborn, stubborn creature understand... Do you know, Magnus, if left to her, she'd say her vows in a drafty barn while wearing leggings and then subject her guests to a nacho bar."

(To be honest, Magnus thought a nacho bar sounded frightening but ultimately delicious, like hot honey.)

"Thank God she had the good sense to put me in charge of all of it."

Magnus pushed the platter closer to her. "That *is* good sense."

"Oh, my good God, you've made blueberry scones. I could smell them baking while I availed myself of your facilities. And—what is this one?"

"White chocolate raspberry. Those two are lemon. The ones on the end are chocolate chip with toasted pecans."

"They're still warm! And *where* did you get clotted cream?" Before he could answer,[16] she rushed ahead. "Oh, it's no use, I can keep up this nonchalant charade no longer!"

He nearly choked on a chunk of white chocolate at the abrupt mood shift. "Are you all right?"

"Do I *look* all right?" she demanded, brushing a hand through her short, ruffled hair. "Well, yes, I do, I was blessed by nature, and with more than intelligence. Even in your workout outfit—and how many times have you washed these jogging pants, they're like velvet—I shine. But that isn't the point. I am in dire, desperate straits, Magnus!"

"I'm sorry to hear that."

"Thank you, darling, it's nice to have my pain acknowledged. I knew you were a good listener the moment we met last spring. And so cute, too. A pity I find bears too much work." This in a tone of genuine regret that Magnus would never know the glory of dating Nadia Faulkner. "The fur alone, gah."

A narrow escape. For both of us, probably. Though he was starting to have trouble remembering exactly *why* he'd kept himself isolated for so long. He couldn't chalk it all up to the nature of werebears. *Was I protecting my heart? Or hiding like a coward?* And why did it suddenly matter?

He knew why. And he hadn't been able to get Sam's pithy observation out of his head: *Is it because the last time you opened yourself up to new experiences and set out to make friends, you unwittingly joined a terrorist cell, which resulted in long-term repercussions including the eventual violent death of your dearest friend?*

---

16. Kowalski's Markets

All roads led back to that, apparently. He could feel his brain poking at it like a loose tooth.

"But I'm getting off track. Thank you, darling, I'll have more tea, and look at these darling sugar spheres! Baby blue, please. So cunning. Now then. I have been pushed, *shoved* very nearly to my limits and am at my wits' end. And you should know I don't throw around clichés lightly."

"I wish I could help," he lied.

"You're sweet. And now that you mention it."

Aw, shite. "Yes?"

"The only venues worth even *glancing* at are booked. Though some credit must be given: for a flyover state, Minnesota has many beautiful wedding venues. And lakes, I suppose, if that floats your boat, pardon the pun. But as I said, anywhere even remotely acceptable was booked months ago. Which is entirely Annette's fault! Who accepts a marriage proposal—and he didn't even get down on one knee, Magnus, he just casually tossed it out over breakfast like he was asking for toast, the great lummox—and then decides to get married within six months? In high summer! The most popular time of the year to 'get hitched,' if you'll pardon the colloquialism. Who? Who? Who?"

"Annette Garsea?" he guessed.

"Well, yes. Nevertheless, I did not hesitate to rise to the challenge because I am a true friend even when I have been set up to fail. Annette is a one-of-a-kind bride and she deserves a one-of-a-kind venue."

That was the literal truth, if what he'd heard about Annette's parents was true. He was fond of his fellow werebear and hoped they would never fight. There was some doubt about the outcome.

Nadia tapped one of her long, sharp nails on the table—
tak-tak-tak!—doubtless sensing his mind was wandering.
"But Aria and the Calhoun Beach Club are utterly, *utterly*
booked. Even though there will be a bare two dozen guests!
Well, perhaps six dozen."

Magnus had a pretty good idea where she was going with
this and took the wedding invitation out again for a closer
look.

Nadia talked faster. "And with Dev being purely impossible, the timeline has been moved up. At least, that was the
reason Annette gave me, but I suspect the true rationale is
that Annette loathes me and wishes I would frazzle myself
into a breakdown, and this was her opportunity, so she did
not hesitate."

"That seems out of character for her," he said mildly.

"Oh, no? When I told her I couldn't possibly pull everything together, do you know what she told me? She said, 'I
never wanted you to have to go to so much trouble. I appreciate all your efforts, but it's fine if we just get hitched in Mama
Mac's backyard.' Right to my face she said that!"

> *Please celebrate with*
> *Annette Garsea and David Auberon*
> *As they begin their best work together*
> *Saturday, July 19, 2:00 p.m.*
> *Terrapin Island, Lake Minnetonka*

"Naturally such a challenge to my organizational skills
and exquisite taste must be answered. Which brings me to
you. And your lovely, lonely island," she finished.

"This isn't Terrapin Island," he said mildly.

"Darling." Nadia's gaze was full of reproach. "You couldn't expect me to use the *actual* name."

"Yes, Assessor's Parcel number 4862-001-010 isn't very romantic."

"Still another obstacle to giving Annette the wedding of my dreams! So will you?" Nadia leaned forward, blue eyes sparkling with…tears? No, it was probably the sunshine. Though he wasn't surprised by the charming histrionics of manufacturing a few sobs if it meant getting her way. "Host this nuptial debacle? Truly, Magnus, you're my only hope. I didn't go to the trouble of flying out here merely for the pleasure of your company." Nadia lowered her eyelids and shifted into flirt mode. "At least, not entirely."

Magnus wondered if the fuss was more of a show than not. Perhaps this was her and Annette and Mama's subtle way of making him feel included.

No, he decided. *Not everything is about me, and assuming otherwise is conceited beyond belief. They're in a jam. And I can either help them or not.*

Six months ago it would have been *or not.*

"What would I have to do?"

She straightened in her chair and beamed, instantly dry-eyed and no doubt sensing triumph. "Ah, yes, like all men, you fear anything nuptial. Just give over your lovely pro tem house and grounds to me and stand back. *Far* back. I shall take care of everything else."

"All right," he agreed, knowing it was a fait accompli the moment she dropped the invitation on him. Besides, he liked Annette and David. And sometimes Nadia.

"Oh, and transport," she fretted, nibbling on another scone. "How to get everyone here?"

"I could rent a houseboat or two. We can use it as a ferry. Some of the newer models can carry twenty people at once."

Nadia clapped her hands, looking for a moment not unlike a giddy child. "Oh, perfect! I knew delivering your invitation in person was the proper way to manage this. How kind and thoughtful you are! Don't worry, I'll never tell a soul about your secret sweetness. So that's solved, then." She smirked and lifted her teacup in a mock toast. "Even better, Annette will be furious, *enraged* to find she missed out on homemade scones."

"But happy that she has a venue, at least?"

"How should I know?" Nadia snapped, treating him to another terrifying mood shift. "She may well be indifferent. The silly creature suggested City Hall, can you think of anything ghastlier?" Nadia set down a half-eaten scone, picked up a new one, inspected it, nibbled. She looked around the deck and said in a tone she may have thought was casual and subtle, "I don't scent your lady friend anywhere."

"No, I haven't seen her since Saturday."

She leaned back, arched black brows. "That's a surprise."

Magnus decided not to be baited. If that's what she was doing. Er...what *was* she doing, exactly? "Why?"

"Well. You've been working together, have you not?"

"Uh, no. Not really."

She ignored him. "You met cute and teamed up. And didn't you just find out a shocking twist? A what do you call it...game changer?"

"Yes," he admitted. He thought about how the blood drained from poor Verity's face when she realized her friend may have been foully murdered. *Game changer is putting it mildly.* His own suspicions had been niggling but relentless, which was why he'd hired David Auberon to see if there was anything to that suspicion. But unfortunately, there hadn't been time to sit down with Verity and explain exactly what—

No. Tell the truth and shame Satan himself: they'd been getting along so well (she didn't mind that he glommed on her Zoom! She let him spend the night!), he didn't want to upset her. In retrospect, a piss-poor call, and he'd deserved the resulting uproar. And she'd actually defended him in front of the other Damp Squibs! So he'd kept his distance since. Lingering or popping up uninvited was a poor way to pay her back.

Though he couldn't stop himself from watching the lake and hoping.

"So, then?" Nadia prompted. "The situation is entirely different now. Shouldn't you be, er, 'going rogue' and investigating?"

"Why would you assume that?" he asked, honestly puzzled.

"Because that's how this goes!"

"This?"

"Magnus, have you not been paying attention? Annette and David had to team up for a case, it's how they exposed and destroyed those syndicate wretches. It's how Caro came to live with Mama Mac."

"Annette is an IPA caseworker," he pointed out. "As her intake officer, I assume you already knew that."

"Sarcasm is not a good look on you, darling." She sniffed. "Though I'm glad to see you actually looked at my business card."

Cards, plural. The day they'd met, she'd tossed a dozen at

him. Nadia treated her business cards like confetti: colorful joy to be spread throughout the world.

"And David's a private investigator who frequently works with IPA," he continued. "So, of course, they teamed up."

"And when Oz had to track down your goddaughter? He and Lila teamed up and thwarted a race war. And then fell in love! Well, it may have been the other way around. But the end result was the same: they're moving in together."

"Oz also works for IPA," he pointed out.

"Yes, well. Lila does not. She's not even a Shifter. Not that there's anything wrong with that."

"Yes, but Lila only became involved because she found Sally in an alley and assumed she was a wild cub. After that, there was no getting rid of her until the matter of Sally's safety was settled to her satisfaction."

"Yes, but—"

"I'm a ferry pilot from Scotland," he reminded her. "Verity is a sniffer of sorts."

"Sorry, what?"

"She smells things for a living. I looked up her job, she's an odor tester. Isn't that interesting?"

"Bit of a niche trade, don't you think?"

"My point is, Verity's not affiliated with IPA in any way. Neither am I. So two civilians getting involved in such an investigation isn't only inappropriate and dangerous, it's potentially illegal."

Nadia pounced like the raptor she was. "Dangerous? Is that why you're staying aloof? You don't want your lady friend to get hurt? Yes, yes." Nadia leaned back in her chair, snapped her fingers at him: *click-click-click.* "That's precisely what it is. It's why you hired David. You can be helpful

behind the scenes, and she can get answers without exposing herself."

"Either way," he said evenly, "Verity's out. And so am I."

"Oh. So I guess David will be the one throwing himself
headlong into danger and fighting the good fight against
woeful odds only to triumph in the end as evil is punished."

"Yes. Exactly right."

"I'm sure David will keep you in the loop as his investigation continues."

"Yes, that was in the contract." He'd never seen a shorter
contract in his life, much less signed one. It was all of three
paragraphs, the gist of which was "I'll search for answers, and
it'll work out or it won't, plus expenses."

He had signed. Of course he signed, and handed over a
generous retainer. Verity deserved answers and so did her
friends.

"So, then. You can reach out to Verity with updates."

He sighed. "Nadia, I see what you're doing."

"That's impossible, darling, I'm far, *far* too circumspect."
She took a final sip of tea, stood, and did some neck flexion
exercises. Typical behavior for someone who was about to
shift and had time to prepare. "I must fly, darling. You don't
mind if I leave you with the cleanup? And thank you for your
hospitality and for bending to my will."

"It just seemed easier," he confessed, and she laughed.
She planted a careless kiss on his cheek, and in the twenty
seconds that followed, disrobed, shifted, and flew away.

Chapter 41

"ROGER, WE'VE BEEN OVER THIS. I DON'T CARE WHAT ARTI-ficial fruit extracts you want to put into nail polish, it will still smell like Satan and a jar of ammonia had a baby. Besides, you don't want toxic polish to smell like fake strawberries. Kids will drink *anything*. Don't make nitrocellulose and butyl acetate enticing! Why are we having this conversation again?"

"Because this time I want you to smell the banana one."

Verity sighed and beheld her colleague, whose white coat was so crisply starched it stood up when he wasn't wearing it. "Literally everything I just said also applies to fake bananas. Roger, you know R&D is with me on this one. It's time to leave the brave new world of fake fruit essence behind and embrace scented paper towels."

He bent closer, and Verity was reminded that cologne was no substitute for a shower. "You bears think you're so smart!" Roger whisper-snapped.

"Uh, no. I just think artificial banana sucks."

She said it to his back, since he was already marching out of the lab. As the only two Shifters to contract with Senses4Hire, it had been unfortunate that they couldn't get along. Almost as unfortunate as his hit-or-miss hygiene. Maybe it was a bear/badger thing. Or maybe Roger was just a flaming dick.

Correction: a prejudiced flaming dick. She'd been work-ing there about a month before she told him the truth: she was a Shifter who couldn't shift. His attitude had done a 180 right before her eyes. He went from bounding into the lab pretty much every day to staying out of her space as much as he could. She'd gone from the top of his list to off his list. He'd tried to use odor testers outside their department then had to admit (but only to himself) that Verity was the best in the building. So he stayed in his cubicle and read her reports instead of seeking her out. Communicated by email, though her part of the lab was eleven feet from his desk and he hated email.

And now: the flouncing out again.

She shrugged it off, which was almost easy. Certainly easier than it had been ten years ago. Back in the day, she would have apologized for her nature. No longer. Roger wasn't the first to assume she was dangerously defective, nor would he be the last. She had been disappointed but not completely surprised.

She felt her phone vibrate in her pocket, fished it out, eyed it, and had never been less surprised in her life. Not even in junior high, when she found all the Christmas presents early and unwrapped, went through the pile, then had to fake astonishment and glee on the twenty-fifth.

"What's up, Magnus fucking Berne?"

"Ah. Good morning. You may be wondering how I—"

"You went to your Stable pal's house and looked at my business card, which a woman I'd only just met stuck to the fridge belonging to another woman I'd just met."

"I stole your card the day it went on the fridge," he confessed.

"Yep. Not alarming at all. Definitely not a red flag."

"And I'm not entirely sure Lila is my—"

"Ugh, don't. What do you want? I've got four different mascara removers to smell, then it's on to vegan 'shrimp,' because I'm the one who lost the bet."

"David Auberon wants to debrief me, and I immediately thought of you."

"That's...sweet."

"I mean—I—I—that is t'say—"

"Take a breath, Magnus."

"I thought you might want to come to the debrief—to the meeting. I'm meeting him at five."

I would, actually. She was still irked that Magnus fucking Berne hadn't sat her down and carefully explained what he was doing with David

(why? he doesn't owe you shit...and would you have listened?)

but she'd also believed what she told the other Damp Squibs: having an independent investigator look into Jerry and Andy's deaths was a good thing.

And she—well, she didn't *miss* the big lug, exactly. She hadn't known him long enough to miss him. But he was interesting to be around. And she liked listening to him; the man could have had a lucrative career recording audiobooks. And he might be unconsciously condescending, but at least he didn't hate her the way Roger did.

Ugh. Pathetic. Get a grip.

Good advice.

"When and where?"

Chapter 42

THE "DEBRIEFING" WAS IN A BIG, OLD, PURPLE HOUSE, THE one they'd passed last week on their way to Lila's place. Or would it be Oz and Lila's place now? *Don't know, don't care. Well, I care a little. How goes the prenegotiated cohabitation?* Stable/Shifter cohabitation wasn't rare, and Shifter DNA was dominant as hell, which is how a Stable and a Shifter produced a Jerry. Verity had always found them intriguing. What would come of a Stable/squib mating?

She parked behind Magnus's absurd car (which exactly matched the house; she'd had to see it to believe it) then got out and started up the walk to the two-story Colonial with dark-purple paint and white trim. There was a birdhouse in the front yard that was a duplicate of the main house, just smaller, a Slip 'N Slide running parallel to the porch, and last year's Christmas tree, an enormous dead thing that looked like it had been attacked by animals every night for a year. Maybe it had.

Magnus waited for her then rapped at the front door and opened it. "It's all right," he told her. "They know we're coming."

"I should hope so." She couldn't tell if the big guy was excited about David's findings, hanging out in a purple house, or (conceited, but still a possibility) spending the rest of the afternoon with her. Probably the first two. Well, maybe the first and third options. Or none of the above. Or all of the above.

"Magnus!" The same tiny woman she'd met last week had all but sprinted up to them. "And Verity dear, oh, let me apologize again for our bad *bad* kit." Verity was pulled into a bony hug that smelled like flour and sugar. Then Mama Mac pulled back and held her at arm's length. "You look lovely."

"I wore my nicest T-shirt."

"Caro is also very sorry."

"No harm d—ack!" Before she could set her feet, Mama Mac was tugging her toward the kitchen, which was full of people. "Okay. Hi, everybody."

"Very *very* sorry," Mama said again, skewering the poor girl with a death glare. Caro averted her gaze but didn't move from her seat at the table. Instead, she slowly reached out and picked up a battered notebook then picked up (even more slowly) a pen. "And so is Dev."

"True," Dev agreed. He was standing beside Annette, looking sulky. Probably trapped mid-lecture. "Very *very* sorry."

"Yes, I"—*I know,* she was about to say then realized Mama Mac hadn't found out the cubs had snuck over to her place a couple of days ago—"appreciate that. Really, it's fine. No apologies necessary." No *more* apologies, at any rate.

"That's kind of you," Annette began, "but—"

"I get knocked down all the time. Honestly, it's weird if I make it to lunch and someone *hasn't* knocked me down. Also I don't think that was Caro's fault. Pretty sure I tripped. So let us speak of this no more."

She heard a snort from Caro's direction, but when she looked, the girl was poker-faced.

"All right," Mama Mac said after a long, suspenseful silence. "We'll let it go, then. Dev, Caro, go wash up, please.

David, did you want to use the kitchen? I can go somewhere else if you need privacy."

"Not on my account," Verity said. "I mean…we all know Jerry's dead. I don't think David's briefing will change that." To David, hopefully: "Will it?"

"'Fraid not," he replied. He scratched his stubble and yawned, and Verity suddenly realized he had bags under his eyes. Working hard on Magnus's dime, then. Excellent. "And I'd rather not move. I brought the whiteboard and everything."

Verity dutifully laughed until he went out to the kitchen porch then came back wheeling a whiteboard. She took a seat, and Magnus, after hesitating for a split second, took the one beside her.

"Okay, so I spent some time talking to the MPD and the SPPD, and some folks from Ramsey County. I'm not done by a long shot, but here's what I've got so far. Andy Bray was killed a month ago, and—"

"So that's definitive?" Verity asked. "You don't think it was an accident? Uh, sorry. You should probably resign yourself to lots of interruptions."

"Don't be sorry. And yeah. The coroner's initial finding was accidental death from blunt force trauma. You knew that much, right?"

Verity nodded. "Yeah, he was supposed to end the evening's shenanigans at Minnehaha Falls. We figured he must have slipped."

"He might have slipped, but it didn't kill him. It's only fifty-three feet to the ground. Nothing's certain, but that's a pretty survivable fall, even for a squib."

Verity gritted her teeth and let that pass.

"It is," Magnus agreed. He turned to Verity. "Sam Smalls survived a plane crash. Broke both his legs and still managed to get out of the wreckage and find help."

"Yeah, I get it." How many trees had she fallen out of as a child? She couldn't remember (hopefully a numbers issue and not a concussion issue), but every Shifter knew someone who'd walked away from an accident that would have left a Stable hideously mangled and thoroughly dead. Squibs might not be able to shift, but they still had the strength, speed, and reflexes of the ones who could sprout fur.

"So it wasn't blunt force anything," David continued. "Someone held him down until he drowned."

Verity sat there and absorbed the info. She had absolutely no idea how to respond, so the sponge route—absorbing in silence—seemed as good a plan as any. After a few seconds, she opened her mouth, but…nope. Nothing.

Andy Bray slipped, and someone was waiting and drowned him when he hit the water.

Or someone pushed Andy off the falls then ran (or jumped) down and drowned him.

Jesus Christ. She could actually feel the hair on her arms and the nape of her neck stiffen and fought down a shiver.

Magnus broke the silence. "But why?"

David shrugged. "If we knew why, we'd know who. I'm meeting with his parents tomorrow, so we'll see if they have any theories."

"Or enemies?" Annette asked.

"He was a cop," David replied, "so he had enemies by virtue of the uniform he put on, if nothing else. But it may be that it's nothing to do with his job. At this point, we just don't know."

"Was he undercover or something?" Verity asked. She

couldn't think of a reason why anyone would need to secretly infiltrate the Damp Squibs; the worst they ever did was trespass. And endanger the occasional minor, of course. Still, she was guided by the weight of what had to be a thousand television shows: cop gets killed in civvies? No one knew he was a cop? Undercover. Killed by someone who found out. TV wouldn't lie to her, right?

David shrugged again. Verity was starting to wonder if it was a tic. "I talked to his supervisor, and his supervisor's supervisor. If Andrew Bray was undercover, nobody in his department knew about it."

"Strange." From Annette, who'd propped her chin on her hand and was studying the (blank) whiteboard.

"Which brings me to Jerry Hart." David's gaze was direct but kind. "It gets a little rough now."

"Do it." Verity hoped they didn't misinterpret her eagerness. It wasn't that she wanted to hear the gory details; that was, in fact, the very last thing she wanted. She'd choose a root canal over knowing. An appendectomy sans anesthesia. Living with her parents until the three of them moved (together) to a nursing home. Problem was, she *needed* to hear them. To understand. She needed to know what his last moments had been like, that was one thing. No one could tell her how Jerry died, that was another.

Les didn't know when he called her with the awful news, and she couldn't bear to ask his parents. Gossiping about it at the memorial would have been beyond crass—ducking out early was bad enough, even if she knew Jerry wouldn't have cared. All she could get out of anyone were conflicting stories that were vague on the details. The secrecy was as frightening as it was maddening.

"His body was found in Summit Overlook Park the morning after Andy's memorial service."

Summit? Jerry's favorite park. Where we took Magnus after he crashed Andy's memorial.

"Bled to death," David was saying, because he took her at her word when she told him to do it. "The cops—all Stables, unfortunately—found dark fur all over him and in the wound. Something was fast enough and sharp enough to take a chunk out of his throat. Jerry had defensive wounds on his hands and feet—"

"He was really proud of his front-shin kick," Verity said faintly.

"—and was able to fend it off, but he bled to death before he could get help."

Verity made a fist, trying to stop her brain from churning out an awful mini movie

(Jerry coughing and wheezing, agony and fear blending into shock as he crawled to safety while the grass grew warm and wet and sticky with his blood)

which never worked, and she didn't know why she tried. She was so numb, she couldn't feel her own fingernails biting into her hands—oh. She was holding Magnus's hand. She had no idea when she did that. Or if she did that. Didn't care, either. She squeezed, and the blockage in her throat eased a bit when he squeezed back.

"Fur?" Annette asked.

"Well, that lets squibs off the hook," Verity said weakly. A piss-poor joke, but it was all she could think of. "Excuse me."

She let go of Magnus's hand then grabbed his collar and hauled him out of the chair. She pushed the screen door open and pulled him onto the kitchen porch.

"Er, lass, if ye want a bit of privacy, you've said yourself that four feet away doesn't—"

She stuck a finger in his face. "Not that it's likely, but if you ever, ever, ever talk to my parents again, you must never ever tell them my squib friend was killed by a Shifter."

"Understood."

"Never *ever*. Ever!"

"Yes, Verity."

"They'll implode in a bundle of fear and paranoia and the fallout will be soul-crushing. And my soul isn't going down alone," she warned. "If my soul is crushed, yours will be, too. And also your skull. Get it?"

"Understood."

"And thank you for hiring David, you interfering POS. Really. I owe you."

"You don't o—"

"Shut up, please."

She shoved the screen door back open and took her seat at the table. "Sorry. We're back now."

"Are you all right, Magnus?" Annette asked with a small smirk. "You look a little gray."

"Fine. I'm fine, lass."

Verity cleared her throat. "So, I was saying that squibs are in the clear."

"Yeah." David was taking her words at face value, hands stuffed in his pockets, head down. Thinking, thinking. "They are. So the cops think a dog or a wolf got him. Obviously, they're leaning toward the former. At most, they'll be open to the idea of a wolf–dog hybrid. They're illegal, but clueless Stables think they make badass pets. Pure wolves aren't so common in Saint Paul," David added. "Well, they are, but not wild ones."

"Except they are!" Verity straightened so suddenly, she almost fell out of the chair. "Jerry saw a black wolf! He told me about it a few days ago. He saw it a couple of blocks from downtown and tried to go over and talk to it, but he never got the chance. He was upwind, so he wasn't a hundred percent sure it was a Shifter, but like David said—what are the odds of a wild wolf running around Summit Avenue?"

"So Jerry spots a black wolf that moves out of range before he can get a scent. And a few days later, a black wolf attacks Jerry in a park about twenty minutes from here," David finished.

Verity wasn't a telepath, but she knew what they were thinking: they all knew a black wolf.

"Did your friend seem frightened to you?" Annette asked, determinedly not looking at the doorway from which Dev and Caro had left five minutes ago. "When he told you about the wolf?"

"N-no." Verity cleared her throat. "No, just intrigued. He thought it was weird, but not in a bad way. He wasn't scared. And he didn't have any enemies. That I knew of, I mean."

"Or that he knew of," Magnus said quietly.

"Right. That he knew of. And then there's. Um." Verity looked up at Caro, a silent presence in the kitchen doorway for thirty seconds or so. The girl was in drab colors—gray T-shirt, gray capris—like she was unconsciously hoping not to stand out. She was looking right at Verity, who rose to her feet.

Verity signed, *Did you kill my friend?*

A slow head shake from Caro, who had more reason than most to bite first and ask questions later where squibs were involved.

Verity studied the teenager, a werewolf with a bite force of four hundred pounds, then nodded, and sat back down. So did David, who had been scrutinizing Caro with an intensity that matched Verity's.

David had said, *I'd rather not move.*

He had said, *I brought the whiteboard and everything.*

Verity suspected he wanted to be near Caro to gauge her reaction when the details of Jerry's death came out. *Memo to me: don't underestimate this guy. Except I haven't, so that's an unnecessary memo.*

"Well. Well, of course not," Mama said. She'd been arranging the pantry and had just now come back up the kitchen stairs. "Caro wouldn't—"

Except she had.

"She doesn't—she's not like that."

Anymore. Maybe.

"She wouldn't just…well." Mama flapped her arms then let them fall to her side. "She said she didn't do it. Case closed."

"Yeah," Verity said, and that was the end of it.

For now.

Chapter 43

"Mama's not being naive. She's looked after a lot of troubled cubs. It's not just blind faith."

Verity looked around, and yep—Annette was talking to *her*. David had hit the loo, Magnus was talking to Mama by the pantry, the kids had vamoosed. No hope for it: she was trapped in a bright-green kitchen with a focused werebear.

"I—I didn't say it was. I mean, I believe her. Them. Caro and Mama Mac."

Verity couldn't have explained why she so stoutly believed the young Shifter and luckily wasn't asked. She knew the girl had been grotesquely traumatized but had trouble believing the teenager could have impulse-killed a man in a public park then gone about her business. Yeah, she'd gone after a squib with lethal intent—one who was directly responsible for subjecting her to years of sustained abuse. That didn't mean she was a squib-slashing serial killer.

Caro didn't attack Verity in the house—she ran away. (Well. Ran *over* her in order to run away.) She hadn't been confrontational, or even hostile, even though she'd had to deal with a squib in Mama Mac's kitchen, one of her few safe spaces.[17]

She hadn't been subtle about sneaking up to Verity's apartment, either. And she had seemed, if not relieved by Dev's interference, at least resigned. When Verity shooed her, Dev, and Magnus away, Caro had left with minimal fuss.

---

17. This is an appropriate use of the phrase *safe space*. Just sayin'.

"It's fine," Verity added, because she assumed she had to say something. Constant nodding wouldn't cut it. Plus she was starting to feel like a bobblehead. "I mean, not *fine*, exactly. It's just. I believed her. Both of them. And I don't know Mama Mac very well, but *naive* seems like it would miss the mark." Especially for a woman who specialized in fostering traumatized cubs.

"Caro would have been covered in blood, that's one thing."

Oh. Annette had an agenda, a little lecture in her head she needed to get out. *Lovely. Well, I'll nod and hope that's the end of—*

"She couldn't have gotten rid of it all before returning to the house," Annette added with not a little urgency, as if Verity was a judge and her client was bound for lethal injection. "Not without access to labs she cannot access."

"None that I know of," Verity replied, because maybe it wasn't a rhetorical question?

"And even a Stable with blocked sinuses would notice if she came back immaculately clean…" Her voice rose as she reeled off points to be made. "…and wearing entirely different clothes and perhaps with wet hair!"

"I get it, Annette."

"And there isn't a mark on her." Gah, Annette's face was only ten inches from hers. Thank God the woman was pro-dental hygiene; her breath smelled like oranges. "Your friend fought back because he was clever and brave, and whatever killed him didn't walk away unscathed."

"I'm going to nod some more now to further indicate I agree with what you're saying and to politely point out that none of it was necessary in the first place."

"Also," Annette added, because *argh*, "Caro couldn't...oh. This is inappropriate. All of it," Annette realized and backed off a bit. "I'm sorry. It's not that I care about Caro more than your friend." She paused, frowned. "Actually, I *do* care more about Caro than your friend."

"It would be weird if you didn't," Verity agreed.

"I only wanted to reassure you that we're not proceeding solely on faith."

"I get it," Verity repeated, because she did.

Annette smiled. A little one, but it was there. "You're very accommodating. Our family is only adding to your stress during this difficult time."

"It's fine. Everyone's just...y'know. Dealing. As best they can."

"Yes, that's just right."

"And you with a wedding to plan."

"I'm not planning it," Annette replied, and the smile widened. "You know how you have a work colleague and over time you realize they've become a friend, a dear friend who will put themself in danger for you? Risk their livelihood and career and personal safety and life for you?"

"No."

"Well, sometimes friends like that are...they can be a bit of a mixed blessing. And it's best to play to their strengths. In my friend Nadia's case, snobbish organization skills. Though I admit I temporarily feared for my life when I moved the timeline up by a few weeks."

"I'll bet."

"I had to!" she cried, because something was going on in Annette Garsea's brain, and Verity had no idea what it could be. "This has been so hard on Dev already. You have to give kits stability. And when you can't, you have to accommodate as best you can. It's imperative!"

"That's what you've gotta do, all right."

"And of course you're invited."

"That's ridiculous, Annette," Verity said, kindly enough. "We've only met twice. Save the chicken entrée for someone you've known longer than a week."

"It's fine, truly. I know Magnus would be thrilled. He's invited, too. But don't let that color your decision," Annette added hastily. "We want you there for—for your own self."

"Again: met twice. You don't know my own self. My own self could be a raging cannibal who loves fracking."

"We want everyone there on their own merits," Annette continued, because she had a thousand things on her mind and listening to Verity wasn't one of them. "Especially the cubs. Though I simply don't know if Dev…"

Oh, God, she's going to do that thing where they tell you even more things that are incredibly personal and then it's so awkward because you don't know them very well and you've got to—

"Ah…never mind. Family business. I hope," she added strangely.

Verity couldn't hide her relief. "Excellent."

"Also, when did you see Dev and Caro?"

"Uh, what?"

Annette made an impatient gesture: *away with your feigned surprise.* "It was perfectly obvious when you came in that they had apologized to you already."

Oh, shit. "It was?"

"Indeed. You covered for them. So, again: When did you see them?"

"You're a little intense right now."

Chapter 44

SOMEONE DROWNED ANDY AND TORE UP JERRY. THE thought kept drumming through her brain like the most obnoxious of earworm pop songs.[18] *But why, why, why?*

Like David said, if they knew why, they'd know who. Which was one of those things that sounded deceptively wise but the more you thought about it, the more you realized was a useless observation.

"It doesn't make sense," she said, arms crossed over her chest as she cupped her elbows. She wasn't physically cold—it was way too warm for that. The chill was entirely internal.

"Not to anyone sane, at least," Magnus agreed.

They were at the scene of the crime, Summit Overlook Park, which had been blocked off with crime scene tape. But no one was around, and they kept their distance.

After Annette had tearfully apologized for being tearful, Verity had made her escape, Magnus on her heels. She'd opened her purse to get her keys and saw a small piece of paper on top of the detritus in her purse. She unfolded it, smoothed it, read it.

Sorry.

C.

"Never even saw her slip this in. I guess Caro could be a pretty fair pickpocket if—wait." She scented the note. "No, Dev's the pickpocket. Caro's just the author."

---

18. We're talking Carly Rae Jepsen and Katy Perry-esque levels of earworm!

"You should see me when I think my cubs are in dang
This with a perfectly straight face and delivered in a perfe
even tone.

Yikes! "Saturday night," Verity admitted. Fuck the kid
she had to save herself from the wrath of Garsea! "But it wa
fine. We ended up having a nice talk over Ding Dongs and
chocolate milk."

Annette looked appalled, either by the junk fare or Verity
getting unexpected guests.

"It was fine," Verity said again. "Only. Uh. Look, in the
interest of full disclosure and because you're kind of terrifying right now, I think Dev is getting ready to bolt."

"Oh, that. Yes," Annette replied. "I already deduced that."
And then she burst into tears.

"That was kind of th'lass," Magnus said, rudely reading the brief note over her shoulder. "She's shy."

"I don't think *shy* even begins to cover it." Verity couldn't seem to stop staring at the note. "A kid like Caro...her notebook...it's almost an extension of herself. Without it, she's mostly mute. Except when she isn't."

"Aye. I've never seen her without it. Granted, I haven't known her very long."

She could barely hear him. She could barely hear herself. "That's right," Verity replied. Her voice sounded far away, like someone was turning down the dial in her brain. "She never goes anywhere without it. Except when she does." She turned to Magnus. "This isn't a movie, and I'm not a detective. I'm not gonna find something all the techs missed. I'm not compelled to involve myself because I think the cops aren't doing a good job. And if I came face-to-face with a serial killer, I would scream and scream and run away very, very fast."

"That seems sensible." This in the tone of a man waiting for the other shoe to drop.

"I just need to see it. The park."

"O'course."

"Resigned isn't a good look for you, Magnus."

"I'm coming with you, lass."

"Magnus..."

"Someone is murdering squibs," he replied evenly. "Someone who brought your number from seven to five in a month. I'm coming with you."

"Oh, jeez, fine, whatever." Too much trouble to argue. And while she wasn't afraid of whatever terrors the crime scene might hold, the thought of Magnus being there was

(argh, so hard to admit)

comforting. It was comforting. She itched to hug him again, only in his current form, not his other self.

No, she wasn't worried about someone staking out the crime scene in order to kill her. She *was* worried about the mind movies her brain would be determined to screen for her. But if Jerry had to go through it, the least she could do was bear witness, in a manner of speaking.

And so here they were, on a beautiful summer day that Jerry would never see, in the park where he fought and bled and died. The bloody grass called to her and repelled her.

Christ, she was losing her grip.

She took a deep, steadying breath, felt a hand on her shoulder.

"This must be especially bad for ye, lass. With your exceptional sniffer."

She had to smile at *exceptional sniffer*. "Don't tell me you buy into that whole 'squibs have super senses even for Shifters because they can't shift' fairy tale."

"I wasn't thinking of that exactly," Magnus admitted. "But now y'mention it, maybe there's some truth to it?"

"Nope. No more than when a Stable goes blind, their hearing gets sharper. Their blindness forces them to pay more attention, so it seems like they can hear and smell better. That's all."

Whether you bought into the "squibs have enhanced senses" SAS propaganda or not, the truth of the matter was the park smelled rich and coppery and meaty to her. There was almost a miasma drifting up from the ground. Like someone in a trance, she began walking parallel to the crime scene tape, parallel to the bloody gouges in the grass, and then swerved right, stepped over the tape—

"Aw, shite."

—and walked right up to the eagle statue overlooking the river valley. She knelt, felt behind it, found the loose stone, pried it aside just enough to slip her fingers into the crack, felt the wadded paper, brought out her prize.

Jerry's battered notebook.

Chapter 45

"SON OF A BITCH!"

It was hours later, and the only thing she had to show for it were paper cuts. "Dammit! There's nothing here. Well, some things are here." A self-confessed "pseudoluddite," Jerry was fond of his phone but only used it as an alarm clock and for the occasional phone call. In all other ways, he preferred his notebook. He'd sketched a number of street signs for some reason, and a few recipes (if charcuterie board assembly could count as a recipe, *and it didn't*), movie reviews (he had not been a fan of the *Mission Impossible* franchise), addresses (but he was a fan of the Panera Bread franchise), and his friends.

Her own face peeked up at her more than once as she flipped through it. Maggie's, too, and Les's. And rough sketches of a black wolf—small and blurry and scrawny, it looked like a stiff wind could blow it over. Jerry had loved to bitch about how no one took weredeer seriously, but he'd held his own in more than one fight. The black wolf had been too skittish to let Jerry get close enough for a whiff or a decent sketch, and it was hard to picture the thing getting the drop on her friend.

In other words, Jerry's notebook was crammed with all sorts of tidbits, none of them relevant to his murder.

"It's not like I was expecting a sketch of the killer with a helpful all-caps caption: 'THIS IS THE PERSON WHO KILLED ME.' But I really thought this was the clue that would crack the case. Ugh, I just said 'crack the case' like someone who watches too much TV. I also watch too much TV."

"I thought so, too," Magnus confessed. "Nadia certainly seemed to think that's how things would go."

"Who the hell is Nadia, and why was she telling you how things would go?"

"Annette's colleague."

Ah. Annette's mixed blessing. The rabid organizer who would selflessly die for Annette but not before carping endlessly.

Verity sighed. "I'll hang on to this. I'm sure his parents would like it back. Hey! No touchy." She lightly slapped his hand when he reached for it. "These fall under the purview of private papers. Jerry'd be mortified if randos were flipping through it."

"If I knew what a rando was, I'd be hurt, wouldn't I, lass?"

She ignored the silly question. "Like I said, this belongs to his parents, but I can't face them tonight. Driving out to Apple Valley will cut into my drinking time. C'mon, let's go back to my place."

He shook his head, either in negation or because he wasn't sure it was an invitation. "You want me to come with you?"

"Desperate times, Magnus. It's pathetic to drink alone twice in four days. You being there will make it slightly less pathetic."

"Then how can I refuse?"

———————

Six shots in, they were in the living area watching *Mission Impossible: Rogue Nation* in Jerry's honor. Verity knew that if she'd been the one to die, Jerry would have hosted a movie night featuring only films she hated.

Well. Verity had six shots. She was pretty sure. In the general area of six, at least. Maybe seven. She had no idea how many Magnus had. It took a lot to get a Shifter drunk, and she was more than up to it.

"You're making that up! There's no fucking way that a) you're drinking your way through every hard cider brand, b) there's such a thing as rhubarb hard cider[19], and c) it's your favorite. Admit you're lying, you liar!"

"Why would I lie about that?" he protested. "Where's the advantage to that?"

"It's *poison*, Magnus, actual fucking poison. And worse— it's a vegetable! A bitter, disgusting, poisonous vegetable. Like asparagus but a zillion times worse."

"So I should never make you asparagus–bacon roll-ups. Noted."

"Just make me bacon–bacon roll-ups." She downed another shot. *Ahh, burns so good.* "Okay, okay, I'll give you a chance to return to sanity. What's your second favorite flavor?"

"Jalapeño lime," he admitted.

She shrieked in mingled dismay and amusement and fought the urge to shake him and yell common sense into his big dumb handsome face. "You've gone completely over the edge, Magnus! If nobody's ever mentioned that, I am now, and your taste buds are trying to kill you. There's no war uglier than a civil war."

"I've been told I'm skating the edge before," he replied with a grin. "That's not a shocking revelation."

"No doubt. Prob'ly started when you decided to learn the secret handshake so you could join Racists 'R' Us."

---

19. There is! Rosie's Pig Cloudy Cider.

"…yes."

"Sorry. Didn't mean to bring down the room."

"No, it's a fair question."

"Wasn't a question. But while we're talking about SAS and their gaggle of speciesist asshats, is that why you've been stuck on me like flypaper?"

Magnus was on the other end of the couch, occasionally taking a sip of whiskey. Now he took another one, and she could tell he was giving what she said careful thought. Which was nice. Most people who knew she was squibby didn't think about what she said, carefully or otherwise.

"If I understand ye correctly, you're asking if I was worried you would make the same mistake I did. But I was worried before I found out you were the Seventh Squib. I didn't want you to get hurt. That was my sole motivation."

"Fifth Squib," she said glumly. "We're down to five."

"But when you told me, I admit I was worried because the SAS ideology can be seductive. For any Shifter, really—most of us don't want to stay in the shadows. They offer a chance for us to stop hiding. They've always been verra straightforward with that part of their agenda."

"SAS: Straightforward Asshat Shitheads. It's got a nice ring to it."

Magnus ignored her devastating witticism. "But especially for a squib, since they've made it plain that they—uh—how to put this—"

"That there'd be room for squibs after the blood apocalypse?"

"Aye."

Verity stuck out her tongue. "Oh, barf. First, I wouldn't trust any of the 'pureblood' crowd. Second, even if I did, their overall agenda is gross and stupid. I'm not the only one who thinks so, either. There's not a single squib who wants anything to do with those turds. Third...I forget the third."

"You have to admit, a group of Shifters who know you can't shift but still welcome you with open arms—"

"No, *you* have to admit that. I think you might be projecting all over the place right now. Just because a group wants you doesn't mean you're jazzed about it. I mean me. Jazzed. I'm *not* jazzed. Would you be jazzed if Holocaust deniers wanted you to join their absurd club?"

"—would be a powerful lure," he finished doggedly.

"I'm not a largemouth bass, fer chrissake. Besides, it's not a lure for me. Little Melly Swiss Cake Rolls, *that's* a lure. Debbie, I mean. Li'l Debbie Swiss Rolls, and I'm like Groucho Marx."

"I'm having trouble following, lass."

"If a club wants me, I don't want them." She paused, but it seemed he had no comment, so onward: "What yer sayin' is essentially you've been bugging me for days because you worried I was doomed to make all your mistakes."

"That's one way to phrase it," he said dryly.

"I doughnut—don—*don't* want anything t'do with them, and maybe, because I've been wondering, d'you think those SAS fuckers were involved in that fucking horrible Shifter trafficking thing that spit Caro out?"

He was leaning toward her, one arm slung over the back of the sofa, focused and intent and just ridiculously sexy; it was irritating, all the sexy. The sofa cushion between them was as wide as the Grand Canyon. "Annette and David were sure of it. The War Wolves, especially."

"Oh, *Gawd*," she hooted. "Don't get me started on fucking

War Wolves. 'Hey, we're unique and special but only because we don't know that mercenaries have been around as long as people have been around, derp.' Can you believe there are people who actually *aspire* to joining the ranks of those jack-booted fuckmuppets? Magnus! I gotta go down to that warehouse. Not this one. The one where all the things happened. T'satisfy my curiosity at least. Um. Not now, though. S'late, and I'm a smidge tipsy. Later. Poor Caro. I'm glad she didn't bite me, but I wouldn't have blamed her if she did. This probably should go without saying, but hashtag Not All Squibs, right?"

He smiled. He really had a very nice smile; it made his eyes crinkle. Before this moment in time, she hadn't found laugh lines even a little arousing. "Not all squibs," he agreed, "but you're a standout even among your elite group."

"I'm not calling us an elite group, and you'd better not start, either. Les will hear it and love it, and next thing y'know he'll have T-shirts made and we'll be expected to wear 'em. And if we don't, he'll get soooooo pissy."

"Noted. And you're not the Seventh Squib or the Fifth. You're your own self. You're Verity Lane, the duck egg in the hen's nest: another creature entirely, who doesn't have to follow the rules of the hen house."

"I love your sexy farm metaphors." She blinked hard, because for some absurd reason, that made her want to cry and kiss him on the mouth at the same time. "M'not calling myself a duck egg, either." She swiveled on the cushion, stretched out, poked her bare toes into his ribs. "Move over, you're hoggin' the whole thing."

"You're on two of the three cushions!" he protested. "And I'm only taking up half of one."

She poked him again, only to feel him seize her ankle and then tickle her foot. She pulled back so abruptly, she fell off the couch. "Terrible warehouse cement floors," she groaned, suddenly questioning every life decision she ever made. "And on top of bein' hard, they're chilly!"

Grinning, he stood and extended a hand to help her up, but instead, she yanked him down. He caught himself with one arm or he would have landed flat on top of her. Which wouldn't have been even remotely terrible. As it was, their faces were just a few inches apart.

"Christ, you're strong." He was so close she could *feel* his whiskey-warm voice. "Ye almost gave me whiplash, lass."

"I bet you say that to all the girls."

"No. Just you, darling."

"*Darling*, I like that. Darling." She blinked up at him and ran a finger along his jawline. His stubble was dark and coarse with—hilarious—a very faint violet tint. "Oh my God, your stubble is purple! Do Stables ever notice?"

"Thankfully, no."

"Right? It sucks to be a major minority—tha's—that's not a contradiction, right? Major minority? Or would it be an oxymoron? We don't have the nummers, but Stables never notice *anything*. Or…or if they do, they make up a fairy tale or scary story about it. Little Red Riding Hood. Or Billie Eilish."

"Stables make up scary stories about Billie Eilish?"

She'd already lost her train of thought. "How should I know? You smell terrific, by the way. In case no one's ever said."

"Thank you, darling."

Maybe it was the booze. Or the lighting. Because at this

angle, Magnus fucking Berne had a nimbus. Like one of those old-timey Renaissance paintings where the halo looked like a flat plate. "I like when you call me *darling*."

His reply was low and intimate. "By happy coincidence, you *are* a darling."

"Nuh-uh. You're the only one who's ever called me a darling, darling." She reached up, seized him by the ears, and planted a kiss right on his astonished mouth. His mouth opened, but that might have been slack-jawed surprise. Who cared? He was warm and smelled like whiskey and cotton and sunshine, and for a hard man his lips were sweetly soft.

"There," she said when he pulled back. "That's out of the way."

"Lass—" He cut himself off as he lowered his head and kissed her back, nibbling on her lower lip while his hand slipped up her shirt and stroked the tender skin of her stomach.

"Oh, excellent," she mumbled into his mouth. "Knew you'd be good at this."

He pulled back to agree, excellent! Except he was pulling all the way back, and now he was sitting astride her hips. "You're lovely. And a wonderful kisser. Glorious in every way, t'be frank. But."

"Let's fuck."

"I can't," he said gently.

"Old war wound?"

"What? No! I meant *we* can't."

"Don't worry, I'm on the pill, and I'm sure there's a box of condoms in the freezer."

He stared down at her, shook his head slightly, then said,

"I don't want to know why you do that to condoms, and I'm not wurred about getting you pregnant."

"Great!" She sat up, and her fingers flew to his shirt buttons. "Let's just get this off you, and then I can rocketh thy world."

His hands caught her wrists, held them. "Verity."

"Don't worry, I'll do all the work. Well, most of the work. A third. I'll do a third of the work. Best and final offer."

"Verity. You're drunk."

"Oh, please, you're just saying that because I had five shots. Or eleven." She tugged to free her wrists, but his grip was firm. "I'm completely capable of consent."

"Disagree."

Wait. What? She couldn't remember the last time she got laid, she wanted some release, *deserved* some release, thank you very fucking much, and Magnus fucking Berne was gonna be the monkey wrench in her gears? Or something?

She scowled up at him. "You've been sniffing up my back trail for over a week, and now when you can have me on a platinum platter—because sex with me is way better than a silver platter—you can't be bothered?"

"That's not it at all."

"What? Afraid you'll get squib cooties?"

He pulled back even farther. If he kept going, he'd be sitting in the hall. "What?"

"Don't pretend you don't understand," she snapped. "You can't tell me there aren't any cooties in Scotland."

"Lass, you're not makin' a whole lot of sense."

"I've never made more sense in my wife! Life, I mean. Y'know, there's mostly just two different kinds of Shifters. The fuckers who are open about hating squibs, and the fuckers who hate us but aren't open about it. You're worse than Roger!"

"Who's Roger?"

"Don't try and change the subject!" She wanted to crawl away and hide. She wanted to hit him with a frying pan, cartoon-style. She wanted to shut up his hot mouth with *her* hot mouth. "All your concern, all the times you said you were 'wurred,' it was only ever because I'm a squib. You'll condescend to crash memorials to 'save' me, but when it comes to real intimacy, you opt out."

The color was draining from his face, which should have been satisfying but wasn't. "That's nae true!"

"And speaking of opting out, get out!"

"Verity." His voice was low, urgent. He leaned forward to take her by the shoulders then pulled back again. Like he'd get squib on him if he touched her again. "Please. It's not like that. I think you're wonderful."

"Shut up!"

"Not because you're a squib, or in spite of being a squib. For yourself, your own special self—"

"Don't start that duck egg bullshit again!"

"And if you were sober and hadn't had to endure a week of loss and pain, I'd count m'self the luckiest lad in the world."

"No, you *could* have been the luckiest lad in the world. But you didn't want to silly—sully! You didn't want to sully yourself with a squib. So now you're just the asshole getting thrown out."

"I would never, *ever* use that word in connection with any part of you. Far from it. Verity, this has been one of the best weeks of my life, all respect to Andy and Jerry, and it's because I had the great good fortune to find ye in my garden. Ever since—"

"No. No!" She wrenched out of his grip. "Don't say that! Not any of it! It's not true, none of it's true, an' it just makes everything worse."

"Verity. Please."

"Just…just get the fuck out." She shoved him, hard, to get him off her *finally*, and stumbled to her feet. He still had the black overnight bag he'd picked up at Target

(*was it only three days ago? two? what fucking day is it?*)

a few days ago, and she started shoving his things at him: toiletries, the bag itself, an empty whiskey bottle, whatever the hell else she needed him to take so he would *get the fuck out already*. And maybe do some recycling on his way out. "And when another squib dies, you'd better not be at the memorial! Just let us sink or swim or die on our own, like the rest of the world does, now *get out*!"

His eyes.

She wouldn't think of the look in his eyes.

She wouldn't think of him at all.

Chapter 46

AGONY FLOWED UP AND DOWN HER SPINE, AND FOR A horrifying moment, she thought she was dying or dead. Then she opened her eyes, saw the blinding white walls but not the cloudy, killer-hiding doors, and realized it was much worse: sometime last night, after showing Magnus fucking Berne the door, she'd staggered into the spare bedroom and fallen asleep on the futon.

The futon! Jesus wept. The only thing going for that sentient and *evil* piece of furniture were the red sheets with a respectable thread count and the plush pillows designed for side sleepers, because only weirdos slept on their backs or fronts. Or would it be back or front, singular? Regardless, she could lie there draped in sheets the exact color of the blood of her enemies and plot her revenge.

Revenge.

"Revenge!" she cried, because just thinking the word hadn't been enough. But saying it out loud carried its own penalties; she groaned, lurched into a sitting position,

(not so fast, not so fast!)

groaned again, and clutched her head. She could count on one hand how often she'd been hungover. Her own fault for hitting the sheets without drinking a ton of water first. A lot of things were her own fault lately.

Then she remembered *why* she'd been determined to inflict the futon on herself last night, and humiliation burned through her while her bile rose. Magnus Berne had showed his true colors at last, but that didn't make it hurt any less. And not that she made a habit of propositioning near-strangers, but she'd never been turned down for sex before.

(And isn't that why you almost never try? Because it's so easy? Because the next morning not one thing has changed? So what's the point? What can a rando give you that Mr. Hitachi can't?)

She struggled free of the futon, which took a minute. Apparently she'd rolled around in the sheets before passing out, turning herself into a burrito the color of the blood of her enemies.

Free at last, she made determined strides (staggered) to the bathroom, passing more than one empty booze bottle, ugh,

(maybe Magnus had a really, really, really good point?)

(maybe shut the fuck up, inner voice?)

(maybe you shouldn't be mad at the guy who wanted to wait for full consent?)

recycling *just* came yesterday morning, so she and the empty bottles would be roommates for a week. Which would have been depressing, but she'd had terrible roommates before. The bottles, by comparison, would be a delight. The bottles wouldn't eat the last Ding Dong and then *lie to her face* about it. The bottles would use coasters!

She stared down at the toothpaste tube and shuddered—the thought of putting anything in her mouth just now was the gag trigger of all possible triggers. But whiskey morning breath was even more unthinkable. So she squeezed out a blob half the size of a pea and got to it.

Soon this would all be a bad memory. Soon she would be alone again, with delightful minty breath. She'd do her own thing and go her own way and pick herself up by her suspenders or whatever the cliché was, mourn Jerry, move on, make new friends. Take a lover, assuming the next guy she propositioned had the sense to see the incredible gift of boning she was offering.

(Or you'll just have another date night with Mr. Hitachi)

Nice try, inner voice, but that actually sounded very fucking great. Just like kicking Magnus out was very fucking great. Sure, she'd had six (fourteen?) shots. But she didn't come on to him because of booze. Last night hadn't been the only time she'd wanted to bone him. It was just the only time she'd asked.

(So whose fault is that?)

Did everyone's inner voice get more sanctimonious when they were hungover? Or was it just hers?

Yeah, Magnus fucking Berne was gorgeous, and he'd made her more than a little horny, but anything beyond a friendly fuck would never happen. Oh, and the friendly fuck wouldn't happen, either. The "oh, golly, Verity, you've had eighteen shots, you might be a smidge tipsy" (or whatever *smidge* was in Scottish), that was just a face-saving excuse.

(Unless it wasn't. Unless his concern was about consent, not whether or not she could sprout fur.)

Nope. It definitely probably maybe wasn't a consent issue. Most likely. Just a way to reject her and still look like the good guy.

Which was fine.

It was all fine.

Chapter 47

SHE WAS THERE AND SHE WAS DEAD, AND THE WORLD WAS ON
fire and
 there was a soft flapping breeze that made no sense
 it was all very puzzling.
 Then another building went up:
 first nothing and then a whooooosh followed by a flump!
 and then one of the walls fell in and he had a thought.
 No, this isn't real, it wasn't as bad as all this, just bad enough
 and he said hold on, I'll carry you to safety.
 And the dead woman opened her eyes and said
 you already did, you silly thing, you carried me
 and Sam looked out for both of us
 that's the part of the story you never like thinking about.
 And he said that's not true, Sam and I are friends now,
kind of
 we are! (kind of)
 and she said the worst and truest thing she said.
 You're not alone because of a lost love
 we were never that
 you're alone because that's just the way you like it.
 And he was wrong there was a worst true thing
 and she said it, she said the worst truth
 while the breeze intensified.
 I was never yours to save.
 And neither is she.
 And you know this you've always

known
this.

He opened his eyes to see Caro staring down at him as she flapped her notebook in his face. "That explains the breeze," Magnus mumbled, not quite sure he was back in the real world.

The teenager scribbled a note, held it out to him.

"Lass, could I please read that five minutes from now? I canna tell if my eyes are open."

"Soup's on," Caro said, smiling down at him.

"Caro?"

"By which I mean cold cereal."

He blinked and needed a second to orient himself. Then the events of the evening came back to him in a mortifying rush, and he groaned and flopped back down on the settee.

Caro smirked. He loved when she talked; they all did. He'd been able to discern no real pattern and wasn't foolish enough to ask her for clarification.

"You talked!" he said before he could stop himself. "Uh. Thank you."

She let out a snort and sat beside him on the settee. This was new territory in all sorts of ways, so he lay there like a lump and told himself to keep his mouth shut.

"It's not always a conscious choice," she told him in a voice low from little use. "Sometimes it is. But. Not always. Sometimes I can't."

Do I make eye contact? I don't want her to think it's a challenge. But not looking at her is an insult, too.

While he internally wrestled, she cleared her throat and continued, "Literally can't. I try, but I can feel my voice box slamming shut. Like how people dry drown. Their lungs lock and won't let even a drop of water in. They still die."

"Oh, aye?"

"But then there's times like this where someone's clearly having a nightmare and you need a good shake. Or a kick. Or…" She waved the notebook at him.

"Thank you for explaining it to me, lass."

"Tell anyone we chatted and I'll kill you a lot."

There wasn't much to say to that, so he didn't try. Just watched her leave, more than a little bemused. Then he remembered where he was, and why he was, and dread replaced amusement, however temporary.

The settee had been a bone of contention. Everything in the past twenty hours had been bones of contention. Nothing could escape all the contention. Not even furniture. He was vague on the precise details leading to Mama Mac's living room settee, but he'd stumbled out of Verity's apartment with no idea where to go and the sickening feeling that he'd ruined it all (again).

And his phone had rung. And it was Annette Garsea. Who greeted him with "I hope I'm not interrupting."

"You're not," he replied, numb. "There's nothing to interrupt. There wasn't and isn't and won't be."

"…okay. Nadia told me about your generous offer of hosting and ferries. David and I can't thank you enough. This solves several problems for us. And apropos of nothing I just said, you sound terrible."

"Fucking allergies," he managed.

"Are you all right?"

He opened his mouth to say "Of course," but "God, no," came out instead.

"Come over" was the instant reply. "Right now. We're all at Mama's."

He opened his mouth to say "I couldn't impose."

"*Right* now," Annette insisted, and he complied. Found his car (he'd only had two shots, which his system had rapidly metabolized). Drove to the purple house with the smaller purple house. Got out. Heard banging coming from the trunk. Unlocked said trunk. Stepped back while Dev Devoss climbed out.

"Aw, hell," the kit complained, squinting up at him. "This completely screws up my plans, Magnus. Hope you're happy."

Dev had been scolded and sent to bed. Caro had absented herself when the scolding started. Mama Mac and David and Oz and Lila listened to the parts of his story he could bring himself to share.

"You did the right thing," Oz said at once.

"She'll never forgive me."

"Dude, you had two alternatives: rape or not rape. You did the right thing."

"But she was so furious."

"Furious and *not raped*," Oz replied. "Get it?"

Intellectually, yes. But her fury and scorn had felt like a sandstorm raging across his exposed skin. The others had commiserated, and Mama Mac made him drink a half gallon of (heinous iced) tea, and Magnus refused to let the cubs give up their beds for him and slept on the settee.

And now there was cereal.

He yawned, stretched, left the settee, found the bathroom. Emerged in time to hear "Thank God Magnus shot

Verity down last night, or who knows when we would have seen you."

Magnus swallowed a groan and tried to figure out how to get back to the living room without being seen by anyone in the kitchen.

"What was your plan, even?" Annette cried. "Hop out and tour the warehouse district in the middle of the night?"

"Among other things," Dev replied. "Look, it's fine. Magnus totally foiled my plan. Thanks again for nothing, *nada, rien,* Magnus! Yeah, I see you trying to creep by." Back to Annette: "Here I am, okay?"

"Very much not okay, Dev!" And just as Magnus thought he had made it safely into the living room... "And thank you, Magnus," Annette called. "I didn't get a chance to properly express my gratitude last night for finding our wayward kit—"

"I didna exactly find him—"

"—and bringing him back to us."

"Happy to help." Accidentally help, but still. He had almost reached the settee, where there were fresh clothes and toiletries. Sweet freedom was so close.

From the kitchen: "And I apologize for the fact that Dev and Caro have decided that stowing away in your trunk is acceptable behavior."

"No problem, lass. I just need to get—"

"It's not about thinking it's acceptable," Dev snapped. "It's about limited options, Annette. When we have to get someplace and you won't help—"

"Then you don't go, Dev! Obviously you don't go! You stay here, and you talk it out with us."

"Talk it out?" The kit's voice cracked, and he flushed. Magnus could sympathize; he well remembered the embarrassment of his deepening voice betraying him throughout adolescence. "What a joke! You've all got your dumb, *estupido*, *stupide* secret plans, and no one else gets a vote. *Talk it out* is just grown-up speak for *here's how it's gonna be, and if you don't like it, too damn bad*."

"First, watch your language. Second, what are you talking about? What secret plans?"

The overnight bag was almost in reach. He'd dress in the living room. He'd dress in the street if that's what it took. He idly wondered where Mama, Caro, and Oz were. Not enough to actually look for them; most of his focus was on leaving the scene of what was a deeply private family squabble.

Aye. That's what you do, innit? Leave when it gets emotionally messy?

He almost snorted. His inner voice, conscience, what have you, was missing the mark this time. Annette and Dev's argument had nothing to do with him. Nothing in this house had anything to do with him.

"C'mon, Annette. It's obvious what you're doing. I'm on the way out, and that's fine, whatever, I never thought this was a permanent thing. But you could've at least respected my intelligence enough to tell me to my snout instead of sneaking around."

"Dev, pardon my French, but what the *enfer* are you talking about?"

"I know you've been seeing my mom down in Stillwater."

Magnus froze in the midst of reaching for a sock. That was—what had Nadia called it? A game changer? He remembered when he'd cleaned up the spilled flour for Mama. Dev had been gone, and Annette had come in and there had been an offside conversation, one he'd kept out of.

Is the one who whelped him causing trouble again?

And Annette's reply had been rather like Annette: straightforward. *The opposite. She doesn't care. Whatever this is, it's not coming from her.*

Annette blinked. "I—yes. I saw her. Dev, it wasn't a secret."

"Good, because you're not slick."

"I wasn't trying to be slick."

"So what'd she say?" Dev wiped his nose, scowled at the floor. "Let me guess. 'Don't look at me, I coulda told you he's a pain in the ass.' Something like that? Is she clean, at least? I know she can get drugs in prison. Everybody knows that but the guys running prisons."

"They know it, too. And yes. She's clean," Annette replied. "She looks good. Uh, comparatively speaking. But I didn't go to her to complain of you, Dev. In fact, I owe you an apology."

"Yeah? Is this one of those deals where the person who screwed up says they owe someone an apology but never actually apologizes? Because I've got no time for that."

"I apologize," she said instantly. "For hurting you—"

"I'm not *hurt*. Jeez."

"—and scaring you."

"I'm not scared, either!"

"I miscalculated."

Dev kicked the table leg. "Damn right!"

"I have no excuse, but—"

"But here comes the excuse anyway."

"I thought it was what you wanted," Annette replied, sounding almost…timid? "Was I so wrong?"

"Are you kidding?" Dev's voice cracked again on *kidding*, but this time he was too upset to be embarrassed. "Look, it's not that I care if you're trading up."

"Again: What?"

Dev ignored the interruption and plunged ahead. "But you could've just told me that's what you were doing. I would've respected that 'cause I'd have known you respected me."

"What?"

"Don't keep saying *what* like you're not even a little clued in to what's going on."

"Dev, I give you my solid, unadulterated, unambiguous word: I am not clued in to what's going on."

Dev threw up his hands. "This is what I'm talking about, the lack of respect!" he nearly screamed.

"I don't understand."

I do. And I can't stand it anymore. Magnus dropped the bag and walked into the kitchen. "I'm sorry to interrupt a verra private matter, but you're both talking about entirely different things."

Annette was still seated at the kitchen table, Dev standing in front of her, hands jammed past the wrists in his pockets, head down. But they both looked up at him and in unison: "What?"

"You both also think the other person is on the same page. So you're just spiraling deeper into misunderstanding. Each of you please ask th'other one *exactly* what it is they're talking about, and I'll go brush my teeth."

"Oh, who cares?" Dev muttered and started to turn away, when Annette's hand shot out and closed over his elbow and gently pulled him back.

"Dev, exactly what is it you're talking about?"

"Let me go, Annette."

"Never. I went to see your mother to tell her about my impending wedding—"

"What, you needed a bridesmaid? I'm sure she was thrilled. Here's a hint, don't give her any money. Whatever expenses she tells you she has, you should pay for them all and hand 'em over. It'll save so much hassle down the road."

"—because I want to adopt you after David and I get married."

Well, hell. I can't leave now. Need to hear how this ends.

To Magnus's surprise, Dev displayed no discernible reaction. Just kept standing there, head down. Not a whoop, not even a smile, or a question. Just stolid silence.

"Dev?" Annette shook his elbow a little. "Do you understand me? When David asked me to marry him, before I told him yes, I told him I want to adopt you. I thought—I thought you would have reali—"

"Don't," the boy said tonelessly.

"You were right, I've been planning things behind your back." Annette had leaned forward, was speaking in as urgent a tone as he'd ever heard. "As a *surprise*. I wanted to have all my metaphorical ducks in a row. All the paperwork filed, the court appearances scheduled, all of it. Judge Gomph and Nadia have been helping me and that's saved some time, but when I started this I wasn't sure how long it would take, and we didn't want to get your hopes up."

"We?"

"David and Mama Mac and Oz and Lila and Nadia and Judge Gomph. We didn't say anything to Caro because—well, she's your big sister. She might not have kept the secret. A miscalculation, I now realize. The secrecy—it wasn't to be sneaky. I didn't want to tell you it would be a matter of weeks if it was going to take longer."

The kit shook his head. "Don't say stuff like that because you got caught sucking at sneaking."

"Dev, you delightful menace, how could I think of starting a new life unless you were in it?"

The kit was rubbing his eyes now and shaking his head harder. Magnus's own head ached in sympathy. No, that was just the headache he woke up with.

"Stop it," Dev whispered into his hands. "Just. Stop."

"Is this why you don't call me *Net* anymore? You thought I was failing you? Getting rid of you? No, sweetheart. Never. I'm entering a new phase in my life and I want you there with me, the wiliest, sweetest, cleverest kit I ever caught, one I've wanted to call my son for...oh, the longest time. I'm so sorry I didn't tell you this before. And I'll understand if you'd rather not join our family. *Stop*, Dev, stop shaking your head and look at me."

Slowly, the kit dragged his gaze from the floor to Annette.

"You've seen too much, and you've been let down by people who should have protected you like you were worth your weight in platinum. I wanted you to have a permanent home, to never again worry about how you'd feed yourself, to never again feel lucky to sleep in a band shell in warm weather—I *always* wanted that for you. From day one.

"But over time, I came to realize that seeing you well-fed and in competent foster care wasn't enough. Because I wanted *everything* for you, the world and all that's in it. I wanted you to have limitless possibilities before you and the security of permanent love and care. A place you could always call home, whether you were twelve or fifteen or fifty. And I wanted those things because I adore you and cannot fathom my life without you.

"I'm so sorry," she finished. "I mismanaged this completely."

Silence from Dev. Annette let go of the boy's elbow and slumped back. "You're overwhelmed. My fault—again. It's fine if you need time to think it over. And if I've hurt you— well, there's no *if* about it, obviously I've hurt you with my bungling. I never wanted that to happen, but that doesn't change what I did. If you can't risk your feelings again, that's on me, not you, and you mustn't feel guilty if you don't want to be adop—"

Dev let out a hoarse bark of a sob and sort of collapsed over Annette, his forehead resting on her shoulder, his small, narrow shoulders shaking as he wept and clung to her shirt with small fists. "Shut up," he said into her shoulder. "Shut up, shut up, *tais-toi, sta' zitto.*"

"I'm sorry. I'm so sorry."

"Nnnfff ssssee nnnsssssn." He raised his head, sniffed, reiterated. "'Course I want to be your son. Wanted it since you scooped me out of that alley. But I never thought—it never occurred to me that you—"

"So we're both silly beyond belief," Annette replied, hugging her wayward kit. "That's all right, then."

Dev pulled back, wiped his face. "I'm sorry. I should've trusted you. You've never screwed me over, and you've never lied. I should've trusted you not to throw me away like a used Kleenex."

"You should have trusted yourself and known yourself as un-throw-away-able," Annette corrected gently then grimaced. "I could not have worded that more awkwardly."

"Don't be so hard on yourself. You definitely could've." Dev giggled, took the napkin Annette held out for him, wiped his nose. Took another napkin, leaned close, dabbed the tears off Annette's cheeks.

"I told you the day we met, Dev: no one with any sense could ever give you up, regardless of cost, no matter how dire the straits. That was true then, and it's been true every day since then."

"And—and my mom said it was okay? She agreed to give me up? Again, I mean?"

Annette's lips went thin. "Yes. She's given you up again. The fool who whelped you signed everything I put in front of her." She sighed. "Though I will say in her defense that she speculated you would be happier with me than you had been with her."

"Well, duh," Dev said, and Annette laughed.

"I suppose I should speak more kindly of her," she admitted. "If not for her incomprehensible actions, you wouldn't be my kit."

"So you'd be my mom and David would be my dad?"

"The former, yes. The latter…" Annette raised her hands and shrugged. "We thought the three of us could discuss it. David wants that—oh, very much! But we didn't want to spring too much on you at once. Regardless, after the wedding, we want you to come live with us in my house in Prescott. I'm sure you remember my roommate, Pat—"

"The baking fiend obsessed with fresh-squeezed juice, yep."

"In Pat's defense, they were obsessed with that long before it was trendy. Anyway, they said if you needed more space, you could have the grain silo for your den."

Grain silo?

"So we'd—the three of us—we'd all be living with Pat, too?"

"Yes, and you've been there. You know there's plenty of room."

"But what if you have a baby? A ton of babies?"

Annette blinked at *a ton*. "Ye gods."

"That's what women of a certain age do when they get married, they toss the BC and get to work."

"First, kindly remove *women of a certain age* from your vocabulary forever. Second—"

"Because you'll want your own cubs. David will, too. Lots, I bet. Werebears are rare bears."

"*Second*, if I have one cub or five or none, you're still my son. Of course you'd still be my son."

Dev leaned down and hugged her again. "Okay," he said into her neck.

"Rude," Caro said right beside Magnus, who jumped and wiped away the lone tear that had escaped.

"Ah, sorry, lass. But you're right. Rude to eavesdrop."

Caro looked into the kitchen. "Told you it would all work out."

"No, you didn't," Dev protested, straightening. "You said I was being a big paranoid jackass and that I should shut up already."

"Nuance" was the reply.

Magnus cleared his throat. "Congratulations, lad. Annette's going to be a wonderful mum."

The kit grinned and hooked an arm around Annette's neck. "*Oui, si, ja, sì, hai, sim!*"

Chapter 48

HE LAUGHED, BECAUSE IT WAS A JOY TO SEE THEIR FACES in this private moment, one he'd felt privileged to witness, and then Caro poked him with something and that was the end of the amusement. When he'd dropped his bag, most of what was in it spilled out. Caro had bent to retrieve the mess and now held Jerry's notebook. With a sinking feeling, Magnus realized that in her urgency to get him the hell out of her home, Verity had shoved everything within reach into his overnight bag. Good God, he even had her remote. He hadn't noticed until now, so intent on brushing his teeth and getting the hell out of Mama Mac's house.

"Lass, ye have to give me that right now. It's private. I've got to return—" The thought of driving back to Verity, who at best found him an interesting nuisance, at worst a creepy stalker, with Jerry's most treasured, private possession in his hands would make the fiercest bear quail. And he wasn't the fiercest bear. He wouldn't face her. No, it went further—he *couldn't* face her. And it was a sucker's bet she didn't want to face him, either.

Hell with it. He'd mail it back. Well, overnight it. And he'd insure it so FedEx would be especially careful. She'd never have to look upon his face again, and that was almost a relief after last night.

Having slept on it, he re-realized he'd done the right thing last night, though quelling the urge to rip her clothes off and kiss every inch of her had been beyond difficult. But he should have come up with a way to reject her without her feeling, er, rejected. He'd bungled it, that was one thing. There was no fixing it, that was another, more devastating thing.

So he'd heavily insure the thing and overnight it to her. Coming up with an actual plan was an enormous relief, not least because he accepted that nothing could induce him to change his mind. They had no future, and he'd been a fool to fantasize otherwise. Her disgust and dismay had been clear.

Case closed.

"Caro, lass, you need to give that back to me right n—"

She had it open to the blurry sketch of the black wolf. Looked up at him with stricken eyes. Tried to speak, but nothing came out but a faint croak. Tapped the sketch, hard, and shook her head over and over and over, her body language plain: *It's not me!*

He softened his tone as he put out his hand. "No, o'course not, lass. I'm sorry if you thought I was cross. That's not why I need it ba—"

Then he took a closer look and, for a moment, understood what it was like to be an elective mute with no overt control over their vocal cords. He needed to speak very, very badly. Couldn't. Everything in his throat locked tight, like an engine that had run out of oil at the worst possible time. And that wanting, that *needing* to speak, made it worse. Everything was ever so much worse.

Finally, he was able to gasp, "No, it's not you, Caro. It's not a black wolf at all. That's a coyote."

Chapter 49

THIS WAS FINE. THIS WAS GOOD! MAGNUS BERNE WAS gone, ne'er to return, and her headache was almost gone, hopefully ne'er to return, and she was thinking about making a runny omelet heavy on the onions and mozzarella cheese and ooh, maybe some bacon, with some chopped tomato on the side, and a healthy sprinkling of fresh basil, because fresh greens were so important, and then she'd go do…stuff.

Somewhere there was stuff to be done, and said stuff only needed the presence of one Verity Lane and then stuff would be done. With a vengeance!

She'd never have to hear a peep from Magnus fucking Berne, he of the killer voice and probable substandard wang.

(I dunno about substandard, you've heard the saying about men with big hands and feet, and Magnus fucking Berne could palm a beach ball with those softball glove–sized hands)

Nevertheless! Today was the first day of the rest of her week, or however the saying went, and she was more than ready to—

"Verity! Verity Lane!"

She groaned. *Please let this be a hallucination brought on by drinking half my weight in whiskey. An audio hallucination. Or a brain tumor. Or any kind of tumor.*

"Verity Laaaaaaaane!"

A temporary break in reality would also be fine.

"I know you're in there, Verity! You have to let me in!"

"Or you'll huff and you'll puff?"

"Veriteeeeeeeeeeeeeeeeeee!"

Jesus wept. "Fuck off, Berne! Today's the first day of the rest of my week! Or however it goes!"

His reply was eloquent. So eloquent, the door was shaking in its frame: *wham-wham-WHAM-WHAMWHAMWHAMWHAM*

"Get bent!" she all but snarled at the door.

WHAMWHAMWHAM—

"Don't make me come out there! Actually, nothing will make me come out there. You're on a fool's errand, Berne! Unless you've brought my remote, you sneaky fuck! In which case, drop it on the mat and get the hell gone!"

—WHAMWHAMWHAMWHAMWH

And then, as if she'd willed it, or he'd passed out from exhaustion, or been silently arrested and hauled away (hard to picture the cop big enough and strong enough to do that) the noise stopped.

A trick? Or did he finally obey her shrieked commands? She'd bet everything in her checking account (-$17.98, thank God this was a payday week) that it was the former. When did Magnus Berne ever do her bidding? Never when she actually *wanted* him to, that was for sure.

Wait. Not all the noise had stopped. She crept closer to the door, quietly so he wouldn't know he'd aroused her curiosity (and a few other things), and heard furtive rustling. If she didn't know better, she'd think he…

Thudthudthudthudthud
Scratchscritchscratchscritch
Thudthudthudthudthud

had taken his other form and was banging his skull against the door when he wasn't clawing at the (metal) door and *Jesus Christ.*

She unlocked it, wrenched it open. Stared up at Magnus fucking Berne, who towered over her on his hind legs. She hoped he didn't make a habit of standing in the open as a bear; he'd give any Stable a heart attack. And more than one Shifter.

"Moron! Get in here before someone sees you. And what the hell is this? You'd better have my remote in there."

He'd dropped to all fours and lumbered into her apartment with the strap of his overnight bag in his jaws, which he dropped at her feet. (The bag, not his jaws.) He nudged it toward her, making deep rumbly sounds of distress.

Her irritation was still in the driver's seat, but concern was starting to be a contender. Something was wrong. Magnus Berne didn't hesitate to show up uninvited (except when he did), but she didn't think he was causing all this fuss just to trick her. He was fundamentally a very good bear.

(wait, what? you've only known him a few days)

(long enough to recognize the fundamentals)

(also maybe focus on current events right now?)

"What's the matter? Because you freaking out is freaking me out. Will you change back and talk to me? Scratch that, change back, leave the remote, get out, and don't even *think* about talking to me. But before you don't even think about talking to me, talk to me. Tell me what's going on very *very* briefly, and oh shit, what's this, now?"

Jerry's notebook.

That was…a weird thing to freak out about. A sweet, weird thing.

She bent and picked up the battered (even more than when Jerry last had it) notebook. *Damn, this thing really gets around.* "Okay, this is…well. I'm giving you the benefit of the doubt again, before throwing you out again, and assuming that you took it accidentally when I threw you out. Which I'll be doing again, in case there's any confusion on that note. And speaking of notes, you could have ding-dong ditched me, left the bag, and a note. And also my remote. None of this weirdness was necessary."

Magnus shuddered back to his other self, and she couldn't help but notice that his dick was anything but substandard. Dammit.

"It's not a black wolf," he panted, eyes wild. "It's a dark-brown coyote."

"It's not a what, it's a what-what?" Because what she thought he said and what he actually said could not be the same thing.

"The face is all wrong." His finger stabbed at Jerry's sketch. "See how the snout is so narrow? And see how big the ears are in comparison to the head? And how small the body? It's nae small because it's a young werewolf like Caro. It's small because it's nae a wolf at all, it's a coyote."

She blinked, processing. "And a Scottish guy knows wolves from coyotes because…?"

He had the utter nerve to look at her like *she* was the naked weirdo in the living area. "They introduced them a few years back. First just a few litters, and they thrived. They're trying wolves next. M'neighbor's a big fan."

Okay. Okay, so…what Magnus said and what she heard *were* the same thing. That was distinctly terrible, and not just because the thought of coyotes running wild in Scotland's moors was kind of alarming. Magnus's observation raised a nest of nasty questions, and she doubted she'd like the answers to any of them.

Nevertheless.

"We know a coyote," she mused.

"One who has never let any of you see his home," Magnus reminded her.

"Is it possible Les has a brother or a dad who really hates squibs?"

"Well," Magnus Berne said, because he was kind of a genius, "let's go ask him."

Chapter 50

"This is daft."

"Says the guy who stripped in the hallway and tried to tear through a metal door."

"I didn't say *I* wasn't daft."

She was driving, and they'd argued every mile on the way to the city of Hampton, though *city* was a gross exaggeration as fewer than seven hundred people lived there. The Mearn house was the last one in town before you hit country roads. It was a sprawling, tan ranch with an enormous fence and, she couldn't help noticing, plenty of room to host Damp Squib meets, even if they doubled their number.

But they weren't doubling their number. Quite the opposite. And perhaps Les—or a family member—could tell them why. If he lived with someone with deep-seated prejudice against Squibs, the *last* thing he'd want would be to expose the Damp Squibs to such an environment.

She understood being mortified by family members—who wasn't, at one time or another? But she wished he'd had enough faith in them to be frank about the problems at home. Whenever she asked him why he'd started the group, he always had vague, empowering answers. And sensing the tension, she'd never pressed.

She should have pressed.

"We've been over this, Magnus. We can't go to the cops, they're all Stables. We can't reach David. So we should wait, but we're not waiting. And I get it, okay? We've all seen the movies where clueless civilians team up and snoop around—"

"Go rogue," Berne interrupted. "Nadia explained it to me."

"Swell. Did she also explain that movies are fiction? Except for documentaries? And musicals?"

"She didn't have to explain that," he replied, exasperated. "And which musical is nonfiction?"

"All of 'em! Well, *Chicago*, mostly. And *The Book of Mormon*. And *Hamilton*. And *The Phantom of the Opera*. And *The Little Shop of Horrors*. And *King Lear*."

"*King Lear* isn't a musical."

"Yes, it is, Magnus!" She paused, heard herself, added, "This is a ridiculous thing to be arguing about. We should be arguing about Nadia's ridiculous team-up rules."

Magnus cleared his throat. "The whole reason I hired David was because I didn't want you to feelcompelledto-investigateonyourownandmaybegethurt."

She needed a second to parse what he'd just blarped out, took her gaze from the road to look at him for a few seconds, then looked back at the road. "Okay. Smart. And generous. I know I thanked you already, but…thanks. I know it's not just a squib thing with you. It's a bad idea for anyone, Shifter, squib, Stable, or other, to go blundering around trying to catch a multiple murderer."

Magnus cleared his throat. "Nadia also said David would be the one throwing himself into danger and th'lad would fight the good fight and triumph."

"I feel safer already."

"And fall in love," Magnus added. "That's also supposed to happen." Verity snorted and Magnus actually flinched. "I know that's not what this is."

"I didn't—" She glanced at him again. Dammit, she wished she weren't driving. At least traffic was minimal. "I wasn't making fun of you, Magnus. Not that time. It's just…" Her grip tightened on the steering wheel. "This is real life. We've got no business being here."

"And yet."

"And yet."

Her GPS chirped at her, announcing their arrival at Les Mearn's house, and she parked across the street. And the reason they had arrived at *casa de Mearn* was because Jerry had written down all their addresses in his notebook, along with his favorite colors, his least-favorite professional wrestler, and a recipe for something called Cullen skink. Or maybe it was a spell?

"Before we go see Les, I wanted to tell you—"

"That we're daft?"

"—sure, but also, last night. When we—uh—" Her knuckles were white on the wheel. Christ, why was this so hard? Couldn't one single thing about Magnus fucking Berne be easy? This was why people died alone! Who needed the hassle?

Oh, owning up to your fuckups is a hassle now?

Yes. It always has been.

That's Magnus Berne's fault now?

Yes. Now shut up.

She took a breath and told the windshield, "It's really good you didn't take me up on my revolting drunken offer."

"It wasn't revolting!" His eyes were so wide in his distress, they showed the whites all around. He looked like a sexy horse about to bolt.

Sexy horse?

I told you to SHUT UP.

"God, lass, don't think that, *please* don't think that. I just couldna—"

She reached out, took his hand, which had locked into a desperate fist. She slowly and carefully pried his fingers out of the fist and smoothed his palm. He watched her like a man who had no idea what was happening but couldn't wait to see what came next. "You don't have to explain. You were a hundred percent right. I shouldn't have made you doubt the wisdom of *not* raping me. I have no excuse."

"That's o—"

"Don't say it's okay. It's the polar opposite of okay. I'm really sorry."

"I could have handled it better," he replied.

"No, you really couldn't have. Anyway, before we go talk to Les, I wanted to tell you in case we get murdered."

"Oh, Christ."

"Right? I've been saying and thinking that a lot lately. But listen. In case we get stomped and bleed out in Hampton, Minnesota, of all places, I'm here because I need to talk to Les face-to-face. But you don't have to be here. Not for any of it. But you are, and I appreciate it. You're coming along not because you think I can't handle myself but so I don't have to do this alone. It's taken me a few days to get that." She paused then coughed it up. "I appreciate you. Every part of you, even the nosy buttinsky part of you."

He smiled and squeezed her hand. "Thank you, lass. And you said it yourself: there's no way to fix it. But we can at least try to get justice for your friend. Or what passes for it. If Les is involved, you have to find out. And I have to help you."

"So let's go find out. I'm calling it now: Les had to grow

up with an asshole older brother who hates squibs, which
is why Les started the Damp Squibs, and his brother's been
picking us off."

Chapter 51

NOPE.

Chapter 52

So there's this movie, *North by Northwest*, where you blink and suddenly everything's a terrifying mess (where before it had been a suspenseful mess): villains are rampant, there's a goddamned *plane* to dodge, and bullets to dodge, and there's a heroine about to plunge to her death… everything goes tits up at once.

All this to say Verity Lane had never seen *North by Northwest*, but given that a dark-brown coyote was intent on killing her, she could relate. Magnus was trapped in the house, and she was trapped in Les's enormous fenced backyard with a pissy coyote.

"Bite first, ask later? Really?"

The coyote jumped for her throat, because he was complacent and forgot that bipeds' throats are too far off the ground. Knowing that hadn't saved Jerry; Verity was determined it would save her. She put her forearm out, and the coyote latched on to it and bit down. The plan, no doubt, was to drag her down until he could get a chunk out of her throat.

Verity's plan was somewhat different, and the coyote's beady brown eyes widened when he couldn't immediately drop the bite. While he was stuck, Verity swung her arm around and bashed Les's big brother (father? uncle? random killer coyote?) right into the trunk of the tree behind her, hard.

"Let me guess," she said, shaking off the dazed coyote.

"You thought, 'Squib, easy meat.' Like all you assholes do. I sniffed out the crime scene, you fucker. I know exactly how Jerry died. You think I wouldn't take precautions?"

The coyote ignored her awesome speech and jumped for her again, giving her an opportunity to smash her gloved fist into his throat. The thing that had killed her friend let out an anguished yelp and fell back, stunned, which worked out nicely. Verity stepped close and kicked him—yep, definitely a him—in the jaw. The coyote flopped over, started to rise, and she followed up with a kick to the ribs that sent it rolling through the grass until it fetched up against a tree trunk.

"Roll of quarters. Steel-toed boots. Padded gloves. Chain mail. Just think, some people believe you can't buy anything good at the Renaissance festival." Her voice wasn't shaking. She was glad. She wasn't afraid, exactly—too much adrenaline for that—but it wasn't as one-sided a fight as she was pretending. She only had to slip once, be too slow once, and she'd go in the ground. (Possible upside: her parents would be vindicated.)

She heard the crash of wood behind her—excellent, Magnus had broken out of the basement, and then the back kitchen door, and then the fence. Also, who keeps a trapdoor in their kitchen? An honest-to-God trapdoor, like in every Scooby cartoon? Thank God she'd been standing a foot to the left.

The rest was a bit of a blur—somehow she and the coyote had ended up in the backyard, fighting for her life: he to take it, her to defend it.

She dealt the cowering thing another kick. The fights she'd been in since she was old enough to understand Shifters thought she was less-than had taught her there was no such thing as overkill. She'd be bruised as fuck, and he broke the skin in a couple of places, but she'd take bruises and blood over a trip to the morgue.

She'd heard Magnus charging behind her, but he skidded to a halt in the grass and stared at the whimpering, trembling thing that had killed Jerry.

"Change back, shitheap," she told it. "We have questions. No, not *you*, Magnus."

It did change back, and Magnus had to clamp his teeth onto the back of her shirt to keep her from killing the thing that was Les Mearn.

Chapter 53

"You utter, complete piece of shit."

"It isn't my fault!" Les yelped, cowering.

"Which part?"

"It was Jerry's fault!"

"So you *want* me to beat you to death. Wish granted—aw, Magnus, leggo."

He did, but only to shift back. Then he stood there, gloriously naked and covered in splinters (ack, one was sticking out of the top part of his *ear*) and not a little blood, and he was scowling. "You're not a *farmadoch*!"

"And also, you lied! What kind of pathetic puke pretends they're a squib so they can kill squibs? Which, now that I think about it, is kind of clever." Verity was reminded of the basic truism in their world: You couldn't prove you were a squib. You could only prove you weren't. It wasn't like they had any kind of membership tests. "But also pathetic!"

"You're proving me right," Les replied.

"I'm definitely not—wait." She reached over and pulled the splinter out of the tip of Magnus's ear, ignoring his yelp. "Sorry, that was really bugging me. And I'm not proving you right, you repellant shit stain."

"Who'd fake being a squib?" Les said, managing a sneer through his rapidly swelling jaw. "Nobody with any pride."

Magnus let out a snarl. "How's *your* pride now that Verity handed you your arse? She's not even out of breath!"

"I'm a little out of breath," she confessed. "That might be adrenaline, though."

"Oh. Good." From behind them. Which would have been alarming if she hadn't recognized David's voice. "You broke and entered without me."

"The door was unlocked. It was just entering. And watch out if you go in there," Verity cautioned. "There might be more trapdoors besides the one in the kitchen."

David had walked through the Magnus-sized hole in the fence and up to their little group. Good thing the Mearn house was practically in the country or they'd have to worry about nosy neighbors. "Trapdoor? For real? Like the kind Mr. Burns has in his office?"

"Exactly like the kind Mr. Burns has in his office."

"My dad was a huge *Hart to Hart* fan," Les volunteered.

"What? Oh, who cares. *This* guy," Verity added, aiming a kick and smirking at the pained yelp that followed, "faked being a squib and killed Jerry. Don't even bother denying it! I can see the bruises all over your shins." She aimed a kick as Annette's words came back to her: *Your friend fought back, because he was clever and brave, and whatever killed him didn't walk away unscathed.*

"Wow," David said, eyeing the greenish-yellow bruises all over Les. "Jerry put up a good fight."

"That's why you ditched his memorial. You had a limp, didn't you, you clandestine motherfucker? He must have clipped you really hard."

"Barely," Les sniffed.

"Hard enough that a couple of days later, you've still got some bruising," David commented. "I'll bet your shins were black from knee to ankle."

"You said it yourself, lass," Magnus added. "There were clues, but only in retrospect."

And isn't that the way it always was? Now that she was seeing the truth about Les, she couldn't believe she hadn't put it together sooner. He'd even explained what he thought of the Damp Squibs: *a tight little pack of malcontents who can't shift.*

If she'd pulled her head out of her ass and paid attention, Jerry might still be alive.

"I ditched his memorial," Les said, because he definitely had a death wish, "because who fucking cares about a dead squib?"

Verity turned her back on him, about as big a diss as one Shifter could give another. *I'm not worried about you at all. I don't even need to look at you. That's how harmless you are.* "So anyway, David, it was all part of some silly, sinister plan and the details will probably be infuriating. Infuriating detail number one, he's blaming Jerry for his own murder."

"It's true, though." Les was carefully palpating his pulped jaw, and Verity was reluctantly impressed he was even able to talk. *Better get that set by the end of the day,* she thought with spiteful glee. *Or it'll mend all crooked.* One of the rare disadvantages of Shifter metabolism. "It's because he—"

"It's because he saw you," Verity interrupted. Damned if Les was gonna get to do the reveal. "You were sloppy, stalking your next kill or soliciting a sex worker or whatever the fuck you do in your spare time, and he saw you. But he wasn't close enough to realize you were a coyote."

"He was, he—"

"He never seriously thought it was you!" The urge to kick him in the face two or seventeen times was getting harder to resist. "It never even occurred to him, do you understand? You killed a sixteen-year-old kid who didn't do anything wrong."

"He was born a squib, wasn't he? Plus he had my address! He left his notebook behind at the Radisson Blu last week, and I flipped through it—"

"Rude."

"—before he came back for it."

Urge to kick rising…rising… "He had all our addresses, you paranoid fuck! He also had a recipe for Chex Mix! That doesn't mean you need to worry about buying up all the Chex!" To Magnus: "Right? That parallel makes sense?"

"Not really," David said as Magnus nodded vigorously.

"And Andy Bray?" David asked. He was eyeing Les with what appeared to be compassion—good-cop routine, maybe? The injured coyote wasn't going anywhere, but he didn't have to confess to shit.

"Was on to us, obviously. He was a cop!"

"Naw. He lied about his job because he was worried you wouldn't include him if you knew. It's small-time, petty shit like trespassing, but still—you're breaking the law. Would you have been so cavalier about it if you'd known he was a cop? He loved what you guys were doing and wanted in."

"Not to give off Psychology 101 vibes," Verity said, "but a squib becoming a cop makes perfect sense." What better way to prove they weren't to be fucked with?

David was nodding. "Yep. I talked to his family first thing this morning. That's why you couldn't reach me. His folks knew what he was doing, but they never approved of him lying to join you. They didn't approve of any of it. They had a hard enough time dealing with his decision to go to the police academy."

"No wonder Mrs. Bray hauled off and hit you," Verity observed. "Good." Not for the first time, she wondered if evil was defeated because good always triumphed or because evil was often petty and careless.

"Then I got your message," David finished. "And here you are."

"That's *two* people you murdered for no good reason, you worthless shithead. What was it even for?"

"I *told* you. It's about War Wolves."

If Les was expecting gasps when he revealed his motive, Verity was thrilled to see he was disappointed in their lack of reaction.

"What are you even talking about, you silly shithead?"

"Lass, I never told ye before, but I love your array of insults."

"Thanks. What can I say? If you're gonna do something, it's worth doing right."

"Don't you remember? We talked about War Wolves, and I said you can't just join." At their blank stares, he cried, "You were both there when I brought it up! How can you not remember?"

"Because you're neither memorable nor special?" Magnus asked with faux sweetness as Verity smirked.

Les huffed. "What I said when you were both *right there* is that to be a War Wolf, you have to earn your spot, just like squibs earn their spots. Except all a squib has to do is be born."

David cocked his head. "So...*not* the way squibs earn their spots."

"And that's not the zinger you think it is," Verity added, "since War Wolves and squibs couldn't be more different."

"But it's irony!" he yelled then winced and wiped more blood off his jaw. "I made you losers feel like you were special, when all the time I was proving how *un*special you are and securing my spot as a War Wolf. Jerry even told me to my face that I couldn't be a War Wolf. I taught him different."

"You know being kicked to death is a thing, right, Les? A thing I can make happen? Look at you trying so hard to pat yourself on the back. You killed a teenager who thought you were a friend. And even that took a bit out of you—a sixteen-year-old deer fucked you up enough that you didn't dare go to his memorial."

"And that's another thing! Where'd Jerry get off hiding his age? That brought IPA into the mix. And *that* guy." Jabbing a bloody finger in David's general direction.

"Ha! You must have shit yourself when David walked into the meeting." Verity remembered how intent Les had been about finding out if she'd known Magnus had hired David. Trying to work out if she was on to him, or if David was. "You killed two people because you panicked. That's it, Les, that's all it is: you jumped to conclusions because you're impulsive, freaked out, killed them for no reason, and brought Stable cops *and* IPA into your mess. What a fucking waste of...all of it, really. Not very War Wolf-y."

"He had no business being a Damp Squib if he was just a kid."

"Wow, you're definitely worrying about the wrong thing here. But sure. Whatever you have to tell yourself to feel like a decent person instead of a walking, talking shitbag."

"No business," Les emphasized.

If Verity rolled her eyes any harder, she'd see her own

brain. "I'm sure this was all part of Jerry's sinister plan to inconvenience you."

"Hey, I know what it's like to live with being different. My fur comes in almost black. Who ever heard of a black coyote? My fur doesn't even match my hair color! My folks hated how we all looked in pictures. She said people were gonna think she cheated on my dad. The contrast was super jarring."

"Truly you have suffered mightily."

"But I overcame all that, *and* I figured out a way to get you freaks to kill each other off."

Magnus started to laugh, which was as startling a thing as anything in the past five minutes. It wasn't a particularly nice laugh, either.

"No. You didn't. You thought up the Damp Squibs so you could pick them off one by one. But they kept surviving! No matter what dangerous task you set for them, they kept proving themselves. You finally had tae cheat to get it done, but all that did was tip off the others that there was something verra wrong. Then, as Verity said, you panicked, killed people who weren't a threat to you, and brought unwanted attention to yourself. You poor shite. You screwed this in every possible way."

"Oh, my God," Verity said, as the reason Andy had drowned was made clear. It wasn't enough to hope the fall would kill him. Les had to make sure, and in doing so pulled the spotlight in his direction. "He's right! And just when I thought this couldn't get more pathetic for you."

"It was working!"

"Yeah, and he would've gotten away with it if not for you meddling squibs," David added with a smirk.

Verity rounded on Les. "How? How was it working, you ridiculous jerk-off? How would the War Wolves even know what you were doing? What, is there an online form? An application process? An interview?"

"Well…I…it's obvious. Or it would be. I didn't finish!" he shouted. "They would have noticed!"

"Jesus wept." Verity could not remember being more disgusted in her life, counting the time Kraft Macaroni & Cheese changed their recipe. "You killed my friend for a *job interview*. Magnus! Hold me back!"

"Why?"

"Yeah, good question," David added. "Because we don't have a lot of options here, and stomping this guy to death would solve a few problems."

"Great! *Don't* hold me back, Magnus."

"Mmm-myou guys canndo shit," Les mumbled, because the swelling was getting out of control.

"Technically true," David replied. "We can't do shit. I don't have any lawful authority. I'm not a cop. I can't arrest you. But you should come with me anyway. I'll hand you over to Judge Gomph, and we'll go from there." To Verity: "He's the unofficial justice we put in place after busting the syndicate ring last year. We couldn't turn any of them over to Stables, for obvious reasons."

"An if I mell oo oo muck merself?"

"If you tell me to go fuck myself, I haul your bony ass to Grove Street, explain to the SPD that you're a cop killer, and let them deal with you. The first time you shift, they'll lose their shit and empty their .40 calibers into you."

"…muck you. Muck *all* of you."

Chapter 54

"OH MY, LOOK AT THIS."

Verity splashed ashore where Magnus Berne was waiting for her with a robe and a smile. And a bird of prey, she realized, getting closer for a better look/scent.

The woman, one of those effortlessly glamorous Brits who seemed to do everything with posh precision, smiled and extended a hand. She was wearing a crisp red suit with a skirt that stopped just above the knee, a spotless white silk blouse, nylons so sheer they were more wisp than pantyhose, and shiny red flats with slashes of black ribbons across the toes. She should have looked silly, dressed to the nines on a tiny island in the middle of a Minnesota lake, but Verity was the one who felt underdressed.

"Oh my," she said again, shaking Verity's dripping wet hand. "I've heard of *you*, Verity Lane. And naked again! Darling, you've got to leave something to the imagination."

"He's seen me like this before," Verity replied. "He *found* me like this before. So what exactly is the mystery? What hidden reveal am I clinging to?"

"Excellent point, you two should embrace the lack of mystery, acknowledge there are no more surprises, and wed at once." Nadia smoothed the 'do that the lake breeze had dared to disarray. "Because 'where is the mystery?' is the siren song of matrimony. And as for your oh-so-charming habit of swimming several miles—"

Verity made a concerted effort not to sulk. "It's not *that* many miles."

"—only to nudely flounder ashore and then pretend you want nothing to do with Magnus, despite every appearance to the contrary—"

"Wow."

"—all I can say to that is: boats exist. In case you had no idea."

"I'm from Florida." She'd been about to finish with *obviously I know boats exist*, but Nadia's expression of dismay was too good and she decided to let it go.

"Oh dear. Well." For the first time (in this elegant woman's entire life, possibly), she seemed at a loss. But then she perked up, and the smile shone again. "I'm sure the stories are exaggerated."

Verity laughed at her.

"Ah…but on the off chance they aren't, you should lock a man down before he finds out."

In fewer than ten seconds, Verity understood why Annette handed over the plotting of her wedding to Nadia. Anything else was exhausting. So much easier to wash your hands of all details and keep out of her way.

"Jesus, Nadia. You're…a lot."

The raptor beamed, showing brilliant white teeth. So scratch that stereotype. "Thank you!"

"I've heard of you, too," Verity continued. "You're some kind of fiend. For matchmaking," she amended. *Definitely not a fiend in general. A very specific kind of fiend. Yep.*

"Among other things, darling."

"Sorry. Only Magnus gets to call me *darling*."

"That's true," Magnus said with a straight face. "It's a rule."

"Pooh on rules. Darling, I practically own the word *darling*. And I must say, darlings, it's lovely to see you getting on so well after all this time."

"It's only been three weeks," Verity reminded her. Three weeks of figuring out exactly what Les had done, and how, and where. (The why, needless to say, had been settled pretty immediately.) Getting Judge Gomph involved. Seeking out the Harts and the Brays and going with David to tell them the truth about why their sons were in the ground. Knowing Les would essentially disappear and not caring. Wondering about all the other Les Mearns out in the world. "Not even a month."

Figuring out what to do next.

"Yes, well, I heard you had a rocky start. But it's lovely to see you've transcended your less-than-stellar beginnings."

"Again: only three weeks. You're making it sound like we've been together for years."

"And we aren't," Magnus put in. When they both looked at him, he flushed. "Together, I mean. I—it's not like that. Verity's just…"

What? Dammit, why did you trail off after just? So not helpful!

Wait, so he's arrogant when he anticipates you, but he's 'so not helpful' when he doesn't presume? Make up your mind, you silly bitch!

She had. Why else would she have swum to the island today of all days?

Despite Magnus's floundering, Nadia remained undaunted, which Verity suspected was a thing with her. "All the more reason for you to snatch him up before someone else realizes what a treasure he is."

"That makes nae sense at all, Nadia."

"And I'm not sure *treasure* is the word," Verity added.

"Ach, ouch."

"All I wish to say is, why wait? Things happen fast out here. In our odd little group, I mean. Oz and Lila, for example. Six months ago, they hadn't yet met. Now they're—"

"Prenegotiated cohabitation. What?" Verity asked at their stares. "It's such a weirdly specific phrase. It's stuck in my head, prob'ly forever." Also, enough chitchat. She turned to Berne, shrugged into his robe. "You guys seem busy."

"*I'm* busy. I've no idea what Magnus is doing."

Verity snickered. "Is this a bad time?"

"Never, darling. Nadia was just leaving."

"Hardly, *darling*," Nadia sniffed. "The wedding is tomorrow, if you recall."

Given that there were banners and decorations and outdoor tables and outdoor seating and a chuppah (built with birch logs and topped with local greens and flowers, beautifully framed with the lake in the background, and were David and Annette Jewish?), Verity doubted Magnus had forgotten.

"And speaking of weddings, I'm thinking of starting a side business, so if you two ever do regain your senses—"

"*Regain* implies we lost our senses."

"Yeah," Verity added. "What he said."

Nadia didn't miss a beat. "—and make the obvious decision, consider calling on me."

"The second we regain our senses," Verity promised. "The ones we never lost. That's when we'll consider calling on you."

"Think of the story for your grandchildren!" Nadia flicked a stray leaf from her immaculate suit. "You found her quite, quite naked, and then you teamed up and solved a murder."

"Two murders," they said in unison.

"Two murders!" she replied, delighted. The smile dropped off her face, and she turned to Verity. "I was so terribly, *terribly* sorry to hear about your brave friend. But you did catch his killer. And you dealt him more mercy than he deserved." Carefully colored eyelids lowered as Nadia veiled her lashes. "Certainly more mercy than I would have granted."

Jesus Christ. Annette devoured her enemies; what would Nadia have done?

"This is the part where I say something about the moral high ground."

"Oh, darling, I'm a red kite." The brilliant smile flashed again. "I *always* have the high ground."

"Okay," Verity replied in as neutral a tone as she could manage, because raptors were scary.

"And now here you are, Verity, the day before the big day. Nothing symbolic about *that* timing, not at all."

"It's just, we both happen to be free today," Verity began, knowing it was futile even before Nadia turned back to Magnus.

"See, Magnus? This is how it goes. Didn't I say?"

"Ye did," he admitted.

"Wise of you to say so. You must listen to me in *all things*, darling. Think how much easier your life will be. And, Verity."

Oh, hell, what now? "Uh, yeah?"

"How in the world did your parents come up with your name?"

"They lost a bet?"

"You do know what it means, don't you, darling?" the bundle of condescension inquired.

"Nope. In twenty-odd years, I never once had any

curiosity about my name and never asked anyone about it and never looked it up."

"Don't tell anyone you're twenty-eight," the other woman cautioned. "And goodness! Check the attitude, if you please."

I will if you will. "And I definitely never found out it means *a true principle or belief.*"

"Especially one of fundamental importance," Magnus added.

"So we all have access to dictionaries," Nadia said, looking more than a little put out. "Lovely." But she brightened almost immediately, like one of those punching bags for kids. No matter how hard you hit the thing, it always popped right back up. Unless you stabbed it. Or set it on fire. "But *why* did they choose it?"

"Their names are Ray and Kay. They wanted a kid who would stand out, so they gave me a name that would stand out."

"That did the trick, I imagine."

"Yep. Of course, they regretted it once they realized I was a squib. Then the *last* thing they wanted me to do was stand out. They figured I'd be safer if I kept my head down. Literally and figuratively."

Magnus had no comment, but he reached out and took her cold hand in his, which Nadia watched with bright-eyed interest. "Well, your parents are awful, darling," she said kindly. "Lovely people, I'm sure, but awful all the same. But don't feel bad. Many parents are. Which is why I myself shall remain unwed and chick-free."

"What a loss to the world, lass." This with an admirably straight face.

"Oh, I know," Nadia replied earnestly. "Believe me, I gave

it careful consideration before ultimately rejecting the very idea of—of any of it. People get decidedly less interesting the moment they reproduce, have you noticed? Perhaps it's the lack of sleep."

"It's definitely the lack of sleep," Verity replied.

"It's quite the phenomenon. I wonder why no one's made a study of it? Regardless, none of that for the likes of *moi*."

"But you're always fixing people up," Verity pointed out. "You always want people to get together. Not just get together—you want everyone around you to get married. It's your thing, right? Your weird, intrusive thing?"

"I'll ignore the cattiness as a lady should and instead point out that solitude is best for raptors. I think Philippa Gregory put it perfectly. 'If I had been the falcon my father called me, I would have flown high and nested in cold, lonely places and ridden the free wind. Instead, I have been like a bird in the mews, always tied and sometimes hooded. Never free and sometimes blind.'[20] Marriage isn't for the likes of me," Nadia finished. "It *is* for the likes of bears."

Verity shivered, and not just because she was wet and wrapped in a robe. Why were they even talking about this? She and Magnus weren't a couple, no matter how badly Nadia wanted to believe otherwise.

"I need to get Verity to where it's warm," Magnus said firmly. "We'll leave you to it, then, shall we, lass?"

Nadia shooed them away like a pageant winner: she waved from the wrist, not the elbow. "Yes, yes, off you trot. You're spending the night, aren't you, Verity?"

"Yeah, so you don't have to worry about me swimming up naked to the wedding party tomorrow."

---

20. Nadia's not remembering it quite right. Check out *The Boleyn Inheritance* by Philippa Gregory to see what the hell she's talking about.

"That is a great relief to me," Nadia replied, and produced a clipboard from who knew where, and crossed something out. Suddenly Verity was dying to see that checklist.

"Nice to meet you," she said, because that was probably true.

Before Nadia could answer, there was a muffled buzz. She pulled her phone out of her pocket, scowled at the caller ID, and answered. "You had better be calling me to tell me the cake will be here by noon sharp tomorrow, madam. Your assistant tried to tell me six o'clock, and I was shocked, *shocked* to hear such nonsense from a Carleton graduate."

"Time to go," Magnus muttered, steering her toward the house.

"And I want the cake to look like rings of birch, *birch*. It should look like three elegant tree trunks stacked vertically. The chuppah is birch, the woods on this island are birch, several things in the house appear to be made of birch, there is birch everywhere, and I *will* have a cake that reflects that!"

"Right now," he added and started tugging her up the short slope to the house.

"I shall have your eyeballs for my gimlet if you tell me two p.m.!"

"Good call," Verity replied, and they scurried for cover like mice.

Chapter 55

"THANKS FOR INVITING ME OVER."

"Thank you for coming."

"I can't believe you're letting them use the island for a wedding. This time tomorrow, your lonely little island will be lousy with Shifters. And I heard David has Stable friends who are coming, too. This place will be packed."

Magnus actually shuddered, which was hilarious. "I'm happy to help a f-friend."

"Hey, you almost got it out without stuttering. Progress."

"Takes practice," he said so glumly, she had to smile.

"You're doing great. You're great. You are...a great guy." *Jesus Christ, spit it out or shut the hell up.* "You—I mean, I know I gave you—give you—a lot of shit. A lot. All the time. Daily."

"It's one of your many charms," he teased.

"But I only do that because I'm pathologically immature. You're great. Argh, I'm bad at this. If I'm not mocking you, I kind of have no idea what to say. Is there a way I can tell you I like-like you while also belittling you?" She hid her face in her hands. "Oh, Christ, I just said like-like."

He gently grasped her hands, pulled them away from her face. "You're doing beautifully. Better than most, under the circumstances. I jumped into your life. Ye had no warning. O'course it was strange and off-putting."

"Actually, I jumped into yours. Well, flopped into yours. Passed out into yours? Naked, by the way. If we're talking strange and off-putting. So why'd you invite me to stay over?"

He blinked at the subject shift. Except it wasn't a subject shift. Not really. "You liked it here. You like the boat. You were coming to the wedding anyway."

"Magnus."

"I wanted to see you," he said baldly. "Badly."

"There we go. Good news is, back atcha."

"Sorry, what?"

They were in the kitchen where he had a pot of Cullen skink bubbling. Verity had made copies of Jerry's notebook for David and Judge Gomph, with an eye toward eventually getting the original back to the Harts. In the process, she saw the recipe for Cullen skink, which Magnus swore to her was delicious, and never mind that it sounded like the name of a space villain.

And it was! (Delicious, but also space villain-y.) Cullen skink was a heavy soup, almost a stew, of something called finnan haddie, onions, and potatoes, all swimming in milk thickened with potatoes and topped with a dollop of butter. It was like clam chowder and bisque had a baby, and they gave the baby a space villain name.

But this was no time to be thinking about her stomach. Also, she had just finished her second bowl.

"And on the subject of boats, Magnus—"

"Were we?"

"—you had to know I'd eventually find out."

Magnus's shoulders went visibly tense. "Find out?" he asked with admirable nonchalance.

"Knock it off. You're not allowed to operate personal watercraft at night in Florida. God, imagine the horrors if you were! But Minnesota doesn't have any such law. I looked it up, after. You could've gone back to your island instead of crashing with me."

"Yes," he said, spearing her with his direct gaze. "I could have."

"And for the record, I think boating at night is a bad plan for any state, not just Florida."

"And yes," he continued, ignoring her view on state water-craft regulations, "I knew you'd eventually find out. I didn't care."

"I figured." She looked down, played with the belt of his robe. "The, um, other thing I wanted to ask you was, when are you going back to Scotland?"

Magnus, who had been leaning forward almost like he was—ha, ha!—drawn to her like he couldn't help it, suddenly straightened and actually took a step back. "I'm not sure. It—it depends on. Ah. It depends on how things go with Sam's recovery and—and other things. I want to spend more time with my goddaughter, too. I had. Ah. I had also hoped we might—but you needn't worry, lass, I won't be showing up uninvi—"

"No, no, *no*. Argh, sorry." She rubbed her forehead and ordered herself to get a grip already. "I warned you I was bad at this. That's not why I wanted to—look, I just—we got off on the wrong foot, you know? The wrong, weird, naked foot. And things just kept getting stranger. And a *ton* of bad shit happened. And nothing's been settled, not really. Les is gone, but so are Jerry and Andy. War Wolves are still a thing, and incompetent douchenozzles are still going to try to join them. The Damp Squibs aren't still a thing, but nothing's really changed for us. Things don't—it took me a while to get it, but things don't magically resolve themselves just because you caught the bad guy. Television and movies have been lying to us, Magnus."

"For decades," he agreed.

"So what now?" She spread her hands and wiggled her bare toes on the kitchen tile. "I don't know, and I'm betting you don't, either. And that's okay. Because I think—hope— we've got time to figure all this out. So I asked about your plans because while I wouldn't blame you for wanting to go knock the dust of Minnesota off your paws and head back home to Edinburgh or Dublin or wherever—"

"I've got no interest in Dublin. And I don't want to go back home. I'm not sure it *is* home. It was just a place I slept. For years. And for no good reason, I now realize. I didn't have to be alone. There was no reason for it." His gaze came up, and he looked right at her. "I was a coward."

"Uh, that's really hard to picture. You *did* blitz through a basement, a kitchen wall, and a fence to help me."

"Physical bravery," he scoffed. "Anyone's capable."

"Not really."

"All that to explain I'm staying," he finished.

She managed a tentative smile, trying to ignore the leap of excitement his words brought. "So, then. If you're going to hang around, I want to."

"You want to hang around?"

Her heart could have cracked at his tentative tone. They'd crossed signals too many times; small wonder he didn't want to risk jumping to the wrong conclusion.

"No, I mean I want to. Spend. Time. With. You." She wasn't emphasizing to be sarcastic. Well, not entirely. More important, she didn't want there to be so much as a sliver of a shred of a doubt.

He stood there for a second then realized she was finished. "Forgive me, lass, but is that an American euphemism for, uh…"

"It's a euphemism for spending time together. Dating. Going out? Whatever you Scots call it."

"We call it *dating*," he said with a relieved grin.

"Can we? Despite our weird beginning? Or because of it?"

"Yes. And yes."

"Well, then. All right. Good. Same page."

"Yes."

"*Finally*." Not really. It only felt like a long time.

"Yes."

A short silence fell, and she saw he was holding himself rigid. Like someone just told him he had to give a speech in five minutes. Or like he wanted to reach for her and didn't quite dare.

"So that's settled."

He nodded. "Aye."

She cleared her throat. "Also, I'm in no rush to get dressed. And I'm halfway dry already. So if you were to, say, touch me, my damp chilly skin would only be a little clammy."

"Verity—"

"Okay, a lot clammy."

"Lass—"

"I haven't had a drop, I swear!" She put her hands up like she was being arrested. "Though when I heard Nadia shrieking at the cake person, I wanted a drink really, really bad. Oh, those poor wedding vendors."

"Same." He reached out, took her hands. Raised one to his lips. Kissed the palm. "Are you sure?"

"Are *you*? You're halfway in love with me already," she teased.

"Yes," he said, perfectly serious.

That brought a pleasant tingle. But she still felt obliged to warn him. "Once we bang, then bang! You'll be stuck. So to speak."

He burst out laughing, and she giggled along with him. "That's the silliest and most erotic warning I've ever gotten."

"Oh, you haven't heard anything yet. Let us seal our pledge to date with a bang to end all bangs."

"Must we call it a *bang*?"

"You prefer *bone*? Or *shag*? Probably *shag*, right? Or is that a British thing? What do Scotsmen call it?"

"They call it the luckiest day of their life."

"But that doesn't even make—ack!"

Next thing she knew, she was divested of his robe, and he was kissing her deeply, and then she had him and his hairy ass pressed against one of the ginormous glass windows in one of the living rooms,

(how many living room/sitting areas/hangout spots did one house on a tiny island need?)

and then they shifted, and she was the one pressed against glass. His mouth was warm, sinfully, deliciously warm, and speaking of delicious, his stubble was divine. Which was not a word she thought she would ever use to describe stubble. Ludicrous! But also true; the friction hardened her nipples and made her wriggle to get closer, which she was pretty sure was a physical impossibility, but fuck it.

She had enough presence of mind to recall there were party planner types crawling all over the grounds and her bare ass was pressed against the glass like dough on a cookie sheet but not enough presence of mind to care.

"Ah…Verity…"

"I know, I know, and *Jesus*, this glass is cold." She was laughing as he scooped her up and carried her through the living room(s) and up the stairs (she had a blurred impression of a long hallway but only three doors), down the hall to the closed door at the end, which he heroically and sexily kicked open—

"Shite! My toes."

"You gotta kick with the ball of your feet, Magnus. Did they not teach you any of the basics in Scotland? Aaahh, that tickles!"

—and into his bedroom, which was blessedly cool and shadowed, and into his bed, piled high with a goose feather duvet, cool and soft, and a man who was neither of those things and who couldn't stop touching her.

They kissed while yanking at Magnus's clothes, and at least two buttons went flying, and several seams tore, and who gave a ripe fuck? Magnus gently pushed her back—

"Don't y'dare move, Verity darling."

—and sat up to frantically tug at his jeans with such horny fury, he almost fell off the bed. Verity didn't dare laugh (well, laugh *more*) because she was perilously close to the edge herself, and maybe they should just give up and make love on the floor. The chilly, uncarpeted floor.

"Christ, *finally*," Magnus muttered, gloriously naked. She'd seen him stripped to the skin (and the fur) before, but it wasn't cool Shifter etiquette to scope genitals outside of a romantic/sexual situation. So this was her first proper look at the man. And once again, the "big hands + big feet = terrific cock" thing was the cock, the whole cock, and nothing but the—

Wait, what?

Jesus, she was almost drunk on the man, his warmth, his urgent tenderness. She ran her hands across his chest, stroked the dark line of hair leading to his cock—the line was basically a landing strip—and she laughed again, and reached for him, and kissed him for understanding she wasn't laughing *at* him.

Because the simple truth was, Verity hadn't felt so light and so free since she was six and had climbed the tallest oak on her parents' property. She remembered clutching the trunk (little more than a branch at that height) in her sap-sticky hands, looking out at the marsh, the branch bending like a bow beneath her bare feet. She was as high as a two-story building, her parents were small and wee and fretful on the ground, and it was exhilarating and it was heady and it was wonderful, and that's what it was like to fuck Magnus Berne.

Chapter 56

"IT'S *NOT* SUBSTANDARD!"

"Beg pardon, lass?"

Shit, I said the quiet part loud. "Just thinking about some of the things I got wrong this month."

"You got many more right," he reminded her, because he was a big sweetie who did not have a substandard wang. "And you were right to warn me of the perils of making love with you. I am definitely more in love with you right now than I was at lunchtime."

"This pleases me," she replied even as she waved away the flattery. "More skink, please. That's also going on a list of sentences I never thought would come out of my mouth."

Magnus obliged then sat beside her on the bench at the end of the kitchen table, hip to hip. The hickeys and bite marks she'd planted all over his neck and chest were already fading—bummer. *I'll just have to reapply. Daily. And nightly. For years.*

"You never did give me all the details on why you were so unsurprised to find what you thought was a dead body in your yard."

"I never thought you were a dead body," he pointed out. "I thought you were a dummy."

"You've got five seconds to rephrase."

"Store mannequin."

"Nice recovery." She scooped up a spoonful of soup and swallowed, relishing the many tastes and textures.

Creamy and salty and starchy, chock-full of umami good-ness. "Does this stuff freeze okay? Because I think we should make a gallon drum of it, parceling it out to our friends and allies over time, but never so much as a drop for our enemies."

"I'm a little alarmed that you've given this so much thought, darling."

"Careful or you'll make the enemies list, and then no skink for you. Anyway, about the dummies."

"Someone kept leaving mannequins on my island in the dark of night for me to find the next morning." This in the tone of a man commenting on the changing of the seasons: *nothing unusual going on here, just keep moving.*

She paused in mid-slurp. "Okay, creepy and weird. They would have needed a boat—you ever hear an engine?"

"No."

"Footprints? Or paw prints?"

"No. The dummies would just appear in the garden."

"Which you would notice the next day, but never really cared enough to pull an all-nighter to see who was doing it."

He shrugged.

"And you'd do what with the things, exactly?"

"When I had a pile—"

"Yikes."

"—I'd run them over to the mainland and drop them off at Mannequin Madness."

She waited, but he didn't elaborate. "You said that like it's a normal thing, but I'm gonna need some clarification."

"There's a company that recycles mannequins."[21]

"Because of course there is."

---

21. It's true!

"So when I had a pile of bodies—"

"Phrasing!"

"—I'd put 'em in the boat and run them to the mainland." Shrug. "Someone from Mannequin Madness would meet me and take them away."

"Why?"

"It's more environmentally friendly to—"

"No, why was someone leaving you store mannequins?"

"No idea, lass."

"And who?"

"Same answer."

"Well. If you knew why, you'd know who. Isn't that the way it goes?" Verity was now scraping the bowl, because Magnus's giant pasta bowls didn't hold enough skink and she would need a refill again. What she needed was a bucket. A nice one, though. Not the kind you'd find on a farm or in the janitor's closet. "When was the last dummy?"

He put a hand over his mouth, and she realized he was covering his grin. "You were the last dummy."

"Guarding your teeth against the inevitable elbow smash, smart," she said approvingly. "And if you haven't figured this out by now, you're the dummy. It's obvious."

"Nadia," he said.

"Nadia the matchmaker."

"And it's nae that I haven't been able to figure it out. It's that there were more important things tae think about."

"Whatever you need to tell yourself, pal. So, Nadia. Obviously Nadia. Birds are light, but strong. She's probably got...what? A five-foot wingspan? Six? And talons the size of breadsticks. It'd be no trouble for a raptor in her prime to fly over and drop the thing. No tracks, no boat engine."

"Just an enticing mystery for the bachelor hermit to think about. Crafty lass."

"*Sneaky* crafty lass."

"I meant you, darling."

"Still applies."

It was hours later, well past sunset. They'd spent the time in bed exploring each other then showered and broke off for Cullen skink. This time they were both naked, and Verity had to admit Magnus wore the all-over tan *very* well.

"This is gonna sound abrupt and out of nowhere—"

"Thank ye for the warning."

"So one of Jerry's favorite movies was *North by Northwest*, because he was a Hitchcock freak. I've never seen it because old movies are boring—ha, I see you wincing. They are, though! Anyway, he blathered on about it soooooo much, so I looked it up on Wiki. And that's what I thought about when things went deeply sideways at Les's place."

"A trapdoor, in the name of Christ!"

"Right? Pretty sure living with a trapdoor is a signal flag for criminal shenanigans. It raises all kinds of questions about his dad." Which in itself raised questions. When David explained to the elder Mearn what his son had done and why he wouldn't be home for years, if ever, the man hadn't been all that surprised. Disapproving, but resigned. In a way, that was the saddest thing about the violent, bloody mess. Mearn had raised a monster and was unfazed when his son did monstrous things. "Anyway, I was thinking how strange it was to have so many terrible things happening at once."

"Les is more than fortunate you didn't kill him."

"Thought about it." She looked down at her empty bowl. "It'll sound hokey, but Jerry wouldn't have wanted me to.

And I wouldn't have wanted me to. How do you hold the moral high ground after you kick someone to death?"

"A question for the ages. And I would think living with the knowledge that the only way he could make progress on his 'job interview' was to cheat, and that he had his arse handed to him by a squib, might be a fate worse than death."

"Plus he lived with a trapdoor. A goddamned trapdoor! Who knows how many people his dad dropped?"

"Aye. Exactly so."

"And if all that isn't punishment enough, I can always track him down and kill him."

"That's not where I was going with that, but as you like, lass. D'you know the other thing *North by Northwest* was famous for?"

"Hitchcock didn't cast yet another skinny blond?"

"Ah…no. He did."

"Of course he did."

"It's famous for how quickly the ending wrapped. The audience finds out what the MacGuffin is, the bad guys get caught and/or die, the hero rescues the heroine, the hero and the heroine get married, and they go on their honeymoon. All in the span of twenty seconds."

"Huh."

"Are you sleeping any better?"

"Where'd that come from?" She stood, took their empty bowls to the sink, and rinsed them, mindful of accidentally spraying hot water on her boobs.

"I thought perhaps that was the main reason you agreed to spend the night. So ye could get a break from the noise."

"That'd be an incorrect assumption, Magnus."

"And I've never been more delighted t'be wrong. But the construction is still going on?"

She nodded. "Yeah, he's stepping it up, even. They're working well after dark. I think the landlord's got a deadline to meet or something. So it's been noisy. Noisier. But to be fair, he warned me from day one. My rotten luck he found skillful contractors who take schedules seriously. What were the odds?"

"Plenty of room on this island for two."

Verity rolled her eyes to cover the way her heart leapt at the words. Which was almost literal! She could actually *feel* something in her chest swell at his warm invitation. Like champagne bubbles. Or the way you felt the afternoon of the last day of school, knowing you had the entire summer ahead of you. "Don't get ahead of yourself, Berne."

"Wouldn't dream of it, darling."

"We've only known each other for a few weeks."

"A few weeks and twenty seconds."

"Yeah, I get you're trying to tie in the *North by Northwest* thing, but that doesn't actually make sense."

"So making sense is a priority now?"

"Hell no," she said and sealed it with a kiss.

Epilogue

"HAVE YOU MET MY MOM? THIS IS MY MOM. HEY! HAVE *you* met my mom? This is Mom. Excuse me! Yeah, you. Come and meet—this is my mother."

That is so fucking adorable, I might cry. Real tears and everything! Like when I left that chocolate cream pie in my car too long and it melted all over my back seat.

Annette Garsea had been Annette Garsea Auberon for about eight minutes, and the bride was ridiculously beautiful. Obviously "all brides are beautiful," but Annette's striking coloring helped her take it to almost but not *quite* over-the-top gorgeous. Her gown was a creamy-white silk column from neck to ankles, the color an exact match to the white tips in her hair, and the cut and fit of the luxurious fabric made her look like one of those statues of Greek goddesses. Right down to her soft leather sandals in rose gold and embellished with crystals.

The groom—well, who cared? People didn't come to these things to check out what the groom was wearing. Though David looked great in a claret-colored, two-button jacket with matching pants, and a white open-throated shirt. The deep brownish-red of the suit set off Annette's hair and eyes; when they stood together, they looked like they were truly made for each other. He sported a purple iris boutonniere, basically a tiny version of the bride's bouquet, and wore the look of a man who couldn't believe his great good fortune.

Verity was dry-eyed—she never cried at weddings—but the tight warmth in her chest made it a close thing. It was an overused phrase, but they looked perfect together. And three was most definitely not a crowd.

"Hi! This is my mom. Have you met my mother? She's right here."

Dev was in a navy suit with a light-blue shirt that made his green eyes sparkle—or maybe the sparkle had nothing to do with the clothing. He'd been one of the first ones on the ferry to the island, had prowled around making sure everything met ~~Annette's~~ Nadia's exacting standards. He stood between Nadia and Caro while Annette and David recited their vows, following everything carefully, and was the first to congratulate the bride and groom.

"Have you met my mother?" he asked Annette's boss while holding Annette's free hand (her other hand clutched a bouquet of deep-purple irises and white tulips). "This is my mother."

Verity briefly considered reminding the kit that Annette knew pretty much everyone there and decided against it.

"Precisely and perfectly planned." Nadia sighed beside her. She took out a small square of lace that Verity felt would make a terrible Kleenex—scratchy!—and delicately dabbed her dry eye with it. "My God, I look incredible."

"Great job, Nadia." Which was nothing but the truth. Somehow Nadia had gotten the entire island decorated and wedding-ready, coordinated the ferries (Magnus had rented houseboats that could carry twenty people), oversaw the food, approved the wedding cake (which had been delivered precisely at noon, thank you very much), got everyone where they were supposed to be, and made it look...well, she *didn't* make it look easy, actually, given the screaming phone calls Verity had overheard. In fact, it had to have been a gigantic pain in the ass. But some people thrived under the relenting, soul-crushing pressure of wedding planning. "You look beautiful."

"Yes." Nadia, as maid of honor and HBIC[22], was wearing a short, sleeveless dress the same claret color as David's suit. The plunging bodice and tight skirt could have been too much (or not enough) for a wedding, but the matching ankle-length lace overlay and scalloped hem blurred and softened the look. The combination made Nadia look sleek and floaty at the same time. "But that was only to be expected. Nothing could have gone wrong, I would not allow it. I would have crushed whatever the problem was, instantly and without mercy."

"Annette's lucky to have you looking after her, I'm pretty sure."

Nadia turned to face her, gave her a long once-over, and finally came out with, "And you look, er..."

"What?" Verity looked down at herself. Red skort, tan blouse, black ballet flats by Toms. She'd ironed the blouse and everything. "I love skorts. Business in front, party in the back. Besides, Annette told me I should wear whatever made me feel comfortable."

"This is not Annette's wedding," Nadia said with a breath-taking lack of self-awareness.

"My mistake." *A lie.* "Won't happen again." *Also, I won't give up skorts for you or ANYBODY. I'll fight to the death if I have to.*

"I suppose it's not such a disaster." Nadia sniffed. "No

---

22. Head Bitch in Charge

one's here to look at you. Except our generous host, of course."

"Damn straight, lass," Magnus said from behind her. He slid an arm around Verity's waist. "You look stunning, Verity darling."

Nadia raised her eyebrows. "That's love, I suppose."

"Not hardly," Verity replied.

"Not yet," Magnus added.

"You remember what I told you yesterday," the raptor told them sternly. "Do not make me bury you in business cards."

"We hear and obey, Nadia," Magnus replied.

"Nadia, has anyone ever told you no?"

"No one still living," she replied sweetly.

"Oh, and you can stop with dropping dummies on Magnus's island. We're on to you! And by *we* I mean me."

Verity had thought the woman might blush or at least protest. Nope. "Well, of *course*, darling. You're here now. There's no point."

"That…doesn't make any sense."

"Now you must pardon me," she said briskly. "For some unfathomable reason, the caterers haven't put out the prosciutto-wrapped dates with goat cheese. Nor is there enough ice for the shrimp cocktail display. My God, we're living in anarchy! Why not just cut all the electricity and abandon the cities and retreat to the woods like hermits? Because that's where a lack of ice leads, people!"

"Poor bastards," Magnus murmured as Nadia darted off.

"Hey. They knew the risks when they entered the cut-throat world of event planning. Man, that woman has *no* shame. I can't decide if that's cool or irritating."

"Hello, have you met my mother?"

Verity turned and beheld a beaming Dev and a bemused Annette. "Once or twice," she replied. "You guys look great. Annette, you're so beautiful right now, it's actually pretty irritating."

The bride laughed. "Thank you, Verity. And thank you for coming."

"I still think you should have given my spot to someone you've known longer than a month, but who am I to pass up free food?" And it was quite the spread, if you excluded the (ugh) dates. Watermelon wedges wrapped in prosciutto, crackers with cheese and sugared cranberries (Verity wasn't aware you could get fresh cranberries in the summer; trust Nadia to find a way), cucumbers stuffed with tomatoes and vice versa, the aforementioned shrimp cocktail, fruit kebabs with two kinds of dipping sauce, bruschetta, caprese salad sticks, platters of carpaccio, grilled scallops on skewers...an embarrassment of riches.

"There you are!" Mama Mac swooped down on them, Caro in tow, and Verity nearly gasped when she saw the young werewolf, having only ever seen her in casual clothing (or fur). Caro's bridesmaid dress was a knee-length crimson dress with cap sleeves and a lace mesh neckline, which did nothing to distract from the long-suffering expression on the girl's face. Annette had instituted a no-screens rule during the ceremony. Not even the photog; Nadia had nearly had an aneurysm on the spot. It was obvious the young werewolf was starting to feel the strain.

Mama Mac was resplendent in a purple midi tulle dress with the most intricate embroidery Verity had ever seen. The contrast made her white curls almost seem to glow. "Oh, Magnus, dear, it's all so lovely. I'm sorry I didn't have time to talk to you before the ceremony. I can't thank you enough for stepping up. And the houseboat was so fancy!"

"They only came in *fancy*," he replied with a straight face.

Verity grinned. "Yeah, he tried to get his paws on a real wreck, but the rental company wasn't having it. Something about not wanting their liability insurance to blow up."

"And you." Mama hugged her then kissed Magnus on both cheeks: *smack-smack*! "Both of you, actually. I was so glad when I heard you're staying in Minnesota at least through the holidays. Wait until you try my Christmas punch."

"Drink a *lot* of water beforehand," Annette suggested. "Mama's punch is ninety-five percent rum and three percent window cleaner."

"Hush, you. Now listen. When Annette and David get back from California—"

"It's Venice, Italy, Mama," Annette said with fond exasperation. "I've told you this at least five times."

"Well, whatever." Mama Mac flapped a hand and waved Venice, Italy, away. "We're hosting a dinner for them when they get back, and you both should come."

"We'd be delighted," Verity said, and Magnus's face lit up. *Note to self: be much nicer to Magnus so he isn't astonished when I'm nice.*

"And then!" Mama Mac actually rubbed her hands together. "Countdown to grandchildren!"

"Good God," Annette muttered.

"It's okay if she has her own cubs," Dev confided to Verity. "I'll always be her kit."

"Yeah, of course," she replied, realizing this wasn't the time to poke fun. "And you won't just always be hers, you'll be her eldest. By definition, there can be only one. Which

I always thought was pretty cool. But then, I'm an only child."

"Thank goodness," Magnus teased. "Who could handle more than one Verity? There's only so much fundamental importance a man can take."

"Yeah, that's enough out of you, Berne."

"Ladies! Gentlemen!" Nadia's shrill voice cut through the guest chatter like a laser through a Kleenex. "Picture time! I need the bride and groom, the bride's son—"

Dev beamed and visibly swelled.

"—the mother of the bride, and our host and hostess."

Magnus took her hand. "We hear and obey."

Verity tried to hang back. "I'm not the hostess."

"Oh, details, details," Mama Mac said.

"No, really! I'm not. I just slept with the host. Oh." She shot a guilty look at Mama Mac and the cubs. "Sorry."

Caro smirked, scribbled, flashed her notepad. *Gross. And about time, too.*

"It's been barely a month," Verity protested.

"Yeah, that seems to be the way they do it around here," Dev said and shrugged. "I dunno. Seems to work out."

"It's *way* too early to determine that," Verity replied.

"So, then." Magnus kissed her knuckles and led her toward a photographer, who was visibly terrified of Nadia. "Don't you want to stick around to see if it works out?"

"That's actually not the worst idea in the world," she replied and kissed him.

Author's Note

Some of my readers might recognize Summit Avenue as the street where Betsy and Sinclair live. It's well worth a visit if you're in the Twin Cities area; it's the longest street of Victorian houses in America and boasts schools, synagogues, and churches. Though it's interesting that Frank Lloyd Wright hated it. He insisted it had "the worst collection of architecture in the world" because he was a mean, grumpy baby.

Unity Church in Saint Paul is a real church. It's a beautiful building with a warm interior (literal and figurative) and well worth checking out. For the purposes of this book, I gave them more convenient parking (in real life, parking is a block away).

All the hard ciders Magnus tries exist; Minnesota is lousy with cideries.

There really is an Earl of Stair, but I've got no idea what kind of a neighbor he is.

About the Author

MaryJanice Davidson is the *New York Times* and *USA Today* bestselling author of several novels and is published across multiple genres, including the UNDEAD series and the Tropes Trilogy. Her books have been published in over a dozen languages and have been on bestseller lists all over the world. She has published books, novellas, articles, short stories, recipes, reviews, and rants, and writes a biweekly column for *USA Today*. A former model and medical test subject (two jobs that aren't as far apart as you'd think), she has been sentenced to live in Saint Paul, Minnesota, with her husband, children, and dogs. You can track her down (wait, that came out wrong...) on facebook.com/maryjanicedavidson, Twitter @MaryJaniceD, Instagram @maryjanicedavidson, and maryjanicedavidson.org.

BEARS BEHAVING BADLY

An extraordinary new series from bestselling author
MaryJanice Davidson featuring a foster care system
for orphaned shifter kids (and kits, and cubs)

Annette Garsea is the fiercest bear shifter the interspecies foster care system has ever seen. She fights hard for the safety and happiness of the at-risk shifter teens and babies in her charge—and you do not want to get on the wrong side of a mama werebear.

Handsome, growly bear shifter PI David Auberon has secretly been in love with Annette since forever but he's too shy to make a move. Annette has noticed the appealingly scruffy PI, but the man's barely ever said more than five words to her… Until they encounter an unexpected threat and put everything aside to fight for their vulnerable charges. Dodging unidentified enemies puts them in a tight spot. Together. Tonight…

**"Davidson is in peak form in this hilarious,
sexy, and heartfelt paranormal romance."**

—*Booklist* Starred Review

For more info about Sourcebooks's books and authors, visit:

sourcebooks.com

THE BEST OF
BOTH WOLVES

Coworkers become something more in this
sexy, action packed shifter romance from
USA Today bestseller Terry Spear.

Red wolf shifter Sierra Redding is on her way to her new job as an art
teacher for a red wolf pack in Portland when she thwarts a break-in. She's
just in time to see the would-be thief and sketch him for red wolf detective
Adam Holmes, earning her a job with the police department as a sketch
artist, and bringing her closer to the handsome investigator…

"Essential reading for werewolf romance fans."

—*Booklist* for *Alpha Wolf Need Not Apply*

For more info about Sourcebooks's books and authors, visit:

sourcebooks.com

THE LAST WOLF

First in an extraordinary new series from
Maria Vale: The Legend of All Wolves

For three days out of thirty, when the moon is full and her law is iron, the Great North Pack must be wild…

Silver Nilsdottir is at the bottom of her Pack's social order, with little chance for a decent mate and a better life. Until the day a stranger stumbles into their territory, wounded and beaten, and Silver decides to risk everything on Tiberius Leveraux. But Tiberius isn't all that he seems, and in the fragile balance of Pack and Wild, he may tip the destiny of all wolves…

"Wonderfully unique and imaginative. I was enthralled!"

—Jeaniene Frost, *New York Times* bestselling author

For more info about Sourcebooks's books and authors, visit:
sourcebooks.com

TRUE WOLF

New York Times and *USA Today* bestselling author
Paige Tyler's STAT: Special Threat Assessment Team
fight paranormal enemies and fall in love once again.

As STAT agent and wolf shifter Caleb Lynch investigates a case of stolen
nuclear weapons, Brielle Fontaine is his hottest lead. Brielle's supernatural
abilities are a force to be reckoned with, making her one of STAT's biggest
threats and a most useful ally. He'll have to get close to her, but when the
team comes under fire from supernatural terrorists, the growing attraction
between them could lead to something much more explosive…

**"Unputdownable… Whiplash pacing, breathless
action, and scintillating romance."**

—K.J. Howe, International bestselling
author, for *Wolf Under Fire*

For more info about Sourcebooks's books and authors, visit:
sourcebooks.com

WILD COWBOY WOLF

Cowboys by day, wolf shifters by night—don't
miss the thrilling Seven Range Shifters series
from acclaimed author Kait Ballenger

Grey wolf warrior Dakota Nguyen has everything she ever wanted, but
when the daily grind gets lonely, her best friend, security technologist
Blaze Carter, always knows how to cheer her up. Lately, she has a feeling
that there might be something more between them. But even as friendship
turns to passion, a hidden enemy threatens to destroy the pack and all that
Blaze and Dakota fight so hard to protect. Now, there could be deadly con-
sequences to acting on their desires...

"Kait Ballenger is a treasure you don't want to miss."

—Gena Showalter, *New York Times* bestselling author

For more info about Sourcebooks's books and authors, visit:

sourcebooks.com

A MOST UNUSUAL DUKE

A delicious mix of Regency romance and shapeshifting
adventure in the exciting new Shapeshifters of the
Beau Monde series from author Susanna Allen

The Prince Regent insists his cousin and fellow bear shifter Arthur
Humphries, the Duke of Osborn, take a mate to ensure the continuation of
their species. After all, Arthur is an Alpha, so he must set a good example.
The duke would very much prefer to continue his comfortable bachelor
lifestyle, but just because he will marry Beatrice, the widowed Marchioness
of Castleton, does not mean he will fall in love, right?

**"Sparkling wit, scrumptious chemistry, and
characters who will go straight to your heart!"**

—Grace Burrowes, *New York Times* and
USA Today bestselling author

For more info about Sourcebooks's books and authors, visit:

sourcebooks.com

BIG BAD WOLF

First in an action-packed new paranormal
romantic suspense series from award-
winning author Suleikha Snyder

Joe Peluso has blood on his hands, and he's more than willing to pay the
price for the lives he's taken. He knows that shifters like him deserve
the worst. Darkness. Pain. Solitude. But lawyer and psychologist Neha
Ahluwalia is determined to help the dangerous wolf shifter craft a solid
defense…even if she can't defend her own obsession in the process. When
Joe's trial is torn apart in a blaze of bullets, Neha only knows that she'll do
anything to defend Joe…even if that means protecting him from himself.

**"*Big Bad Wolf* is a perfect urban fantasy for the times:
clever, romantic, heroic, and filled with hope for a better
future. Suleikha Snyder has crafted an amazing world."**

—Award-winning author Alisha Rai

For more info about Sourcebooks's books and authors, visit:
sourcebooks.com

Also by MaryJanice Davidson

BeWere My Heart

Bears Behaving Badly
A Wolf After My Own Heart
Mad for a Mate